A LAVENDER TRIP

SASHA MOORSOM

A
Lavender
Trip

THE BODLEY HEAD
LONDON   SYDNEY
TORONTO

© Sasha Moorsom 1976
ISBN 0 370 10593 1
Printed in Great Britain for
The Bodley Head Ltd
9 Bow Street, London WC2E 7AL
by Unwin Brothers Ltd, Woking
Set in Monotype Imprint
by Gloucester Typesetting Co. Ltd
First published 1976

I

As soon as you start up the narrow road that leads to the village it always seems as if you are climbing into a dream. Once past the church of Saint Jacques the ground falls away to the left with a steep drop down to an outcrop of those big grey stones that lie about everywhere. On the right, field after field of lavender stretches towards the lower slopes of the mountain. When they have been trimmed the bushes look like crouching humps of animals, and then in June, with the flowers out, a waving sea of mauve and grey as far as the eye can see.

There are very few cars on the road. Those you do pass are usually going much too fast as if their drivers hardly expect to meet any other traffic, and every curve and turn of the road is so familiar they could drive it blindfold. The strangers did not have such bravado. They clung to the inside curve on the way up and hooted tentatively at every corner. Philip was circumspect. He prided himself on his safe driving and, although Hannah was often a nervous passenger, she had learnt to relax with him. They were looking for somewhere to have lunch.

At the top of the hill the road straightened out to run alongside the last, long valley that ended in the wooded edge of the mountainside. A track led off the road into the fields. Hannah touched Philip on the shoulder.

'Let's stop. Can we?'

Philip ran the car a little way up the track and turned off the engine. They got out. The scent of lavender was everywhere. As she bent to pick a few sprigs the smell caught at the back of her nose. You could get high on it, she thought. Philip was examining a spider's web strung between two bushes. The web, broad at its circumference, narrowed into a spun-glass tunnel where the spider crouched. A large, yellow butterfly was caught on the outer edge. It flapped its

5

wings desperately but could not take off. Gently easing his finger underneath, Philip extracted it from the sticky web. It stayed on his finger for a moment, then slowly fluttered away, hovering over the flowers.

The fields were divided by low stone walls, half fallen down, covered with lichen. At the far end of their field was a round hut shaped like a beehive made of the same grey stones. A borie, said Philip, the simplest kind of construction, no one knew how old.

Hannah picked her way between the rows of lavender to explore it. The entrance was a low arch. She crouched to get through, then stood up in the dim light inside. The walls curved up to a domed roof, one stone balanced on top of another as a child might build, symmetrical and satisfying. The floor was dry earth. It looked as if someone had been staying there – two sacks laid over a pile of loose straw, an empty tin of cassoulet, sheets of yellowing newspaper. Last month's date. So this landscape was inhabited after all.

*

That's it. Hannah is me. I'm Hannah. Or at least some part of me is Hannah. Then why am I telling this story in the third person? I don't know. I seem to be relating these events to myself in the third person. It makes it easier, somehow. To narrate it. Is it a way of being more honest, of saying things I wouldn't be able to say otherwise, or more dishonest, of leaving out the parts I don't want to remember?

At least it's a way of beginning. This distancing of myself helps me to get started. I can follow where it leads. I keep thinking of Harry saying, 'How do I know someone isn't dreaming me?' I never can think of a convincing answer.

What about Philip? Notice the neat way he's introduced: 'Philip was circumspect'. At first I put, 'He was nothing if not cautious'. Later I crossed it out. How unfair. Was I trying to prejudice people against him from the start? Anyway, why is he circumspect? Mightn't it be because Hannah is a nervous passenger, at least partly?

He's considerate. Or is she just used to him? His particular style of driving?

He is considerate.

6

He releases the butterfly.

It's yellow. Hannah's favourite colour.

*

At the end of this long valley of lavender the road curved round to the smallest village Hannah had ever seen. On three sides of it the mountains rose abruptly like giant hands in whose palm the village lay cupped, the soft, washed-out colour of earth. And there the road came to an end. Or rather it divided in two – a narrow alley sliding between houses built so close together you could not tell where one ended and the next began, and a dusty track skirting round the outside.

They parked the car in a field next to a Citroen farm van, in the shade of a lime tree.

Quite quiet. The sacred hour for lunch. They started up the alley, peering at each window for a sign of people.

A woman came out of her doorway and shouted roughly, '*Micheline – à table!*'

A small girl came running down the street, gave them a startled look and disappeared inside. In the shadowy kitchen the table was laid for three. A man in blue dungarees was already seated, holding an enormous loaf of bread against his chest and slicing it towards him in a concentrated manner. On the table was a bottle of wine and a large sausage. They began to feel hungry.

'*Excusez-moi* . . .' Philip hesitated in the doorway. 'Is there a café in this village?'

He enjoyed displaying his French. The man looked up, surprised, and gestured with his knife. 'Further up the hill. Madame Pinet.'

'*Merci. Bon appétit.*'

The alley widened at the next corner and they saw the place he meant – two iron tables outside. They stepped through a bead curtain. Inside, the room was small – three more tables, a bar at one end, the smell of Gauloises and coffee. A woman was putting cups on the counter for two men sitting together. One of them was cleaning his plate meticulously with a wedge of bread.

'Is it too late to order lunch?' asked Philip.

7

'Soup? Omelettes? Tomato salad?'

She rattled it off without smiling and waited for their order, her eyes expressionless and shiny as black grapes that have lost their bloom.

'That sounds excellent. But no soup. Have you any sausage to start with?'

Seeing the man in dungarees had given Philip an appetite for the coarse sausage of the district, garlicky. He came to France to eat – at least partly; this was also a business trip.

'And two pastis, please.'

She nodded, served the pastis, and disappeared into the back without a word.

*

A business trip. Busy-ness. Never was man more busy. He never goes anywhere unless it's for work. He's saturated with travel – international conferences, consultancies. His idea of a holiday is to spend the whole week-end in bed. At home. He invites the children to a game of Mah-Jong, like a Chinese Happy Families, only more complicated. Instead of Mr Bun the Baker there are White Dragons and East Winds. I know how to play but I'm no good. Even Harry is better. They lay the pieces out on an enormous tray, keeping their scores in a notebook so that Sarah, in particular, can refer back to previous games and see where her strategy went wrong. They shout a great deal and argue about the rules which Philip settles with a complicated reference book.

Before the children were born I went to one of those conferences. I could see how it worked. It wasn't really the papers that people came for – they could get off-prints of those sitting in their offices. It was all the junketing in between, chatting in bars, late-night visits to seedy clubs they'd have been embarrassed to patronise in their home towns.

Philip meets the same international network every time, so they can all offer each other work, invite someone to join them on a special sub-committee of a committee to consider the problems of light-weight, prefabricated structures for disaster areas, knowing they'll be

8

invited in their turn as consultants to some continent other than their own, jetting past each other in mid-air. Philip likes the sun. He's never anything but brown. I imagine that's why he specialises in the civil engineering of hot countries. The Marseille trip is a good example of what I'm talking about. He has a French friend who's trying to land some big development contract in Tunisia. He's brought Philip in on it.

'A long week-end. I only have to spend Friday with Jerome. We can hire a car from Marignane airport – the fee will cover all that, and it'll give you a chance to find a house for the summer holidays. I expect Jerome can tell us some likely places.'

A long week-end's all I can manage. Although I don't work full-time it's awkward in the staff room if I miss a session. Remarks like: 'It's all very well for part-timers, not everyone can take a day off when they feel like it.' I never do unless one of the children is too ill to be left. It was the first time he'd pressed me to go with him for years. He knows I hate rushed visits. And then his idea of the holiday house. That gave it some point.

'A holiday in France? All of us?'

He looked embarrassed.

'I'll probably be away most of August. The Libyan plans have to be completed by September so there'll be a lot of negotiating to do on the spot. You might as well be somewhere pleasant with the children rather than hanging around in London.'

Busy. He'd be busy. That's what he was saying. And he didn't want to feel too guilty at being away so much. Perhaps he thought I wouldn't notice if I was away myself. He may have been right. He really is thoughtful. And busy.

*

Lunch was perfect. Everything tasted fresh, of itself. Philip could not help praising the omelette – the best he'd eaten for years. For the first time Madame Pinet suppressed a smile.

'Do you like goat cheese?'

She lifted a glass jar onto the counter and scooped out a soft, white

9

round. The jar was filled with olive oil and herbs, their flavour seeping into the cheeses. Philip was lyrical. He ordered coffee and cognac. He pressed Madame to a drink herself. Cognac? She was smiling openly at last. She preferred *marc. De la région*. The cheese was of the region too. The old man kept goats. Hannah wondered which old man. She spoke as if he was the only one – *Le Vieux*. Perhaps his age was as rare as his cheese. The men at the next table stayed on and on, enjoying Philip's enjoyment. How about a *marc* for them? They shook their heads, smiling. They had to start work very soon. Philip insisted. All right. Just one. They wouldn't say no.

Hannah sat back watching the scene. She admired Philip intensely, at that moment. His open delight in the meal had spread to everyone in the room.

Hannah had none of his ease with strangers. She could talk French as well as Philip but she held herself back, always afraid people would not like her. She did not know how to begin. Except when she was with Philip. Then she could follow. His exuberance included her in the delicate circle of communication.

Madame was leaning forward on the bar, lifting her glass to them. It was a good moment to ask – did she know of any house to let for the summer holiday?

She drew back looking puzzled. A house to let? Where? *Dans la région*, said Philip, feeling it was a word she approved. In this village perhaps? She looked across at the two men, repeating Philip's words musingly. One of the men nodded his head. It could be. There was the house of Marc Bonnieux's aunt. More precisely Monsieur Marc's house since his aunt had died. Now it was Madame's turn to nod. It was as if she had been waiting for the suggestion to come from one of the men, to show their approval.

She turned to Philip. 'The owner did talk of letting it. He doesn't need it himself. He has another studio in the village.'

'Could we see it?' Philip sounded casual. 'We're only here for a few days, I'm afraid.'

She hesitated again, glancing at the other table. The men were smiling over their glasses.

'Why not? The key's upstairs.'

She disappeared for a few moments and they heard her heavy steps above their heads. When she came back she placed a key on the counter, a piece of wrought-iron sculpture. Philip picked it up to feel the weight. It was longer than his hand.

Asking one of the men to mind the bar, Madame Pinet led them up the street to the top of the village where it ended in a small square, in the middle a fountain of three stone fishes dribbling trickles of water.

It stands at one corner of the square set slightly back with a courtyard in front. A vine grows over the front door in a waving curtain of green. The afternoon sunlight shines onto faded grey shutters. They are closed. The house looks asleep, closed eyes waiting to be touched into life again.

Hannah is inexplicably drawn to it. She had not expected anything in particular but now she feels a shock almost of recognition.

Madame Pinet has difficulty with the heavy door. She pushes her weight against it, breathing hard, and they step into darkness.

'Just a moment. Let me open the shutters.' Creaking, and then a sudden rush of sunlight into the room.

They are standing on red, hexagonal tiles in a kitchen with white walls.

'There's another room through that door.'

This time Hannah wants to open the windows for herself. She gropes her way across the darkened room to push back the shutters. A lizard quietly sleeping on the stone sill is dislodged onto the ground. Instantly a black cat, liquorice thin, pounces on it. The lizard gives one desperate wriggle and is gone, back up the wall. But something is left, twitching in the dust. As Hannah stares, the cat pats the tail, catches it up into the air and lets it drop. The tail flickers again, then stops. The cat eats it.

Hannah shivers and turns back into the room. It is as if it was still lived in. Books on all the shelves. A divan bed covered with a brown Moroccan rug. The Provençal fireplace with its curved chimney-piece and wide raised hearth laid with logs ready to light.

'When she couldn't manage the stairs any more Mademoiselle Grant lived in this room. She had everything she needed, her books and papers, the table for her work. At the end I even brought her meals in here.'

The staircase leads straight out of the kitchen to a small landing. Two bedrooms, one with French windows leading onto a tiny terrace, a private look-out over the tops of the other houses to an endless landscape.

The eye cannot take it all in at once. Their back is to the mountains now, as they look down into the valley they came up that morning. Beyond it the hills rise again, and behind them more hills, then mountains, range upon range, diffusing as they become more distant into a soft blue light so that finally you cannot tell where the mountains end and the sky begins.

'On a clear day you can see the Alps.' Madame Pinet is breathless from climbing the stairs. 'You have to wait for the *mistral* to get a clear day. That's all you can say in its favour.'

The room is furnished sparely – a bed with a white cotton cover, a solid chest of drawers, wood darkened from long years of polish. Madame Pinet draws her fingers across its dusty top and wipes them on her apron.

'She used beeswax. She got it from Monsieur Terrain. He keeps bees. But he didn't prepare it for her, just gave her the empty comb. She liked that,' Madame Pinet snorts with a kind of affectionate disdain. 'All the old ways of doing things. A lot of work. Marc cleared out the chest but I kept this.'

She opens the top drawer to reveal a wedge of golden-yellow wax resting on brown paper. Hannah leans forward and sniffs. In an instant memories of her own childhood engulf her, her grandmother melting beeswax in a metal bowl.

The wax is liquid but not too hot. Her grandmother carries the bowl to her dressing table and places it on a felt mat. Then she paints the wax above her upper lip, layer upon layer, coating it with a stiff, golden sheen.

'What are you doing, Granny?'

'I am removing my moustache.'

She speaks indistinctly, unable to move her mouth properly.

'Why are you?'

'Because this morning when you got into my bed you asked me why I had one.'

'Why do you?'

'Some people are afflicted in that way, particularly as they grow older. I don't wish to be reminded of that.'

She takes one end of the golden coating and with a swift movement pulls it away. Her upper lip is now red and hairless, her eyes bright with tears.

'Does it hurt?'

She nods. Hannah clasps her passionately.

'Oh Granny, why did you do it? You shouldn't hurt yourself. I liked your moustache, it was beautiful. I wanted to stroke it.'

Her grandmother pats her head.

'It will grow again. Only too soon.'

At seventy she was meticulous about her appearance. Hannah, now half her age, often found herself peering intently into the mirror for signs of her own hairiness. If it should come this summer the bees-wax would be handy.

She began to laugh. Philip, giving her a curious look, stepped out onto the terrace. There was a lot of noise below. They looked over the parapet. An old tractor was being driven into the square pulling a trailer. An old man, older even than the tractor, was walking towards it leading a brown goat. He lifted it into the trailer awkwardly, legs sticking out at all angles, then climbed up with some difficulty, for he was very bent, to sit beside it.

'The old man must be taking her down to the billy at Saint Jacques,' said Madame Pinet. 'He doesn't keep one himself.'

The tractor contorted itself round the fountain to go back the way it had come while the goat stood proudly looking round like a queen in procession.

'Greetings, cheese.'

Philip raised his arm in homage. The goat appeared to acknowledge him with a sudden jerk of her head.

'Well?'

Madame Pinet had left them and started slowly down the stairs to close the shutters again. Philip put his arm round Hannah's shoulders as she stared at the limitless landscape. She inhaled deeply as if to absorb the beauty of it with her breath.

'Will it do?'

She nodded.

'Let's try and arrange it with Madame, then.'

13

'Only I wish . . .' Breath drifted out of her in a long sigh.

'What? What's wrong with the house?'

'Nothing, it's perfect. That's why. I wish . . . you could be here too. With us.'

'It's impossible. You know that. You know my commitments.' He kissed her hair lightly. 'I've enjoyed these few days. Pity we can't do this more often.'

*

So little time together. Why? All the intrusions. The children wanting as much attention as they can get, my job at the school. Philip's work. That more than anything.

Commitments. The progression seems inescapable. So and so will lead to so and so that depends on so and so developing into so and so. If he lets one drop the whole construction might tumble. People are ladders to climb on.

It exhilarates him to exercise his own particular skill at creating viable structures out of what seem like irreconcilable demands. Is that what drew him towards his profession – a need to harness tensions?

Engineering. The orchestration of stress.

How relieved his voice sounded. He can't tolerate uncertainty. He's solved the summer holiday. More than anything he hates problems nagging at him.

*

They had another cup of coffee at Madame Pinet's.

'My wife would very much like to take the house if you can arrange it.'

Madame Pinet did not commit herself. 'It may be possible. I'll write to Monsieur Marc.' She made notes on the back of an old bill. 'How many in the family?'

'Four.'

'Monsieur will be the tenant?'

'No. My wife. I'll probably be abroad most of that time.'

'Your wife's profession?'

Hannah ventured her French. 'I'm a counsellor. No, just a moment . . .' She turned to Philip, laughing, reverting to English again. 'She can't put counsellor. He'll think I'm some kind of deputy-mayor or something. Better say teacher. Isn't that what I am?'

Philip shrugged. The niceties of her profession did not concern him.

'*Je suis maîtresse.*'

That sounded odd, too.

Madame Pinet wrote it down. She would inform them as soon as she had a reply.

2

Walking into the school on Tuesday Hannah knew immediately what was for lunch. Cabbage. A smell like old farts drifted along the corridor. An olfactory cliché. Why do schools always have to smell of cabbage? And what else? Onions. Probably that glutinous mince.

The tiny room allocated to her was next to the dining hall and the clashing of china and the noisy exchanges of the helpers often made it hard to hear what the children in her room were saying.

Officially it was a Parents' Room. A frayed notice on the door drawn by one of the children announced that 'Parents are welcome in this school'. Below the words was a picture, supposedly of the head-mistress, very spiky-looking, shaking hands with a parent. The parent, half her size, had on a red hat with three green feathers sticking out of it and, by a stroke of realism, her face was black. Below was written 'Please Walk In'.

The door was always kept locked. This was because the room contained filing cabinets of medical record cards and these cards were officially confidential. They had overflowed from elsewhere. Every term Hannah suggested to the Head's secretary that they might be moved. She always agreed to try to find somewhere else to put them. But Hannah's room was one of the few that could conveniently be locked except when she was in it or when someone felt ill. There was a couch at one end where children could lie down in emergencies. It was also used for medical examinations. Then Hannah had to sit in the corridor.

She went to fetch the key from the board in the staff room. Jim Finnigan was lying back in one of the armchairs reading the *Daily Express*. He looked sideways up at her.

'V.D.'s on the increase. Did you know that? Some figures here just been released. The bugs are getting too cunning. They actually thrive on antibiotics – adds a little touch of spice to their normal diet of succulent sexual juices.'

'Oh dear.'

'Oh dear. Oh dear it is. Ever had crabs?'

'Do women get crabs?' She was not absolutely sure what they were. Something eighteenth century? Did Boswell have them?

'Do women get crabs? My God, Hannah, you are the most innocent bitch that ever graced this establishment.'

He looked round hopefully for an audience and caught the eye of the only other woman in the room, Mrs Shadgrove, who looked away frowning.

'I'll say women get crabs. Where do you think men catch them from? Real devils to get rid of. You have to pursue them with . . .'

Hannah, half out of the door, called back faintly, 'Good hunting.'

*

It's always the same with any group. I feel on the outside. Worse because I'm not full time. It makes them suspicious of me. Or is that just my paranoia? My present role is typical, half teacher, half counsellor, nothing definite, always on the fringes, not really committed to anything. Commitments are what Philip has. A part-timer.

No one seems to know what a counsellor does. I try to sort out children's troubles with their parents or put people in touch with the right social services. Mostly I do remedial teaching. Basic literacy. A lot of the teachers regard it as a rest cure.

I dread going into the staff room at break, that crowded, fuggy room, gossiping voices, four of them always playing bridge in the corner. The coffee cups are all dirty by the time I get there. Usually I end up perched on the window sill.

The one person I like the look of is Nick Gates. He's only been there a term. Remedial, like me, but full-time. I think he must be from Yorkshire by his voice. I once went unexpectedly into his room to borrow a book. Inside there was chaos. It frightened me. At one end of the room some boys were making a makeshift den. There was a tiny entrance that could only be breached by crawling on all fours, too small for a teacher. Nick was helping them rig up a lighting system of batteries and torch bulbs. I couldn't help asking, 'What on earth is all this, what are you doing?'

'Eliminating negatives.'

'What . . . do you mean?'

'Can't do it. Don't know how. That's what these kids say all the time. I'm working on that.'

*

The worst kind of day. Drizzling. To the scent of cabbage was added a smell like wet dogs. Children were pouring into the school, all shapes, sizes, colours. Damp hair, sodden coats and jackets. The floors were already streaked with dirt. Hannah always wondered how the building could contain them all. They flowed in and in, an endless stream, till the whole place was vibrating with restless human energy. *I had not thought death had undone so many.* Early summer. Yet they had a wintry air about them that comes so easily on a grey day in London, as if the dirt in the air had washed down onto their faces.

The bell clanged. People began hurrying in different directions. Mr Blagdon stood at the head of the staircase shouting, 'No running.'

He put out an arm to restrain a boy dashing round the corner. The boy's shoulders hunched. His arm came half way up as if he was about to swing a punch. He looked at the figure blocking his way, saw who it was, how big he was, and his arm dropped. He walked on with the stream.

What restrains these children? Why do they submit to the hectoring voices, the intricate ritual of containment, day after day? They could tear the place to pieces if they wanted. And yet they don't. They play along with the illusion that it means something, that it is – as they're continually assured – in some obscure way for their benefit. The willing suspension of disbelief. Hard to suspend mine.

Hannah unlocked her door and, balancing on a chair, strained to open the window a fraction, not wide enough for the rain to come in. She just had time to get a box out of the cupboard and put it on the table. There was a knock.

'Come in.'

The two Indian girls she was helping to learn English slid smiling round the door. Even the drab green uniforms hardly disguised their grace. Beautiful white teeth, dark plaits hanging either side of burnt umber cheeks.

'Hallo Sita, Amarjit, please sit down.'

'Hullo Mrs Straight. I'm sitting down.'

'Look in the box. What can you find?'

'I can find table. Here is table.'

'A table.'

'Here is a table.'

And so on through the ritualised game they played together each morning Hannah was at the school.

At first they had sat anxiously staring at each other, unable to communicate. The box was an inspiration. Clearing up with her own two children, Hannah had come across the old doll's house. She brought some of the furniture and the pipe-cleaner people to school to act as interpreters between them. It was a magical key that unlocked their tongues and led them, intriguingly, through things they could touch and move, into the mysteries of the new language.

'The man sits at the table.'

Amarjit propped a tiny, male, pipe-cleaner against a chair.

'He's hungry.'

'Where's his food?'

'Woman cook his food.'

The man was always hungry, getting cross, eating his food, going to work. The woman was always cooking, cleaning the room, washing the clothes, looking after the baby. Sometimes Hannah teased them, standing the man at the stove and asking,

'Is the man cooking his food?'

Whereupon Sita vigorously shook her head, whisking him away from this indignity, and put him firmly back in his chair.

'No. The man not cooking. He sitting at table.'

Hannah enjoyed their time together, particularly the change from silent, locked-in strangers full of fears they could not express, to these laughing, intent girls. She was sorry when the next knock came and she had to put the box away and get out books for someone else.

It was Sean. His attendance at the school was irregular. Hannah never challenged him about it. She merely said, 'I'm sorry you didn't come yesterday, Sean. I had something for you.'

'What's it, then?'

'I'll see if it's still in my pocket.'

She would bring out some object – a pure white pigeon's feather, a card from a cereal packet, or a magazine with photographs of animals.

Sean liked anything to do with wild life. Living as he did in the decaying centre of a huge city, animals and birds, strange creatures whose existence barely touched his own, represented some freedom he could never reach. He was in the middle of a family of seven. Irish Catholic. He had once transfixed Hannah by asking, 'D'you believe in the Holy Mother of God?'

'The Holy Mother of God?' Hannah had repeated wonderingly.

'The kids in my class, they don't.'

Long pause.

'You mean Mary, the mother of Jesus?'

'Yeah.'

'I think Jesus had a mother called Mary . . .'

She wondered where this was leading her when luckily he interrupted: 'Me sister's called Mary. We call her Molly. She's daft. She's at this school. One of them weirdos.'

Sean was illiterate. The school had some remedial classes but he was beyond them, so fiercely ashamed of his ignorance that he refused to join a group of slow learners. So they had come back to something very old-fashioned. Learning the alphabet by means of mnemonics, jokes, games that he was far more inventive at than Hannah.

'My Mum makes maggots miserable.'

She would not let him breed them in the kitchen for his fishing. He was slowly filling an exercise book with drawings – an elaborate animal dictionary.

That day after Hannah came back from France they had got up to 'p'. As he was working on a purple parrot someone knocked. Sean looked up indignantly.

'S'not time yet. I only just come.'

Hannah opened the door a crack to find two girls outside, one supporting the other.

'Please Miss, Mary's queer. Mrs Shadgrove said for her to lie down Nearly fainted, she did.'

'Bring her in. I'll get a blanket from the cupboard.'

The girl leaning on her friend was pale as paper. She had long, dark-red hair half hiding her face, lids drooping, a Pre-Raphaelite air about her. Sean jumped up. 'What you doing here, Molly?'

'She's sick. Get out the way, Sean,' said Mary's friend.

Hannah could see his fist clenching. 'Is it your sister? The one you told me about?'

'Yeah.'

'It's all right, Sean, she needs to lie down.'

Hannah covered the girl with a grey blanket and told the friend she could go. Sean stood awkwardly at the end of the couch. 'What's wrong, Moll? You hungry?'

Molly made an obvious effort to open her eyes fully. Blue-green, shimmering. She looked at Hannah in some kind of appeal and tears began to drop slowly out of them.

'Sean . . .' Hannah put her arm lightly round his shoulders. 'I think we'd better go on later. Could you come back at one thirty? I'm sorry to have to change things.'

'S'all right.'

He walked to the door reluctantly. Hannah smiled at him. 'Thanks a lot, Sean. See you later.'

His exit released a spasm of sobs from the girl on the couch. Hannah pulled a chair near her. 'Would you like me to try and get a doctor?'

The girl shook her head. Her sobs were groans, torn from deep inside her. Words came slowly, in gasps. 'I . . . don't know . . . what to do.'

Hannah sat silently. The girl's head was turned away, hair hiding her face. 'I've got to tell someone.'

Hannah tentatively passed her a tissue. 'Tell me if you want to. I'm supposed to be a sort of school counsellor as well as a teacher. That's partly what I'm for, to talk to.'

'You won't tell no one?'

'Not if you don't want me to.'

'Not the Head, not Mrs Shad, no one?'

'No.'

'You swear?'

'I promise.'

'Holy Mother of God?'

Hannah smiled. Sean's sister all right. 'Holy Mother of God.'

'Got any more tissues?'

Hannah passed her several. The girl pulled herself a little way out of the blanket and half sat up. She spoke in a whisper. 'I'm pregnant.' Hannah stared at her. 'I got to tell someone.' *Her voice was ever soft, gentle and low.* Not Irish but a touch of something un-English, a lilt. Inadvertently Hannah's eyes dropped to the girl's stomach, half covered with the blanket.

'It doesn't show yet, does it?' She pulled down the blanket anxiously and Hannah shook her head. Since she did not know her she could hardly judge.

'I feel dead sick in the morning. Today it was worse. I went all icy cold in the classroom. I thought I was going to fall.'

'Does no one know?'

'No.'

'Are you sure about it? Sure you're pregnant, I mean?'

'I sent a test by post. They said it was positive. Told me to see a doctor.'

'Have you?'

She shook her head, the hair falling across her pale cheek. 'Don't know where to go. I can't go to that old Dr FitzPatrick. Tell him something and the whole street knows. He's always in the boozer. Anyway, he'd be no good to me.'

'What do you mean?'

'I want to get rid of it, don't I?'

Hannah is suspended in mid-air, paralysed by the uncertainty of what her reaction should be.

'Are you shocked?' The girl leans forward anxiously, peering into her face.

'No . . . I don't know. It's a bit of a surprise.' Hannah manages to smile.

'Well, I can't have it, can I?'

Hannah looks at her, older than Sean, softer, on the edge of some flowering, the beginning of a woman yet still a child. She shakes her head slowly.

'I don't know where to go. Can you help me?' Softly. 'Please can you?'

Hannah moved her hand instinctively to touch the girl's. 'I'll do anything I can. I don't know much about this kind of thing. I'll try to find out.' Find out – how did you begin? She had a feeling of dread. 'Molly . . .' she used the name her brother used. 'Do you know how long it is?' The girl shook her head. 'I don't know for sure. I missed two months. It must be two months I think.'

Two months. It might be more. Hannah had a vague idea that three months was the deadline. For an easy abortion.

'Molly, what about your family?'

'My Dad would kill me. He's not my real Dad. He's dead. My step-Dad's his cousin. He's got the same name so everyone thinks he's our real Dad. But he's not. All he does is shout and knock us about. He'd chuck me out if he heard a word about it.'

'And your mother?'

'Mam? She's so many troubles already. She'd just cry.'

'Molly . . . how old are you?'

'Fifteen. Sixteen next month.'

'I think you'll have to tell her.'

'What for?'

'Because I couldn't help you without her knowing.'

Molly stared at her, afraid.

'I couldn't, Molly. She's your mother. She's legally responsible for you. I'll have to talk to her first.'

'She's Catholic.'

'Aren't you?'

'When I was younger they made me go. Mam's dead scared of priests. Always trying to please them. I'm not bothered now. I stop in bed of a Sunday morning.'

'Would you like me to tell her?'

Molly's hands, white with long, pointed finger nails, smoothed the grey stuff of the blanket over and over till there was not a wrinkle. At last she said, 'I'll do it. She'd be more ashamed for it to come from you.'

'Shall I come and see her after? I think it should be soon.'

'All right. Come tomorrow. That'll make me.'

'It'll have to be in the lunch break.'

'I'll make sure the other kids go to school. I don't want them hanging around.'

*

A bad night. Waking suddenly I sit stark upright, my throat aching as if I've been screaming. I'm soaked with sweat. Something frightening, to do with Harry. That's all I can remember. Did I really scream? I can still hear the sound in my ears. I look down at Philip, solidly asleep. I can't have made any noise. I get out of bed and creep across the landing to Harry's room.

He's lying on his back, his face towards me. I bend down to hear his slow breathing. A lovely smell, like a puppy, warmth rising from his soft cheeks. My own breathing slows in response.

A faint light from the street lamp outside comes through the curtain. It falls on the four creatures propped at the foot of Harry's bed. His guardians. A bear, an old doll, a kangaroo, a cat.

A year ago Harry had nightmares. He woke up screaming nearly every night. He couldn't give a coherent account of his terror, just 'Monsters, monsters are coming.' I had to search through every drawer to reassure him there were no horrors lurking among the socks. Then one evening he thought of the guardians. His own idea. He ranged them like soldiers at the end of his bed. From then on they offered complete protection.

> *Matthew, Mark, Luke and John*
> *Bless the bed that I lie on . . .*
> *One to watch and one to pray*
> *And two to bear my soul away.*

Where is Harry's spirit? Is it in this softly breathing room?

My grandmother sang me that song when I was four. The year my father was killed. Why do I think of it now? It's made me afraid ever since. Her voice was high and keening. She stroked my head while

24

she sang. They said the Germans killed him. I thought their names must be Luke and John.

Is Philip a kind of guardian, his presence in the bed? Only the magic isn't working any more. The nightmare was more powerful.

3

The streets around the district where Molly and Sean lived were all named by Wagner. Hannah walked down Lohengrin Street past a huge tenement – Valkyrie House – into Parsifal Road. Some crazy councillor had managed to foist his addiction on the entire neighbourhood. It was rapidly decaying. In Parsifal Road all the houses on one side had been boarded up with corrugated iron. The last one was already half demolished, exposing a wall of pink-flowered paper, the dado marked with a change of pattern chosen with love some twenty years before.

Molly's house was opposite, curtains half-drawn behind smeary window panes. Hannah rang the bell, leaning her ear against the door to hear if it was working. No sound. She banged with the flat of her hand. At length Molly opened the door.

'Sorry. I was out the back.'

Her purple velvet skirt hung to the ground – crushed velvet, very crushed, a marvellous colour, the patina of age. Above she wore a man's dress-shirt, collarless, with numerous tiny pleats down the front, and a waistcoat of dull black silk. Her feet were bare and dirty.

'I like your skirt, Molly.'

'Look at this.' She drew Hannah into the passageway and banged the door shut. 'Look at this lining.' Turned back, the edge of the waistcoat showed a soft green. 'Feel. Silk, Miss, isn't it? I got it last Saturday at the Catholic jumble. Seven pence. Imagine giving it away. Some people must be daft.'

They went into the kitchen and Molly called out of the back door, 'Mam, she's here.'

The room was jammed with furniture – a kitchen table with a packet of sliced bread on it and a greasy margarine paper, a huge old television in the corner, eight chairs festooned with the litter of nine

26

people's lives – broken toys, comics, clothes. Damp. A pan on the stove gave out a smell of boiled bones. Molly lifted the lid and made a face.

'Scouse! Mam's putting out the washing. She couldn't get it dry yesterday.'

Mrs Malone came in. The same red hair but where Molly's glowed, hers was dull-looking, like a dead bird. Her skin was stretched so tight over her temples that the effect was skull-like. Molly had not told her one thing – her mother, too, was pregnant. She wiped her hands on her swelling belly.

'I've heard about you from our Sean.'

From behind her skirt peered a small boy. When Hannah smiled his face instantly disappeared from view.

'Come on then, Johnny, give us a kiss,' Molly coaxed.

'Let him be,' said her mother. She turned to Hannah: 'He's queer-like with strangers. Will you have a cup of tea?'

'Thank you.'

With the four of them the room already seemed crowded.

'Sit down, won't you?' Her voice was Irish. Soft, like Molly's.

Molly jerked her head towards her mother as she put the kettle on. 'I've told her.'

Mrs Malone abandoned her effort at social niceties and sat down abruptly at the table, her head bowed as if the weight of this knowledge was forcing it down. She rested her forehead on her hands, her shoulders swaying.

'It's a terrible thing,' she whispered, 'a terrible thing.'

'I'm very sorry about it.' Hannah's sympathy overcame her awkwardness. 'I'll do anything I can to help you.'

Mrs Malone lifted her head slowly, grey eyes brimming. Hannah noticed a yellow bruise round one socket. Had she been punched?

'It's a sin. She's done wrong and now she's after doing more wrong. It's sin on sin.'

Hannah dropped her eyes. The words meant nothing to her.

'Come on, Mam, don't carry on.' Molly was standing behind her mother. 'I've told you I'm not having it. Not if I can help it.'

'There isn't very much time, Mrs Malone.' Hannah spoke quietly. Their soft voices were catching. 'I think Molly should see a doctor as soon as possible.'

'Not Dr FitzPatrick?' Alarm showed in Mrs Malone's face. 'I'd never be able to keep it from her step-father then.'

'I thought of asking my own doctor. But I couldn't without seeing you.'

'Will it cost money?'

'Not to see him. But afterwards . . . I don't know. It may do, I'm afraid.'

At this Mrs Malone began to cry. The little boy echoed her noisily. He pulled her by the arms and tried to climb onto her knee. His nose was running. She picked him up and began to rock him from side to side, wiping her cheeks on his hair.

'Here, Mam. Have your tea.'

Molly shook her shoulder roughly and put the cup down in front of her.

'I'm afraid of what her step-father would do if he found out. He's a hard man. I couldn't tell him.'

'Shall I make an appointment as soon as I can? Would you like me to try and . . . arrange something?'

Mrs Malone nodded, looking down at the table in embarrassment. 'I wouldn't know what to do at all.' Suddenly her voice rose hysterically. 'Who was it, Molly? Tell me that. Who was the wicked fellow done such a thing?'

'Oh, Mam. You've asked me that already. It's no one you know. I said before – I can't tell you nothing.'

'You're a wicked girl, Molly.' She turned to Hannah. 'She's wild, Miss, wild. I can't do a thing with her. Just look at her clothes. She walks down the street in that rig-out for all the world to see.'

*

A counsellor. Ludicrous word. Who am I to offer counsel? Teacher? Social worker? Busybody? Voyeur? I invite confidences – 'I'm supposed to be there to talk to' – and then, what do I register? Shock. Nothing but shock. Total ignorance of what to do.

Why did I involve her mother? Molly didn't want to. Was it cowardice on my part, a fear of being held responsible if something went wrong, of losing my job perhaps? Or was it some stock idea of what a mother ought to be? The mother. A loving, supportive figure.

Molly knows another kind. Someone exhausted, struggling, more helpless even than herself. Someone not protecting but to be protected. That's what she was trying to do. Protect her. I spoilt it.

*

'Molly . . . why did you leave it so long?'

The news was bad. Molly was more pregnant than she had thought. Hannah's doctor would not say how many weeks. That was a job for the specialist.

'What were you thinking of doing?'

'I don't know.' Molly's face was turned away.

'If only you'd told me sooner.'

'I couldn't, could I? I didn't know you. I wouldn't've come then only Mrs Shad sent me down.'

'It's going to make it much more difficult.'

They walked on in silence. Suddenly Molly burst out: 'Why don't you ask me, then?'

'Ask you what?'

'Who the fellow is. I bet you want to know. Why don't you ask?'

'What difference would it make? I imagine you would have gone to him for help if it was going to do you any good.'

'You're dead right. It won't do me no good. Shall I tell you, then?'

Hannah said gently, 'It's up to you. If you want to.'

'There's these guys live round the back of the flats. One of them used to be at school. He left to go to art college. They said they were going to have this party for a whole lot of friends coming down from the Leicester Poly. My Dad was on night shift so I took the key and told Mam I'd be late. It was great. They had it all going, music, some kind of light show. One guy from the Poly, he really seemed to go for me. He was a bit of a nutter. He said . . .' she paused, puzzling over the words, '. . . he said my hair was a figment of his imagination. What do you think he was on about?'

Hannah shrugged her shoulders, laughing.

'He got a hair brush and brushed it so hard it stood on end, like it

29

was all electric. I danced a lot and then I got dead thirsty. He fetched me a Pepsi. After that everything began to go weird. I thought it was the lights. Like fireworks, flashing right inside my head, as if I was all made of electricity. I began to fly.'

Hannah looked at her wonderingly. 'Fly?'

'I seemed to be floating about near the ceiling looking down on all the other people in the room. It felt like . . .' she frowned then suddenly went on, '. . . like I was God. I really loved them.'

She turned to Hannah with a look of surprise at what she had just said. 'That's funny, isn't it? I never felt like that before.'

Hannah was listening intently.

'I picked out this guy way down below me. Seemed like he was the one I was meant to go for. So I landed on him, like a bird. Just folded my wings like I really was a bird. After that it's all a dream. I was flying along with him. That's all I can remember.'

She shivered. 'When I woke up I was lying on the floor. There was a lot of other people round but it was dark so I couldn't see them properly. I was dead cold. I think that's why I woke up. Then I heard the clock at the Catholic striking three and I knew I better get home quick.'

Hannah let out her breath. 'Did you see him again? The fellow from Leicester?'

'No. They went back next day. I didn't go for him all that much. Not really. I prefer the guy who gave the party. Anyway I don't know who it was, do I? Not for sure.'

'And you didn't want to tell him? Your friend, I mean?'

'Tell him?' Molly looked at her scornfully. 'What would I say? I got done at your rave up and I don't even know who the guy is?'

They sit down on the bench by the bus stop, one at each end. Molly slumps, staring at the ground, her shoulders hunched. Hannah, glancing along the bench at this isolated figure, feels for the first time a confused anger erupting inside her. Anger that something of such importance can happen to someone almost without them being aware of it; anger that the female body is so mechanistic, that it needs no participating spirit to conceive. An object to which things happen. Passivity, not passion.

Molly turned to her with a look of real fear. 'What if it happens when you've taken drugs – the baby might be queer, mightn't it?' She began to cry. 'I'm sure he put something in that Pepsi. Most likely acid. I know they had some.'

Hannah moved to put her arm round Molly's shoulders. She tried to speak with a conviction she did not feel. 'We've got the doctor's letter to the hospital for next week. It may be all right, Molly. Try to stop worrying.'

Her doctor had suggested they try the National Health. 'If the girl's got no money it's always worth a go.'

*

The clinic was packed with women in all stages of pregnancy sitting in rows facing the nurse's desk. Strange to see so many together. Hannah and Molly took their places at the back and the women moved forward like players in a game of slow-motion musical chairs as the nurse read out their names. They waited an hour before Molly was called. Then she was gone ten minutes. When she came out, her drooping figure drowned in a hugely flowered nylon gown, Hannah could tell she was trying not to cry.

'What did he say?' Hannah asked quickly, taking her hand.

Molly shook her head, whispering, 'It's no good. He says I've got to have it.'

'What do you mean?'

'It's too late.' She began to sob openly.

Hannah pushes past the nurse and walks in. The doctor's head is bent over the desk as he writes.

'Just lie on the couch. I'll be with you in a moment.'

She tries to hide her nervousness. 'I'm not a patient. I'm with the girl you just saw. Her mother couldn't come so she asked me to. I'd like to know what you said to her.'

He looks up quickly, eyes cold behind half-rimmed glasses. A bland face.

'I'm just booking her a place in this hospital to have the baby. I'm afraid there's no question of termination at this stage. It's well over three months.'

31

Hannah gasps. 'Over three months? What do you mean? How can it be?'

'Sixteen weeks to be precise. These young girls all make the same mistake. Incurable optimism. As I explained to Miss Malone, the length of pregnancy must be calculated from the beginning of the last menstruation. They seem to think it's the conception date that's all important. It isn't.'

'But she doesn't want the baby.'

'That's hardly our business. She should have thought of that at the . . . er . . . time. I'm afraid there's nothing I can do at this stage.'

'But can't it be taken away?' Hannah is conscious of a lack of medical precision. Should she have said 'aborted'?

'Termination at this late stage would mean a full-scale operation. We cannot justify such an action unless the mother is clearly incapable of having the child for physical or psychological reasons. That doesn't apply in this case. We'll arrange for her to see the social worker on her next visit. I understand she's a Catholic. There are several Catholic homes for unmarried mothers.'

'But it's monstrous!' Hannah is shouting. 'She's only a child herself.'

'I'm afraid I'm a very busy man. I must ask you to leave.'

A nurse moves forward, propelling Hannah towards the door. Hannah pushes her off, shaking with anger. She is near to tears herself.

Molly is already dressed, her face white and afraid. They walk out into the street.

'If I have to have it, I'll have to. But I can't stay at home. He'd never stand for it. He'd see me in hell first.'

'I'm not giving up yet.'

'What else can I do?'

'Try a private consultant. I'll ring up Dr Coates and see if he can suggest someone.'

*

Four days later they are in Harley Street. Mr Van Leer, elegant, smiling, shakes them both by the hand. 'Which is my patient?'

32

Hannah indicates Molly, saying hesitantly, 'Shall I stay in the waiting room?'

'No, no, dear lady. You can sit here. I shall examine Miss Malone behind the screen.' A slight foreign accent, like an actor in an old film playing the part of a distinguished consultant. 'Would you mind taking off your shoes, Miss Malone?'

Molly is wearing old leather boots. She tries to get them off. In a panic she turns to Hannah. 'They're stuck.'

Hannah tugs hard. Molly's feet come out with a plop. No socks. Her feet smell very strong.

She disappears behind the screen. Mr Van Leer murmurs softly, like a lover. Hannah hears Molly cry out, twice. A tap is running.

He comes out and sits behind his desk. Molly struggles with her boots again. He smiles as if he had good news. Hannah moves to the edge of her chair, her mouth quivering, ready to break into an open grin as he starts to speak: 'I'm afraid it's too late for me.'

She catches her breath, staring at him. He folds his hands on the desk. Olive-skinned and smooth, clinically clean finger nails. Hannah's eyes smart. 'You can't do anything?'

He shakes his head. 'I'm afraid not.' He stands up, still smiling. 'That will be twelve guineas.'

'Twelve . . .' Hannah feels herself go red with embarrassment. She gets up. 'Will a cheque be all right?'

He inclines his head. She stumbles to write the cheque, leaning it awkwardly on the edge of his desk. 'Is there anyone who could . . .?' she asks incoherently.

He shrugs. 'I'm afraid I cannot say.'

*

They went into a café for a hot drink and sat staring at the endless row of people passing outside. Some of them stared in. Which, she wondered, were providing a show for which? The window framed the passers-by for her, just as it framed her for them. Only they were giving a moving show. Hers was static, a tableau.

Struggling to think if there was anyone else whose advice she could

33

ask, she remembered a woman who worked for a Citizen's Advice Bureau. A long shot, but worth trying.

'Stay here a moment, Molly. I'll just try and telephone someone.'

Margaret's voice sounded businesslike. 'Citizen's Advice Bureau. Can I help you?'

'Margaret, this is Hannah, Hannah Straight.'

'Hullo Hannah, how are you? How's Philip?'

'Fine, fine. Look, I'm in a telephone box so I must be quick. Can ask your advice?'

'Of course.'

'I want some help for a friend of mine. She's pregnant and she doesn' want to have the baby. Do you know of anywhere she could get help?'

There was a pause. 'A friend of yours, did you say?'

'Yes. A young girl.' Did she think it was her?

'How pregnant is she?'

'Over three months. That's the trouble. We've tried a hospital and a private consultant and they both say it's too late. But I can't believe it. There must be someone in the whole of London who does thi kind of thing.'

'There's a voluntary bureau for pregnancy advice in Birmingham and one in London but they're usually very booked up. From wha you say I think it would be too late for them. Just a moment, I'll loo up the card index.'

She went off the line. Hannah could hear the office typewrite clattering in the background.

'Hullo, Hannah? Still there?'

'Yes.'

'There's only one place we have a note of that might be able to help It's a commercial agency. I'm afraid we don't know much about it We've just got a card with their address.'

Hannah wrote it down.

'Let me know what happens, won't you? I'd like a report on it.'

'Yes, I will. Goodbye.'

Even to have a new address made her feel once more optimistic 'Come on Molly. We'll take a bus down Oxford Street. I've got an other place to try.'

Molly looked at her in amazement. 'You don't give up easy, d you?'

Up two flights of narrow stairs into the Bureau. A poky little office. The woman behind the desk had on a baby-pink jumper. Hannah described the situation with despair in her voice. The woman patted her hair – like candy floss, almost edible. Her face, by contrast, was hard and businesslike. Inedible.

'Don't worry, I'm sure we can help you.'

Hannah and Molly exchanged unbelieving looks. The woman's voice was clipped, refined.

She spoke at great speed. 'We have a panel of twenty-four gynaecologists on our books. The one I'm thinking of is a top Harley Street man. He specialises in advanced terminations. I don't think there'll be any problem. We only send people to the very best. He has his own private nursing home in South London with fully qualified staff.'

Hannah sat back in her chair with a feeling of bewilderment. There must be a snag. Suddenly she remembered. 'What will it cost?'

'Our fee is ten guineas.'

'What about the doctor?'

'I'm coming to that.' She was filling in a form with Molly's particulars. She looked her over from head to toe, dispassionately. 'Student are you?'

'She's still at school.'

'Oh dear, oh dear. You've had a bit of bad luck, haven't you? Father's occupation?'

'He's on the building.'

'I'll put labourer. Is your mother working?'

'What, with seven kids? You're joking.'

She went on writing for a moment and then looked up. 'We recommend a fee to the consultant. In this case I'll keep it down to the minimum. One hundred pounds. He won't go lower than that.'

'A hundred?' Molly gasped.

'Over three months it's usually one hundred and fifty. But in your circumstances I hope he'll make an exception. You have to take the money with you in cash. Payment's in advance of course. Will tomorrow afternoon do?'

Molly looked at Hannah, speechless. Hannah nodded. 'Yes. Tomorrow afternoon. Where do we go?'

She gave them a card. 'Any time after two o'clock. We have a block booking for Fridays. So many girls come over from the continent, we can never be sure of the numbers.'

Hannah leant forward; she could not help asking, 'How do they know where to go?'

'The taxi drivers at the airport know where to bring them, don't they, dear? They all have our card. They come straight here.'

Is it really as simple as that? If you know the ropes everything is always simple. And if you have money. A smooth-running, commercial affair. What a miracle she had thought of ringing Margaret up. What a fool not to have done it earlier. But how could she have known?

On the way out she paused. 'How is it this surgeon can do it easily when the one at the hospital said it would need a full-scale operation?'

'I told you, dear, he's the top man for this. He has his own vacuum method. People come from all over the world to study his technique. Your friend won't have a thing to worry about. She'll be all right.'

Outside, Molly grasped her arm. 'But I haven't got a hundred quid. Where will I get that sort of money?'

'I'm thinking about that, Molly. I'm thinking as hard as I can. I've got seventy pounds on deposit at the bank. You can have that. Has your mother any money at all?'

'I don't know exactly. She's been trying to save up for a holiday in Ireland. She hasn't been home for five years. She keeps it in her stocking at the back of the cupboard – where Dad won't see it. She might have a few quid.'

'You go home and ring me when you've seen her. I'll try and borrow some.'

'Oh, Miss . . .' Molly was half laughing, half crying, 'I'm scared.' She clung to Hannah's arm.

'Please don't call me Miss. You can't after all this. I'm Hannah. Call me Hannah.'

'Do you think it'll be all right?'

Hannah put her arm round her. Molly was trembling.

4

Molly's mother managed eleven pounds. That left nineteen to find. She would have to ask Philip for a loan. He already knew about Molly. She had said Hannah could tell him the week before. Then, he had tried to persuade Hannah to tell what he called 'the authorities'.

'What authorities?'

'People at the school with the responsibility for dealing with this sort of thing. The headmistress, for instance.'

'I can't. I promised Molly.'

'What d'you mean, you promised?'

'Not to tell them. She'd never have told me otherwise.'

'But you didn't know, then, what was involved.'

'I can't go back on it.'

'Hannah,' he said impatiently, 'Don't take on too much. Aren't you going rather beyond the terms of your job?'

She did not know what the terms of her job were.

Now she approached him reluctantly. His reaction surprised her.

'Thank God you've found someone. I was afraid we'd end up having to adopt it.'

Hannah stared at him.

'Don't look so amazed. Hadn't you thought of it?'

She shook her head slowly. She had never consciously considered the idea. Now that Philip threw it at her so baldly she realised that deep down inside her the possibility must have been there.

'You're always a soft touch. And you believe in Fate. You would have thought it was Meant. I could see it all coming.'

Of course. His mind's like that. Click, click, click. A quick run-through of all the possible permutations. Then bang. A decision.

I'm never like that. I can't think of more than one solution at a time. I go at it slowly, plodding all round the situation and getting bogged down, painfully trying to find a way out. Then working on to the next thing. What else does Philip know about me that I don't know myself?

*

It was ironical to be back the next afternoon in Harley Street. The waiting room was crammed with girls, some with young men. Heads close together. Whispered conversations in many languages. Three smart receptionists moved them in and out like heifers on a conveyor belt at the slaughter house – urine test, blood test, doctor's examination.

Molly was called. When she came back she handed the money over and sat down again. 'I have to wait to go to the nursing home.' She was shaking.

'You mean . . . he's going to do it this afternoon?'

'Yes.'

Hannah tried to disguise her surprise. 'Don't be nervous. I'm sure it'll be all right. How long do you have to stay?'

'They said I might come out tonight.'

'Tonight?' Hannah stared at her. 'Are you sure?'

Molly nodded. 'That's what they said.'

It all seemed more and more extraordinary. No major operation. Perhaps not even an overnight stay in the nursing home.

One of the receptionists gave Hannah a number to ring that evening and within the hour Molly and three other girls – a Belgian, a Canadian and a German – climbed into a taxi and headed for South London. As Hannah waved from the pavement a middle-aged man in a dark striped suit with a gleaming white collar over which his neck bulged, came down the steps and got into a chauffeur-driven Rolls which crept softly away after the taxi. The abortionist, thought Hannah, staring after them.

*

At home Sarah had taken an urgent telephone message from Philip. The man from the World Bank was free to come to dinner that night with his wife.

'Daddy's gone to meet him at the hotel. They'll be here about seven. He says we've got to be tidy and respectable and make a good impression.'

'Oh, God!' Hannah had quite forgotten they might be coming.

'Harry's not to swear or muck about. That's what Daddy said.'

'It's Mama that says fuck mostly, it's not me,' said Harry indignantly. Hannah looked at him in surprise. Did she? She had not been aware of it. It seemed . . . out of character. She sat down feeling depressed, dreading the evening. 'Mr Moneybags, that's who he is, the man from outer space.'

Philip likes to invite people at least twice a week, for his work. He hopes this man will give him a research grant for a feasibility study of his lightweight structures for disaster areas. He has some good ideas but he needs money to work out the practical details, make prototypes, test them. Disaster areas. Parsifal Road is a disaster area. Shall I give them scouse? Molly's mother sitting hunched at the table, her eyes running. Nine Malones sitting round the table eating scouse.

'Mama, what's for supper?'

'I got fish fingers for you.'

'We had fish fingers for lunch at school.'

'Oh Lord, did you? I'm sorry. I couldn't know that, could I?'

Harry muttered, 'Fucking fish fingers.'

'Harry!' Sarah looked at her mother.

'It's all right, he's not here yet is he? He hasn't got long-distance ears,' said Harry sourly.

Hannah looked at her watch – five o'clock. No time to do anything elaborate. She must go to the shop and get some pork chops. No. He might not eat pork. Lamb. That was safer.

For the next two hours she worked non-stop. A robot. Sweep the floor of the kitchen-dining room.

'Harry, put away the coats and gumboots.'

Hoover the sitting room. Feed the children. Wash the kitchen table. Prepare the hors d'oeuvres. Peel the potatoes. Make chocolate mousse.

Put out the drinks and glasses. Turn on the central heating. Americans like it seventy-five at least.

A servicing machine. Philip presses the button.

Philip needs this machine for his work. His work's important, everything is subsidiary to it. Mine isn't work. It's occupational therapy. A release of tension that might otherwise clog the machine?

Last year Harry was six:

'Philip, I'd like to get a job.'

'Why? Haven't you enough to do?'

'I'd feel less . . . useless.'

'Useless? What do you mean? You keep the whole thing ticking over. We depend on you, you know that. You help me enormously in my work, entertaining people . . .'

'I want to earn a bit of money . . .'

It's humiliating to depend on someone else for money. Philip likes very careful accounts kept. He goes through them once a month. As soon as he comes home in the evening he turns out what he calls unnecessary lights. Once I fell downstairs in the dark. The switch is at the bottom. I'd been in the lavatory.

He agreed reluctantly to a part-time job. One that wouldn't clash with the children's holidays. Nothing too demanding, nothing that might preoccupy me at the expense of this other primary functioning.

Interlocking networks. Philip creates them. Do they rest on me? He throws the ball in my direction. What if I drop the catch?

Change my clothes. Uniform of hostess-wife. Long embroidered skirt. Silk blouse. Earrings. A touch of scent. Clogs. The current deformity. Philip bought them. He's sensitive to such images. The teacher-counsellor – grey jersey trousers, dark green sweater, sensible, unobtrusive – lies in a crumpled heap on the bedroom floor. No time to hang her up now. Oh Lord, yes, not even the bedroom will be private. Mrs Moneybags might want to touch up her nose. Stuff everything under the pillow.

Harry calls out, 'Come quickly, there's a spider in the bath. He's got a broken leg, I think. He can't walk.'

'I expect he can. Spiders have too many legs anyway. Maybe he's having a rest.'

'Come and see.'

The spider is sodden, half-cooked. I put it onto a piece of lavatory paper on the window sill to dry off.

'Will it be all right?'

'I expect so. It'll probably be gone by the morning.'

Oh God! He still believes whatever I say. I must remember to remove the dead body when I go to bed. Should I protect him like this?

Harry squeezes the sponge onto his belly to make a waterfall, singing in the jolly, high-pitched tone of the commercial jingle:

> *Trebor mints, stick 'em up your bum*
> *And they last a bit longer.*

His voice changes to a husky drawl:

> *Fry's chocolate creams –*
> *Everyone deserves a little piece,*
> *Fry's chocolate creams –*
> *They turn relaxation into an art!*

He slides sensuously under the water. I pull out the plug.

Harry's in his pyjamas, rosy from the bath, Sarah beside him in a long-sleeved nightdress, her black hair brushed into a halo round her head. Perfect children. That's what Philip wants. The front door opens. They run down stairs.

Philip's voice in the hall. 'Hullo, Funny Buttons. Come and meet Morton Fuchsover.'

I must have heard it wrong. He can't be called that.

'Hi, kids!'

Hannah switches off the bedroom light and stands for a moment looking out of the window.

> *I am the astronomer, for me*
> *Light is not sunlight but the light of stars*
> *I watch in darkness. Even moonlight mars*
> *The coruscating brightness that I see.*

When had she thought of that? So long ago, when she was seventeen, standing in her grandmother's garden in Suffolk one night of no moon. Her father's passion, so her grandmother said, had been to study the stars. All she could remember of him was the prickly feeling from his moustache when he kissed her, carrying her in his arms into the dark garden to look at the sky.

Harry stood on the stairs. 'Is your name really Mr F . . .?'

'Yes,' Hannah interrupted quickly, following him down. 'That's right, Harry.'

'Ow!' said Harry. 'Don't poke me.'

'Sorry. I was trying to tuck in your pyjama jacket. Would you like to get some nuts out of the tin to pass round?'

'Hannah, this is Morton Fussinger.'

So that was the name. Thank God he had repeated it.

Mr Fussinger shook hands vigorously. Black hair. Square glasses, an affable, friendly man, eyes cold above his smile. Out of sync, his mouth and his eyes.

'This is Carol.'

The timeless powder-blue suit, skirt just above the knee, crimplene, uncrushable, washable, travelable, fresh white blouse, primrose yellow hair . . . maybe that, too, was crimplene, uncrushable, wash . . .

Philip led the visitors into the sitting-room. 'What'll you have, Carol? Morton?'

'Scotch on the rocks. That's twice. If there's one thing we agree about, it's liquor!'

As Philip went to get the ice, Hannah followed him, shutting the kitchen door behind them.

'Philip, there's a problem.'

'What's that?'

'Molly. She went to have it done this afternoon.'

'I'm delighted to hear it.'

'But they may not keep her in.'

'So? What's that to do with us?'

'I told her mother she could stay here . . . if necessary.'

'For God's sake, Hannah!' He banged the ice-cubes impatiently into the bowl.

'I've got to ring the nursing home. I may have to fetch her tonight.'

'You can't do it now.' He kept his voice low, muffling his irritation.

'I'd much rather you didn't bring these problems home with you. Do we have to have the wretched girl here?'

'It would only be one night. I'm sorry. I didn't know what else to do. Her mother's so afraid of her step-fath . . .'

'You'll have to wait till the Fussingers go. You surely don't mean to walk out in the middle of the meal?'

'No.'

He handed her the empty ice tray. 'Better fill this up. The table looks nice. Is the food ready?'

'All but the chops. I'll put them on now.'

'Sorry,' he said, leaning to kiss her cheek before opening the door. 'But you do see this dinner matters, don't you?'

He went into the other room as Harry was asking, 'Do you know any swear words?'

'Well . . . yes, son, I do know a few words of that sort, I suppose . . .'

With a glance at Philip, Harry cut him short. 'I don't.'

Soon the children went up to bed. Harry took the nuts upstairs with him, calculatedly.

Hannah hovered between the kitchen and the sitting-room, keeping an eye on the grill as she waited for a signal from Philip to serve the meal. He was in no hurry. His visitor liked whisky. Philip put the bottle beside him and after a while he began to help himself. The cat leapt onto his knee, rubbing her head against his chin.

'This is a nice friendly animal. Hey, Carol, why don't we have a nice, cuddlesome animal like this?'

'We've got the craziest dog at home,' said Carol, turning to Hannah. 'She's so sweet and loving.'

'Only to you, she is, not to anyone else.'

'I'll admit she's a bit of a watch dog, but you need one nowadays. It's a real violence-orientated situation back home in the States. We had to put up a fence to keep her in. She sure hates strangers. She gets so mad at them she tries to bite holes in the wire. My, is she cute!'

'That precious dog! Did I tell you, Carol, the day we left Mr Brewis next door phoned me at the office – at the office, note you well, not chez nous, he must've been afraid to get you on the line – to say that if we don't control that dog's barking he's going to have to take out an injunction.'

They were locked in some old ritual, sparring across the drinks table like two gladiators in the arena. Hannah tried to divert them with a dish of olives. Mr Fussinger put out his hand and knocked the bowlful flying all over the floor. He knelt down awkwardly, groping to replace them in the bowl. Thick white fingers, barely divided, like pig's trotters. Hannah bent down beside him, glancing at his wife as she did so. The expression in Carol's eyes was triumphant.

'Shall we eat, Hannah?' Philip was wondering what had gone wrong.

'It's all ready.' She took the garlic bread out of the oven and lit the candles.

Mr Fussinger came stumbling into the kitchen. 'Well, fair lady, where shall I sit?'

How could he gave got drunk so quickly? Hannah pulled out a chair. He swayed slightly, clutching the edge of the table, and collapsed into his seat. Carol paused as she came in behind him, looking at a small reproduction on the wall.

'Is that a Monet?'

'Yes,' said Philip eagerly, 'the beach at Etretat.'

'Isn't it a darling? The colours are unusual – so mellow. I just love Monet passionately.' Her fingers hovered over the print, stroking the air. 'Do you know the Leningrad collection? We were there last fall.'

'It's a fine collection,' said Philip, 'but I always think it's a pity they're so badly hung. The lighting's terrible, didn't you find?'

Had Philip really been to Leningrad, Hannah wondered? Oh yes. After that conference in Moscow. He went on, 'Of course you've got the best ones in New York. I envy you those.'

Carol bared her teeth at him in ecstasy. Gallery buffs. Philip seated her on his right and poured out the wine, the only good bottle they had in the cupboard. She waved aside the garlic bread. 'No carbos. I'm on all-protein.'

Hannah took three pieces. She kept thinking distractedly about Molly. Mr Fussinger toyed with his food. He was preoccupied with the generation gap.

'You're lucky your kids are still young. That's the best time of your lives. The golden years. You don't have the trouble we've got.' His son, Wallace, was a university drop-out, living in a commune, no job. 'I just can't understand that boy.' He swayed towards Philip. 'He's against the establishment.'

44

Carol interrupted, 'No, dear, not the establishment, the system. He's against the system.'

'I said the establishment,' he shouted. 'I meant the establishment.'

Her wine glass was empty, his was still full. She leant across the table and took his glass, replacing it with her own. Not once did she look at Hannah during this transaction. Why are they married, thought Hannah? What horrible necessity keeps them together? A caricature of all warring couples. She felt quite sick, watching them. Wasn't her role as audience part of their satisfaction?

Each course of the meal was a scene in the unfolding drama. Everything Morton said Carol took him up on. Everything she said he contradicted. Unity of time, place and action, Aristotle's classical formula. Morton left his chop untouched. He stubbed out a cigarette in the chocolate mousse. Carol looked at her tiny watch, inset in an elasticated gold bracelet. Ten o'clock. They had an early plane to catch back to the States in the morning, could they ring for a cab?

As soon as they left Hannah hurriedly telephoned the nursing home.

'Oh yes, Mrs Straight. Miss Malone said you'd be phoning. She's all ready to leave.'

'To leave? Then she's not staying the night?'

'She's not booked in. You can call for her at any time.'

'But . . .'

There was a click as the woman put the receiver down.

Molly was sitting impatiently in the hall, her face tense. 'Let's get out of here. This place gives me the horrors. That doctor, he's like Count Dracula.'

'I went to see your mother. She said you'd better spend the night at my house. She's afraid of your step-father asking questions.'

'Friday night? He'll be pissed. He's never back till gone eleven.'

'She seemed . . . frightened.'

They got into the car.

'Was it all right?' asked Hannah. 'Did it hurt?'

Molly shook her head. 'I never felt a thing. They put me right out.' She was silent for a moment and then went on, 'It's funny. The nurse told me I was calling out all through the operation, and the tears were pouring down my cheeks.'

A mile or so further on Molly asked her suddenly to stop the car. She was violently sick on the pavement.

*

The next morning, Saturday, Hannah's children were excited to hear there was someone in the house.

'Can I take her some tea?' asked Sarah.

She carried the cup carefully behind Hannah into the sitting-room. Molly was on the sofa. It was long enough to act as a bed. When Hannah drew the curtains she sat up. She had on a black petticoat, her red hair curling in tangles round her neck.

'Is that your nightdress?' Sarah asked, staring at her.

Molly looked down sleepily at herself. 'I don't know. I wear it in bed sometimes. Could be.'

Harry, leaning against the doorway, said slowly, 'She wears it at night so it's a night dress.'

Sarah went red. 'It's not. It's a petticoat. It's not a proper nightdress.'

Hannah said with embarrassment, 'Do you keep things in separate compartments in your mind, Sarah? Everything in its proper place, ready for its proper usage?'

Harry speculated: 'If we could cut her head open we'd see how it is. I bet she has everything hung up on coat hangers like her cupboard upstairs.'

Sarah said angrily, 'And I bet yours is a filthy mess. Smelly socks, football cards, bits of chewing gum – all stuck together.'

Molly stared from one to the other. 'What are they on about?'

Harry went out to get his breakfast. Sarah, catching Hannah's embarrassment, sat down on the edge of the sofa. 'Please, I didn't mean to be rude. It's just that . . .' She fingered the blanket then went on in a rush, 'I've never seen anyone sleeping in a petticoat before. I think it looks lovely. I'm going to wear one tonight.'

Molly burst out laughing. Her teeth were uneven. 'What a funny kid.'

It was the first time Hannah had seen her laugh. Her face, though pale and exhausted, looked also more child-like that morning. She

46

finished her tea and lay back. The Lady of Shalott this time, floating on the pillows. 'Smashing bed. You won't get me out of this in a hurry.'

Over a late breakfast, Hannah glanced at the back of Philip's *Times*. He had already gone to a meeting. In the 'wanted' column she read: 'Jasper is 4. He needs someone to look after him and his two dogs and his home in Chelsea while his Mummy and Daddy are at work. He's very considerate – own room, colour T.V., nearly every evening off. If you think you would make a good housekeeper and love children (especially Jasper) phone his Mummy after 8 p.m.'

A vision of Molly's mother as she had seen her the day before suddenly burst into her mind – heavily pregnant, her little boy hanging onto her hand with his head bent against her belly, her face stretched into a mixture of horror and relief as Hannah told her about Molly's abortion. Molly had escaped. The bars of Mrs Malone's cage would never open. As Hannah read the advertisement, the sickening clash of Chelsea with Parsifal Road overwhelmed her. She put her head down on the newspaper and began to cry.

*

For the next few weeks she could not shake off her depression. She had been so preoccupied with the need to help Molly before it was too late that she had pushed everything else out of her head. Now the implications obsessed her. The image of the foetus kept coming into her mind, of Molly with the tears streaming down her face, crying out, the nurse had said. She kept telling herself she was not involved. She was merely helping to carry out a decision that was Molly's. But it was no good. She felt degraded. And sad.

She caught glimpses of Molly in the corridor with groups of other girls, confined once more in the ugly green. She was often laughing. Quite carefree, it seemed. Their eyes would meet in a fleeting acknowledgement. It was bizarre, this retreat into being strangers.

One Saturday, just before the holidays, when Philip had already gone to Libya, Molly came round to the house. Sarah discovered her on the doorstep.

'Mama, come quick, it's your friend. She's got a lovely blue dress on.'

In a moment, away from the restrictions of the school, their old relationship returned. How beautiful she was, thought Hannah, how free and inviting.

'I've come to tell you I'm leaving school,' said Molly, 'I'm going out to work. I've got to pay back that money.'

'Who said?'

'Mam. She said hers was a gift but yours was only a loan and I must pay it back.'

Hannah shook her head. 'I'd rather you didn't.' She felt awkward. 'I'd much rather you paid your mother back.'

They were both embarrassed. Hannah tried to go on: 'I mean it, really.' She knew suddenly she could not bear to receive spasmodic payments of a debt she did not think of as one. Each time Molly came with a few pounds in her hand she would feel degraded all over again, her complicity extended month after month into the future. It would destroy any possibility of friendship between them.

'Please,' she took Molly's hand awkwardly, 'I'd rather forget it.'

Molly looked puzzled. Hannah tried to distract her: 'Have you found a job?'

'As a temp, in an office. I've got my typing from school. Mrs Shadgrove wrote a letter for me. I've been for interview. Looks dead boring.'

'Will you stay there all summer?'

'I don't know. Maybe not. That guy I told you about, lives round the corner, he said they might be hitching around France in August, him and some friends, just to see how far they can get. I might go along.'

On an impulse Hannah tore a piece of paper from the kitchen pad. She wrote down the address of the house in Provence. 'We'll be in France. If you get this far come and see us. You never know.'

They smiled at each other. For the last time Hannah forced herself to revert to her old role. 'That surgeon, Count Dracula, did he tell you how to avoid it all happening again?'

'Yeah,' Molly drawled casually, 'told me to take the pill. He gave me a prescription and told me to go to some clinic when I need more. I've got the address.'

Hannah looked questioning.

'Don't worry. I'll go. I don't want all that again, do I?'

'What about your mother?'

'She's had the baby. Another boy. Six pounds. Skinny little bugger. I tried to get her to go to the clinic herself but she won't listen. Says she'd have to tell that Father Casey. It's against the law of God, she says. Says she'd rather trust the Catholic way. I don't know what she's on about but whatever it is, it's not much use to her.'

5

After driving down that endless motorway from Arras to Marseille you cannot stop. You go on driving in your sleep. Your feet press imaginary pedals under the bedclothes, the engine still humming in your ears.

Hannah had never driven so far on her own before but she was determined not to spend more than one night on the way. She pushed on till dark then turned off at a small town where they could find a cheap room. She was almost too exhausted to eat. Later, through the window of the hotel room, she could hear the throbbing of the cicadas. They were already in the south.

They arrived at dusk the next day. The house was just as she remembered. Again that odd feeling of recognition. It was as if she had left it only the day before. She got out of the car and sat on the stone step of the fountain. She felt light-headed. The children, full of bounce after their confinement, ran off to explore.

The oddest thing was the silence. None of the usual noises of the city settling down for the evening that she associated with this hour at home – car doors shutting, engines starting up, voices calling to each other. Just silence apart from the trickling water.

She must have sat there a long time. After a while, from far away, she heard the tinkling of a bell. It came nearer and nearer and then a brown goat came into the square – perhaps the same goat they had seen before – leading three others. The old man, bent over his stick, walked slowly behind. He wished Hannah a good evening and opened his barn. The goats went in. She heard him murmuring roughly to them, the squeal of some other animal – could it be a pig? – then he closed the door and went into his house next door. Quiet again.

She got up at last, feeling the cold stone through her cotton trousers, and walked down to the café. Madame Pinet was obviously expecting her. She must have seen the children. The key was ready on a nail behind the bar.

'I've opened the shutters and put blankets on the beds. You'll find everything in order. Would you like to eat here tonight?'

Soupe, pommes frites and *saucisson*. Hannah was relieved not to have to get it herself. She could think about buying food later.

Next day she saw the vine over the lintel had grown even longer. It reached the door handle. Every time they went in and out it swept across their faces and became trapped in the door.

'You'll have to cut it.' Madame Pinet pulled off a crushed tendril. 'It should have been done in the spring but nobody bothers when a house is empty. I'll ask the old man for his step ladder.'

Hannah found some secateurs wrapped in an oily rag in the kitchen drawer. She balanced on top of the ladder while Harry held it at the bottom. She had never pruned a vine before and she felt nervous of cutting too much. There were footsteps up the alley and she heard a voice below her, speaking English. It sounded amused.

'Don't lean so far out, you may fall.'

Clutching the vine stem, she looked down into a face that struck her first of all as ugly. Sharp bones, fierce black eyes, a little mad. The man had on a pair of faded trunks and a dark blue shirt. His black hair was matted with bits of white dust like plaster. He wore goggles pushed up on top of his head. Had he stepped off a motor bike?

'It's like cutting hair,' he said, 'beautiful green hair. You ought to think about the shape, to cut it like hair, don't you think?' He held the ladder firmly. 'Come down. I'll do it for you. Not much of a landlord, am I?'

Monsieur Marc. Hannah had not thought about him as a person at all, only a landlord. She was startled now to find him such a tangible presence.

'I hope you don't mind. It was getting damaged. Madame Pinet got me the ladder.'

As she climbed down she saw he was hardly taller than her, thick-set. Only his feet bare on the ground were extraordinarily delicate. Straight brown toes in the dust.

'Anything Elaine Pinet suggests is sure to be right. She looks after the house for me. I don't know really what to do with it myself. When she wrote to me in Paris I was glad she'd found a tenant.'

He took the secateurs from her and climbed up to trim the vine. 'Step back a bit to see if it's right. We don't want it to look too naked.' He left the shorter tendrils untouched so they formed a fringe over the doorway. 'All right?'

She nodded. He came down again and carried the ladder back into the barn. Sarah and Harry picked up the fallen shoots, entangled in greenery.

'Give them to Claude's rabbits,' he said, pointing to a shed across the square. 'Now, let's try the door.'

It swung clear and he walked inside. 'Is it all right for you? Have you everything you need?' He spoke with a slight accent but his English was surprisingly fluent.

Hannah answered softly, 'It's perfect.'

She was afraid his presence might break the spell, that it might somehow interrupt her communion with the house to have the owner there. She did not feel he was the owner. He glanced at her sharply as if seeing her for the first time. He had been speaking casually, performing his duties as a landlord, a role in which he had no interest. Now his voice, too, softened as he looked at her.

'You really like this house?' His eyes held hers.

She nodded. 'Very much.' She looked down, embarrassed to show how much she cared about it.

'That's good,' he said slowly, 'my Aunt would have liked that.' He turned his head abruptly as if to shake off some emotion and pulled the goggles down over his eyes. 'I'm in the middle of cutting some stones.'

'Stones?'

'For jewelry. My workshop's down the alley at the back of this house.'

He went outside again. Hannah was glad to be alone. She could continue her slow involvement with the house.

*

It was strange to step into someone else's place, as if Mademoiselle Grant had gone out for a walk and would be back any moment.

Hannah sat at her table and looked out onto the square as she must have sat so many times, learning its human geography.

In the far corner lived the boy called Claude. The father went off every morning by car to work in the market town nearby. His wife was a schoolteacher and, since it was the holidays, she spent a lot of time tending rabbits in an old shed adjoining the house. Harry, invited by Claude, took the vine shoots in there and counted thirty-nine rabbits.

'He was a farmer,' Madame Pinet explained, 'but they couldn't make it pay. They sold most of the land but he didn't want to leave the village. He keeps those rabbits to remind him of the old life but he's had to take a job in the canning factory. They've got two cars now. Of course she's earning too.

'The big farmer on the outskirts of the village, Monsieur Terrain, the one who keeps bees, he's bought up most of the land worth culti-vating. He's moved some of the walls to make fields big enough to grow grain. The rest he's planted with cherry trees for the crystallised fruit business, and lavender. He's nearly as old as *Le Vieux* but he has three sons to work for him and a wife and daughter to keep his home comfortable. They run the farm like a business.'

Would any young man now choose the hard life of the small-holder? Already many of the terraces on the hillside were overgrown, the stone walling that supported them crumbling, the aromatic scrub of the mountainside encroaching nearer and nearer to the village. *Le Vieux*, next door, was the only one who still kept to the old way of life, helped by his son, Georges, a strange, silent man of at least fifty with thick glasses magnifying his squint. Now that Madame Pinet had formally introduced them the old man never failed in his greet-ing. When Hannah told him she liked goats he took her into the barn to see them.

The adults were in one pen. Separated in a much smaller stall were three babies with hardly room to move. She stroked their heads. Through the short fur she could feel the bumps of horns. One of them sucked Harry's finger like a teat.

'Why are they kept away from the mothers?'

She spoke French slowly. She had not yet recaptured her old fluency as a student when she spent every summer in France. The old man rolled his r's so thickly it was hard to understand him. He had to keep them shut up in the small pen, he explained, otherwise they would play about too much and get thin. Then they would not fetch a good price.

In another compartment was the cleanest pig she had ever seen. Through its white bristles she could see the sheen of its skin. There was barely even the smell of a pig coming from the straw on which it stood.

'For the market?'

'No, no. That's for ourselves. For the winter.' He scratched the pig's back with a stick and it grunted with satisfaction.

Outside, above the barn, was a pigeon loft, the front wired so the pigeons could only flutter from perch to perch. The old man looked at them with pride.

'Pretty birds, aren't they? Some for us, some for the market.'

Each day he climbed the wooden steps and swept out the loft. Bird dirt and feathers fluttered down into the square. To this he added the animals' straw, shovelling the whole lot onto a barrow, and wheeled it along the road as far as his vegetable plot.

Watching his careful husbandry, Hannah felt sad. A way of life that must have continued for thousands of years was coming to an end. Had Mademoiselle Grant felt the same?

Her collection of books intrigued Hannah. They were the only clue to her personality. They seemed to be divided roughly into sections – on witchcraft and mythology, some in French, some English. Even more on the history of Provence and associations with that countryside. Caesar's Gallic Wars in Latin with the English translation beside it. Some had slips of paper between the leaves to mark a significant passage. She opened Van Gogh's letters at one of the slips. Letter 603, to his brother Theo:

I'm enclosing a sketch of the cicadas here. In the hours of great heat their song has the same fascination for me as the cricket on the hearth at home. My dear fellow, let us never forget that it is the small emotions that are the captains of our lives and that we obey them without knowing what we do.

*

Standing on the balcony in the dark listening to those same cicadas the whole air hums with different notes. Is song, I wonder, the right word for the sound they make? Some chirp with regular pauses, others burr continually like a door bell. What is it they do with their wings? Vibrate? A musical vibration. They have good vibes. Then there's another note – high, intermittent, much louder. A small owl, probably, out hunting.

Time has stopped. That's the sensation. At least it has for me. Everything a now. It's not just a question of leisure – I've had that before. I've moved into another dimension, as if I was floating under the sea, rocked by the gentle movement of water at my sides.

In London everything is routine. 7.30 the alarm goes. Call Sarah and Harry to get up. Harry's quite often already eating cornflakes in the kitchen. Put the kettle on and pull *The Times* out from behind the curtain that covers the front door. The newsboy only pushes it half way through the letter box so the curtain sticks out as if the door was having a mild erection. Make breakfast and take the paper and a cup of tea up to Philip. He can't wake up without it. The room's fusty. He smokes at night in bed.

7.45 shout at Sarah again to get up. Wash. Get dressed. 8.05. Philip's shaving at the basin in the bathroom. First the right cheek, then the left, then his upper lip. A soft hum from the miniature machine mowing his face. He brushes his teeth vigorously, the movements always the same, leaving spittle all over the mirror. He insists on a clean shirt every day. First the left arm then the right. Downstairs to his breakfast, leaving his pyjamas on the floor, the bed unmade.

Open the window, make the bed, fold the night clothes neatly under the pillows. 8.20.

'Harry, are you dressed?'

The regular morning tension begins to mount, searching for things they must remember to take to school – football boots, library books. Sarah shouts, angrily, from the front door.

'Harry, I'm going without you.'

The front door bangs, once, for her exit.

'Wait, Sarah . . .' Harry wails.

A few seconds later . . . bang . . . for Harry.

Philip's finishing his coffee.

'Are you in for supper?'

The stock question. One he never asks me. He looks up the answer in his diary – yes or no – each page crammed with large, elegant writing. The source book of his life. He consults his watch, it tells the minutes as his diary does the hours. Self-winding. 8.30. Up to the lavatory.

Wash up, wipe over the table, feed the cat. She's miaowing with exaggerated intensity, driven by the precise clock inside her own stomach. Philip shouts goodbye from the door. Bang. From the kitchen window I can see him driving off. Upstairs to clean my teeth. First the left side then the right. Always the same movement. Shut the bedroom window, collect the things I need for school and leave the house. Bang.

Do we really need to be awake to follow these well-worn, daily tracks of our lives?

*

In the village at first the children were mildly bored. Gradually they began to expand into the space around them, like small animals that venture every day into territory a little farther from home.

Sarah started to make a map. Initially it showed only streets, a rough marking out of the terrain. Then houses began to be sketched in with the names of their owners. Far more important to Harry than the people were the animals. Sarah agreed, reluctantly, to include them. They would give the map to Philip, when he came, so he would know everything about the village the moment he arrived.

Hannah wondered when he would. He wrote, briefly, from Libya. They were working against time to get the plans ready, he said. He was not sure if he would be able to get away.

Hannah's initial regret at the moment of finding the house, that Philip would not be there with them, had faded. She felt all the time on the edge of some new discovery. The lack of pressure in her days seemed to release a new dimension of awareness.

She went up the Roman road with Harry in the early morning. Sarah was still asleep. At least the villagers said it was Roman, the shortest way over the mountain towards Aix – Aquae Sextiae – paved with flat stones set on end in the Roman style like a wall built into the ground. Some were loose. Grass and mosses had sprouted in the crevices but wherever they scraped away the soil they could see the stones laid elegantly side by side.

On the left a stony bank followed the track with ferns growing out of it. Snails were creeping along the damp leaves. The spiders' webs glittered with dew, more brilliant than any jewels, some as much as a foot across. And the spider at one side like a golden basilisk. Harry blew one of the webs to see what would happen. The spider rocked threateningly then hurried across to find out if he had trapped some insect in the sticky threads.

They rested on two flat rocks to look down on the village, curved like an ear in the hollow of the hillside. Carved out of stone. From this height they could see four other villages perched on the hills in the distance. A civilisation of village fortresses, of dry stone walls, stone houses. The austerity of the landscape made each flower miraculous. By the side of the track they found a huge, yellow-green thistle, sprouting seemingly out of the rock, low on the ground like a pale, dried sunflower. There was one hanging above Madame Pinet's bar. Very difficult to pick, she said, you needed leather gloves and a sharp knife. But once gathered it would last a year or longer.

As they came down again, they could see from a distance old Monsieur Terrain taking out his sheep. How many of them? They could not count. The sheep were perfectly camouflaged against the corn stubble, only the sound of their bells gave them away and their lowing, scattering movement as they crossed the field. There were two dark forms among them, one a young goat, the other a dog running low towards the flock then back to his master.

I want to relate the moments as they pass as if, by doing so, I'll discover their significance. Images, resonant with some hidden meaning. Or perhaps none – just images?

Generally the village is quiet. The only sounds are murmurs from the pigeons floating up to the balcony where I sit reading, or the four goats bleating as they return from their morning walk. I'm aware that although my own rituals have been suspended there are as powerful ones ordering my old neighbour's life.

Early in the morning, drowsy in my bed, I hear the sound of his first call of the day – the flushing of the public lavatory. Then he goes back into his house. At about seven he leads the goats out for their walk, hooves tapping on the roadway. At eight, their first grazing over, he comes back for his own breakfast. Then, in the late afternoon around six when the air is cool and often a slight breeze blowing, it's time for their evening walk. The bell is rough but musical, stopping whenever the leading goat stops to eat, then jangling again as she trots forward. Movement reflected in sound.

The fidelity of the old man's routine touches me profoundly. Why do I find his noble, my own so lifeless?

He is what he does.

Hannah isn't.

Alienated almost to the point of extinction. A sleep-walker.

I'm looking at her through the wrong end of a telescope, very far away and tiny. She moves without seeing where she's going.

On the church roof opposite small birds gather in rows. Their aerial skill is dazzling as they swoop and turn round the grey stone arch of the church. House martins. Or are they swallows? I can't see their tails precisely. One perches on the wrought iron cross and preens himself. Still not near enough. Then one bird glides in silhouette against a white cloud. A perfect outline. Definitely a house martin. The certainty delights me. But why does it matter? The flight is just as beautiful either way. The human passion for naming – like Harry and Sarah in their inventory of the village. It even shows in the Christian's idea of the creator:

And God called the dry land Earth; and the gathering together of the waters called he Seas . . .

immediately propelling Adam into the same game:

Out of the ground the Lord God formed every beast of the field and every fowl of the air; and brought them unto Adam to see what he would call them; and whatsoever Adam called every living creature, that was the name thereof.

Perched on this terrace so high above the square I have this God-like view all around me. Naming. Naming of birds. Naming of Hannah. Zombie.

Suddenly there was the wail of a child's crying. Claude came

58

sobbing across the square. He opened his front door and slammed it back against the wall. Then his father's angry voice, shouting from the garden by the house, trying to control his son's wild emotion from a distance. The sobs continued. He shouted again. They died down, hesitated and stopped.

Hannah's body went rigid at this display of so much violent emotion. She became aware of it after the sobs stopped. Her breath came out in a great sigh as she rubbed the back of her taut neck with one hand.

She did not like Claude. He killed the bees that came to drink at the shallow *bassin* in his father's garden. He whacked at them with a stick, then flicked their shattered bodies onto the ground. Perhaps one had stung him. Her sympathy was with the bee, yet Claude's anguish moved her deeply. An image. Her detachment, she realised, was the merest illusion. Not God-like at all.

The sun had reached the balcony fully. It made her sleepy. She pulled a blanket and pillow off the bed and spread them out on the terrace. If she lay down she would be invisible from the windows nearby. She took off her clothes and stretched out in the warm sun, her body sopping up the sunlight like soft, absorbent stone. Danaae in her tower. Trickles of sweat began to slide down her skin.

Suddenly, she was startled by a slight noise on the roof tiles. Her eyes flew open. There crouched on the parapet of the balcony was her landlord. His eyes looked directly into hers. She shut them instantly, transfixed where she lay, truly turned to stone. How long had he been there? She had nothing to cover herself with. In any case it would be prurient. She felt totally exposed. He had been watching her without her knowing, the enemy who creeps up unawares and takes his prisoner sleeping. Perhaps if she kept her eyes shut he would disappear. Thaw and resolve himself into a dew.

The sun burnt down onto her lids, filling her inner world with a scarlet light. She heard a light thud as he jumped down onto the balcony. Her breathing was minimal as she strained to catch every sound that would tell her what was happening. She could not open her eyes – like a child who shuts her eyes in a game of hide and seek convinced that no one then can see her. As idiotic as that. But she could not open them. She felt a touch on her right nipple. Moist. His tongue licking her gently. He must be kneeling. Delicious. She kept quite still. His tongue moved over her breast then down across her

59

belly to her navel where it probed delicately. She put her right hand on his head to stroke his hair. Rough, like a dog's. Her fingers travelled round his ear, massaging the lobe. He began to slide upwards over her body, mouthing his way over her skin leaving a wet track like a snail's behind him. She was shivering. He reached her face where his mouth crept softly over hers hovering like a hawk moth with barely perceptible vibration of wings, then settled to extract the last drop of nectar.

Half an hour later Hannah still had not opened her eyes. If she did the dream would be broken and she would have to face a reality in which she did not know how to behave. She was lying next to a total stranger. A man she had spoken to once – glimpsed a few more times crossing the square. Their sweat mingled to form a damp patch on the blanket. One of his arms still rested across her belly, his face close to hers. She could hear his slow breathing by her left ear and feel cooling draughts from his nostrils on her cheek. Perhaps he was asleep. She half opened her left eye and peeped through a shaking curtain of lashes. Both his eyes were open – so dark as to be almost black. He was smiling at her. She opened her eyes fully. She felt herself smiling all over her body from her toes to her eyebrows. Were her eyes as shining as his?

One of them had to say something. Without moving she murmured, 'Do you come here often?'

He burst out laughing, rolling onto his back. He sat up, turned to look at her, and started laughing again. She smiled up at him. He stroked her hair back onto the pillow. 'I used to come here a lot, when my aunt was alive.'

She looked at him in some surprise. He began to laugh again. 'No. Not what you're thinking. Not . . .' he waved his arm over her body, 'not like this. My aunt was fifty-five. I loved her very much. More than my own mother. When I was staying in the village I always had coffee with her. In the summer she usually brought it up here. My roof terrace is just over the tiles. It's much quicker to come this way rather than use the stairs.'

He stopped speaking, looking at her hesitantly, then went on, 'I was . . . curious. I kept wondering what was happening in the house, if you had your coffee on the terrace like her. The house has been empty since she died last year. It's . . . strange to have someone in it again.'

He frowned and his thumb pressed into her shoulder, massaging the top of the bone. 'I had to climb over. I almost thought I might find her sitting here. I couldn't help myself.' He looked down at her. 'Do you mind?'

She shook her head. She could not mind anything about him. She was totally intrigued. By the savagery of a face that softened only when he smiled. By the smooth brown skin of his body, pale round his thighs, the area covered by the shorts he habitually wore.

'Mama . . . where are you?' Sarah's voice soared upwards from the square. He got up and pulled the shorts on, then jumped lightly onto the parapet and disappeared over the tiles.

Sarah and Harry had found a dog. An extra one, unaccountable in the register of village dogs. She did not belong to anyone.

'She's a stray,' said Harry. 'She must be. No one owns her. We asked all round.'

'Madame Pinet calls her Bi-Biche. She feeds her,' added Sarah.

It was a mystery how the children managed to communicate so well with Madame Pinet. Sometimes they ran to Hannah to ask the French word for something and then hurried off muttering under their breath for fear they should lose it before reaching the person it was destined for. Madame Pinet played Dumb Crambo with them. She stuffed imaginary food into her mouth to ask if they wanted something to eat. Folded her hands neatly beside her head to signify bedtime.

Bi-Biche was medium size with dusty, black fur, and pleading eyes. She jumped up to rest two scratchy paws on Hannah's belly.

'Do you like her?' asked Harry anxiously.

'She's lovely.'

'Can we look after her then?'

'I don't see why not.'

She found plenty of occasions to bend down and run her fingers through the dog's fur. It's roughness delighted her.

6

Late that night Hannah lay in bed wondering what had happened to her. Had anything? She felt in a dream-like state, intensely conscious of everything going on around her and responsive to it.

What was she doing lying here alone in a small white bed in a place where she had no connections, dropped like a pebble into the sea? And where was Philip? Lying alone in another bed somewhere in Libya? Perhaps not alone. She felt completely detached from him.

What was there between them? For the time being she could not make a connection. She forced herself to imagine the house in London, herself and Philip lying side by side, the blind down. Two bodies in a bed. In other rooms children, the fruit of those bodies. What linked them all together if not feeling? And the feeling in her seemed to have got blocked up as if the small necessities of daily living were gradually choking her. A drain through which the household rubbish had to pass. Was that why Philip avoided the domestic so skilfully? The two bodies turned to each other in the darkened room and caressed each other. They clung together, affirming each other's presence, then lay back again. Often they were too tired even for that. There was no deep release of emotion. That came, if it did, unpredictably. Like the first time she had stood on the balcony here when affection for Philip had suddenly touched her.

Something had indeed happened but its origin was mysterious. It was not the physical experience of the day, her surrender to something totally unexpected and sensual. That had happened, but only because she was in a state to receive it. It could not have happened a week earlier in London. No. It was something to do with the landscape, something to do with the house, something to do with the total change from her ordinary circumstances. And that was why everything, the house martins, Claude crying, the goat bell, seemed o matter so much. She was tuning in, like the cicadas, to something both inside and outside herself. Listening once more to their vibrations, she drifted into sleep.

The next day after breakfast she was restless. She wondered if she would see Marc. How should she prepare herself for their next meeting?

The children caught her mood of restlessness. Sunday. No different, on holiday, from any other day. But there were small differences in the village. Claude's father was sweeping out the rabbit shed, whistling a tuneless noise as he did so, very content. For *Le Vieux*'s son, Georges, it seemed to be washing day. Round his waist he wore a makeshift apron of thick, pink plastic tied with string. The plastic had green writing on it – part of an old bag of fertiliser. He washed silently, rubbing the clothes up and down on the stone edge of the *lavoir* next to the public lavatory at the corner of the square. Then he squeezed them out and took them to the trees behind the church where a line was suspended.

Le Vieux, watching from the doorway of the barn, followed him towards the trees and held out the clothes pegs as Georges pinned up the washing – four shirts, two pairs of trousers, a faded blue jacket. The jacket was neatly repaired in several places. Who, Hannah wondered, stitches those meticulous patches? In honour of Sunday, *Le Vieux* was wearing a clean shirt with a small spotted handkerchief knotted round his thin neck. She remembered similar cravats round the necks of old men in the East End of London.

Sarah tugged at her hand.

'Let's go out. Let's go somewhere today.'

'What sort of somewhere?'

'Swimming, couldn't we go swimming? It's so hot.' It was. When you stepped into the square you felt the presence of the sunlight immediately, baking the stones. There was a public swimming pool down the valley on the way to the market town. They had stopped there earlier in the week after a shopping expedition.

'All right. We'll go swimming.'

She looked regretfully down the alley, still half hoping to see Marc. No sign of him. Only Bi-Biche lying in the shade outside his door. They got in the car and started the long descent to the valley. Hannah could never imagine getting tired of that view. The difficulty was to keep her eye on the road. Suddenly there was a bumping noise and the car seemed to be moving unevenly on one side. She stopped and got out. The back tyre was completely flat.

'Oh Lord! We've got a puncture.'

She stood looking helplessly at the wheel.

'Do you know how to mend it?' asked Harry. 'I'll help you.'

'I'm not sure. Philip always does it.'

She found what she supposed must be the jack and examined it. She could not make out which way up it was supposed to go. Where should she fix it? As she squatted peering under the boot, she heard the sound of a car. She stepped half into the road holding the jack in her hand. An old *Deux Chevaux* came round the corner and stopped beside them. Out jumped a woman in grey, linen trousers.

'You are from G.B.? English? On holiday?'

She fired her questions with a strong accent making English sound a violent, unpredictable language.

'You have troubles?'

'I'm afraid it's a puncture.'

'I arrange it.' She smiled delightedly. 'Leave all to me.'

'You mean you know how to change the wheel?'

'Naturellement. I am very ... *mécanicien*. All machines ... they love me, I love them.'

She seized the jack from Hannah, and fitted one end into a groove at the side of the car. As she jerked it up and down the wheel lifted. Harry craned out of the window, full of admiration. From then on it was easy. When the nuts resisted her she gave them a masterful tap with the spanner.

With the spare wheel snugly in position she straightened up and pushed wings of grey hair back from her forehead revealing clear grey eyes, unnaturally bright.

'*Voilà! C'est fini.*' She wiped her hands on a silk handkerchief and held the right one out to Hannah. 'Madame Corneille.'

'I'm Hannah Straight. You've been wonderfully kind. I don't know how to thank you.'

'You come to my house for coffee? Yes?'

Since this seemed to be the answer to how they could thank her Hannah agreed.

The 2CV led off down a sandy track to a stone farm house. A small fox terrier came yapping to meet them.

'My little Fox. *Chien de pure race.* An English breed, isn't it?' Madame Corneille cuddled the struggling dog to her grey hair. 'Very nervous, aren't you, Fox? An aristocrat.'

Her house was cool.

'Do you like old furniture? That is my passion. I am a dealer in *antiquités.*'

She opened the shutters. In the middle of the room was a huge table and spread out on it, half completed, the largest jig-saw puzzle Hannah had ever seen. Harry picked up one of the pieces.

'No, no.' Madame Corneille flew towards him in agitation. 'Not to touch!'

He dropped the piece as if it had stung him.

'Too difficult for children. Very, very difficult. All the pieces are specially disposed. They must not be touched.' She pushed Harry towards the door. 'Go outside, children, outside in the garden. This is not the house for children. Too much precious things.' She shooed them out, her movements sharp and peremptory, like a bird of prey, then turned, smiling, to Hannah.

'You will take coffee? An apéritif?' She drew forward a chair and patted its cushioned interior invitingly. 'Sit down, Madame Straight. You had a shock from the car accident.'

Hannah sat down, surprised. She had no sense of shock, only amusement.

As she poured the coffee Madame Corneille let off a barrage of questions, like staccato bursts from a gun, barely leaving space for Hannah's replies before coming in with the next round. Where was she staying? Did she have a husband? Where was her husband? Again her clear eyes looked straight into Hannah's. Hannah veiled hers and looked to one side. She felt faintly embarrassed. Madame Corneille put her hand lightly on Hannah's knee.

'I will present you all the pleasures of Provence, I will guide you in her hidden mysteries.'

Hannah stood up abruptly, knocking over the coffee cup.

Madame Corneille flew to retrieve it. 'Sèvres. The handle is broken. *Quelle catastrophe!*'

Through the window Hannah could see Sarah's grimacing face

mouthing at her, hands beckoning in agitation. Hannah seized on it
'I'm so sorry about the cup. I'm really very sorry. I think I'd bette
go. The children want something.'

She edged towards the door. Madame Corneille recovered hersel
enough to put out a detaining hand. 'Never mind. I can repair it
Must you go so soon? I will come and visit you in the village. Made
moiselle Grant was an old friend of mine. We will explore together
. . .'

Her voice followed Hannah outside. Harry was in tears.

'Harry! Whatever's wrong?'

Harry cried louder, screwing up his face in agony. Sarah pointed
to the middle of the courtyard where a huge earthenware pot lay
shattered on the ground. 'Harry broke it.'

Madame Corneille was transfixed. Her eyes flashed at Harry as i
she would shatter him to pieces, then she darted towards the po
moaning.

'How on earth did it happen, Harry?' asked Hannah. 'What wer
you doing?'

Harry still could not speak. Sarah said, 'We were playing hide an
seek. Harry hid in the pot – you know, like Ali Baba . . .'

'How could you be so stupid?' Hannah asked angrily.

Madame Corneille was trying to fit the pieces together. 'It is irre
parable. Children are my enemies. They break everything.'

Hannah tried again to apologise. She offered to buy a new pot
No, said Madame Corneille, it was an antique olive jar. She woul
never find another. Hannah took the children's hands and led then
to the car as Madame Corneille stared after them with horror i
her eyes. She said no more about coming to visit Hannah in the village

Half way down the hill Harry's tears had dried up completely.

'Are you very cross, Mama?' he murmured.

'It was an idiotic thing to do,' said Hannah. 'What possessed you?

'It looked such a good hiding place. I was trying to jump inside bu
when I climbed onto the rim it just fell to pieces,' Harry explaine
sadly.

'I told him to cry,' said Sarah.

'What do you mean, you told him to cry?'

'I thought if Harry looked very upset that French lady might no
get too angry. And you wouldn't be so cross.'

66

'But he was really crying.'

'Oh yes. Once he started he couldn't stop.'

'I wasn't too cross, was I?'

'No.'

'I couldn't be. I'd just broken one of her cups myself.'

Harry brightened up immediately. 'You did? You broke a cup?'

'Yes. I knocked it over.'

He could hardly believe it. 'How awful.' He smiled broadly at his mother.

Hannah began to laugh. 'It was. Awful.'

'Awful. We're awful.' Sarah took up the theme.

'Awful . . . awful . . . awful,' they chanted loudly as the car followed the road downhill into the town.

After they had left the wheel at the garage they went to the swimming pool. It refreshed them. They ate fresh bread and ham in the shade of the trees, sunbathed, swam again and returned lazily to the village in the late afternoon.

Marc was sitting in the fountain, naked except for his shorts, his feet resting at the bottom of the basin, his head held sideways to catch the trickle from a stone fish. The water made dark rivulets through his dusty hair. Harry rushed out of the car to join him. Hannah got out more slowly, carrying the shopping and the wet towels. She felt shy. Marc smiled at them. He showed no embarassment.

'You've been swimming?'

She nodded.

'I wish I'd been with you. I've been soldering. It was so hot I couldn't bear it any longer. I'm trying to cool off.'

Harry stuck his thumb into the fish's mouth and squirted a fine spray over Marc's face and shoulders.

Marc laughed. 'Wonderful. I'll hire you to do that!'

'We had a puncture,' said Hannah, watching them.

'A puncture? Where?'

'On the road to Saint Jacques.'

'Did you manage all right?'

Hannah shook her head. 'No, I was no good at it. But we got some help.'

'Who from?'

'A Madame Corneille. Do you know her?'

'La Corneille? She changed the wheel for you?'

'That's right. And invited us for coffee.'

Marc sang softly as he splashed his feet:

> *'Will you come into my parlour?'*
> *Said the spider to the fly.*
> *'It's the prettiest little parlour*
> *That ever you did spy.'*

'It was. Very pretty. Only not exactly to my taste. I broke a cup.'

'She must have loved that.'

'It was self-defence.'

Marc laughed, shaking the water out of his hair. 'Madame Corneille's garden is fertilised with the remains of young women. You were lucky to get out intact.'

'What do you mean?' asked Sarah anxiously.

Marc jumped out of the fountain and pranced after her, his voice a shrill falsetto. 'She's a vampire. She entices them into her parlour and sucks their blood.'

Sarah screamed and ran into the house. Harry shouted with pleasure. Laughing, Hannah said, 'She was going to show me all the mysteries of Provence. But I don't think she will, somehow. Harry broke her antique pot.'

'Congratulations.' Marc shook him by the hand, 'My felicitations.'

'She said she knew your aunt.'

'She did. My aunt was well above the danger age. She used to go with her to sales of old furniture. La Corneille can't be faulted on that. She knows everything about restoring wood. And she admired my aunt because she was English.'

'English? Your aunt?'

'Yes. La Corneille's crazy about everything English. Smokes Players. Did you see her bloody dog?'

Hannah nodded. She was thinking about what he had just said. 'I didn't know Mademoiselle Grant was English. I hadn't seen her name written down. I thought it was Grand – something like that.'

'Yes. English.' He looked at her. 'Like you.'

He swung Harry down out of the fountain. As he bent to put him gently on the ground his faded shorts slipped down at the back a little way and Hannah could see the sharp dividing line where his skin turned from brown to white. She felt her body imperceptibly curve towards his as if she had no control over it. Avoiding his eyes, she forced herself to turn towards the house.

On the ground by the front door she noticed a circle of small stones carefully arranged with a line dividing them, a meticulous design. Some child, she thought, making patterns in the dust. Her foot dislodged them as she walked into the house.

*

Around nine-thirty there was a knock. The children had gone to bed. When she opened the door Marc walked in, his arms full of papers, loose-leaf files, small notebooks. They reached to his chin. Bi-Biche slipped in behind him.

'My aunt's papers,' he said. 'I've brought them for you to look at.' He walked into the living room and dumped them on the table.

'What are they?'

'Notes mostly. She'd been collecting stuff for years – anything to do with this region. She read everything. She talked to everyone. Maybe a kind of oral history? I don't know. Perhaps she didn't. It was just a passion – something she couldn't help doing. She spent hours with *Le Vieux*, my grandfather.'

Hannah sat down in bewilderment. She could not get this network straight.

'*Le Vieux?* He's your grandfather?'

'Yes. I thought Elaine Pinet would have told you.'

How odd there should be a connection between this savage young man and her frail old neighbour.

'You don't know anything about us, then, about my family?'

Hannah shook her head. 'No. Nothing.'

'For once Elaine seems to have been unusually discreet.'

He sat down on the couch. Since he had come into the room Hannah had been trembling. It was as if the air all around him was charged with some force that sent little ripples of shock towards her.

69

He was not wearing shorts but a pair of old jeans and a worn blue jacket over his shirt. His hair was still standing on end. Perhaps he never combed it. He began talking.

'Helen Grant and my mother were twins. Identical. It's not true they were completely English. Their grandmother was French and they spent every summer with her. After France fell in 1940 they offered their services to the resistance from England – a useful combination, twins who could speak perfect French. Unless you knew them very well you couldn't tell them apart. Or so people tell me. Of course I could. They smelt different, for one thing. That's what I remember first . . . their different smell . . .'

He seemed almost to have lost the thread of his story. Bi-Biche jumped up onto his lap and sat there, very upright, her furry cheek pressed against his, her paw on his sleeve. He put his arms round her.

'They were dropped near Lyons. They had identical papers and a job in a factory. One job between them. That was the point – a perfect alibi. They took it in turns to go to work. That left the other free to go on night jobs or liaison work and sleep all day if she was tired.

'My father was in charge of one of the resistance groups nearby. That's how they met. No one knew there were two of them. The idea was that if one was caught, the other could carry on. Even the people working closely with them didn't know. Safer that way. Any information had a way of leaking out.

'It worked. No one suspected anything odd. Except, after a while, my father. He knew them . . . in a different way. He was their lover.'

Hannah could not stop staring at him.

He went on: 'It must have been extraordinary – gradually finding out the person he loved was not one person but two. The different smell. That must have puzzled him. Finding out he loved two people. Because that's what happened. They both fell in love with him. It was war time. They couldn't worry about the ramifications. They just had to live with it. Keeping alive was the main thing. The three of them were never together at the same time. My father didn't have to choose between them.

'Then the war ended. Everything was different.'

'How do you know all this?' asked Hannah. 'Did your mother tell you?'

'No. My aunt. My mother never speaks about it. I'm not very close to her. I suppose what happened was inevitable, like a Greek drama – the chain of events that cannot be stopped.' He paused. My mother got pregnant.'

'On purpose?'

'Who knows? My aunt thought so. They were identical twins but very different in temperament. My mother's much more impatient. She can't wait if she wants something. She has to go out and get it. She may have pushed things to a crisis because she couldn't stand the strain. I don't know.'

He shrugged. 'Anyway, my aunt withdrew. She went back to Croydon where their parents lived. My father married my mother. What else could he do? They came to live here.

'Four months later he was killed. A head-on collision on his motor-cycle. It was six weeks before I was born. My aunt thought . . .' he paused and stroked the dog roughly against the lie of the fur, '. . . it wasn't an accident. Not that he meant to do it, consciously. But he couldn't stand the division in himself. He had to find a solution. There wasn't one.

'The odd thing is he'd made a will. I think that's what made her reach the conclusion she did. He'd left this house to her and the one next door to my mother. His mother had left them both to him when she died during the war. Georges will get the farm from *Le Vieux*. Why would he have made a will? It's an odd thing for a young man.'

'Have you made one?'

'Of course not. That's what I mean. My mother went back to Croydon and I was born in England. Technically, I was British. I had dual nationality. Later, I chose French. My mother never liked it here. She came sometimes for holidays but she always felt . . . I don't know . . . uncomfortable. My aunt loved it. After a few years she came to live here all the time. She earned money by translating and teaching English. She couldn't stand Croydon. My mother married another Frenchman and went to live in Paris. She's divorced now but she still lives there with my half-sister, Janine.

'I was brought up between them, my aunt and my mother. Very convenient for my mother, having someone to leave me with. Especially when she married again. I was some kind of pendulum swinging between them; I knew I mustn't fall to one side or the other but go on swinging. *Perpetuum mobile*. I could never let go, quite. I had to be on guard. Against what I . . . don't know.'

'A child is often that – the pendulum. But usually between a husband and a wife.'

'Don't forget they were identical twins. That goes very deep. But they couldn't trust each other. The trust had gone. My mother never comes here now. Since my aunt's death. I think she's relieved not to have to.'

He looked puzzled, as if he still had not unravelled the meaning of the story. And vulnerable, as he sat, very upright in the chair, his arms still clasped round the dog. Hannah wanted to put out her hand and touch him, but she could not. It might have been an intrusion.

She touched the notebooks on the table instead. 'Can I keep them for a while?'

He looked past her, thinking about something else.

'The notebooks,' she leant forward slightly. 'Can I keep them?'

His eyes focussed on her. 'As long as you want. Perhaps you can tell me what to do with them. I don't like to throw them away. I'd like your help.'

Hannah was intrigued. It was the kind of exploration she would enjoy.

As he was going out of the front door he said, 'They're buried in the cemetery.'

'Who?'

'My father and Helen.'

The cemetery is enclosed by a high stone wall. Small ferns and creeping plants grow out of the crevices. There's a heavy, wrought-iron gate that creaks as you push it open. A very small cemetery, like a room furnished with headstones. At the far end, two imposing family vaults for *La Famille Terrain* and *La Famille Pinet*. Madame Pinet's husband must be in there. The other memorials are humble – carved angels, crosses festooned with intricate black beadwork in the shape of flower and leaf patterns. The wire that holds the beads together has rusted so the beads dangle out of shape, shedding small glass droplets onto the ground.

Helen Grant's gravestone is the most recent. The earth looks freshly raked and the weeds haven't yet had time to spread. A stone of plain, pale marble, just her name and the dates of her birth and death.

The plot next to it is marked with an iron cross. In the centre a photograph. The face is so like Marc's that I drew back in shock, then forced myself to look again. Marc, but older. The same black hair only short and well smoothed down, the same eyes, the same full mouth, but less savage-looking, more in control, sadder. On a plaque at the base the name:

'*André Bonnieux, fils bien-aimé de Marie et Henri Bonnieux, 1919– 1948. Avec Dieu dans le repos éternel.*'

A bush of rosemary is planted on the grave, grown so big and rambling it covers the whole surface. A bee buzzes among the tiny blue flowers.

7

Next day Hannah sat down to examine the notebooks. Clear, sloping hand-writing. She could read it easily. On the cover of each book a name – one for Madame Corneille, another for Elaine Pinet. Three marked 'Henri Bonnieux' – *Le Vieux*. Hannah opened one with some curiosity – it seemed to be a record of conversations. One, dated 'March 16, 1952', started:

'Henri wants to talk but doesn't know how far to trust me. He learnt all he knows from his wife Marie. She was a folk healer. I've seen the bunch of herbs hanging over the doorway. He helped her Can't pass the knowledge on to Georges – he's too "*dérangé*"; Marc too young, no longer "*dans la tradition*". The Lycée's seen to that

I'm patient. His wife was the same. Some women have the power to wait. Must reassure him my interest is only a scholar's Does he think I'm going to set myself up as a rival? Show him books I'm collecting on history of region. How far does the tradition reach back? See Theodor Mommsen's "History of Rome" Vol. I on the Roman Provinces, more particularly Provincia or Provence, on the type of religion the Romans found:

"It would be vain labour to seek to give any conception of the internal character of the Druidic doctrine, strangely composed of speculation and imagination ... The power of speech was symbolically represented in a bald-headed, wrinkled, sunburnt old man who carried club and bow, and from whose perforated tongue fine golden chains run to the ears of the man that follows him."

Le Vieux, thought Hannah with a sense of shock.

' "There is a continuous traffic in secret remedies and charms, in which priests played at the same time the part of physicians and in which, alongside of the conjuring and the blessing, human

74

sacrifice occurred, and the healing of the sick by the flesh of those thus slain." '

Hannah shivered and closed the book. As she went outside to get some sunlight she noticed again the same symmetrical circle of stones on the ground. This time an arrow pointed out of the circle towards the house. She called to Harry who was arranging a dirt-track for model cars on the far side of the fountain.

'Harry, did you make this pattern?'

He came over and looked down. 'No. Nice, isn't it?'

'It must be Claude.' She crouched to touch the smooth white stones with her fingers. Something inviting about them. She changed them into an arrow pointing away from the house.

Suddenly she was aware of someone watching her. Georges, half-hidden in the doorway of the barn. When she looked up he quickly withdrew inside with a muttered greeting. She had never exchanged more than a '*Bonjour*' with him.

She went to the door of the barn. '*Monsieur Georges?*'

In the half-darkness of the interior she could not see his face properly. He stood silently waiting to know what she wanted. She had a sense of his being afraid. An animal fear. She asked if they had any goat cheese for sale. She would like to buy one. Shuffling sideways with his back to the wall, he came out of the barn and opened the door to his house. Looking up, Hannah's eye caught the bunch of dried herbs above the door. She imagined a faint, balmy smell coming from them as she crossed the threshold.

Le Vieux was sitting at the table cutting up beans with a short knife. He gave Hannah his usual childlike smile. No teeth. When he smiled, his face folded into a deep crease.

'*Entrez, entrez.*' Pink gums like a baby's. If you put your finger against them, thought Hannah, they would be hard. Good for grinding up food.

The room was bare and comfortless. A wood range in one corner, the table at which he was sitting, a sideboard with an ancient radio on it.

'*Asseyez-vous.*'

She sat at the table. Georges said, his face turned away, 'She wants to buy some cheese.'

75

Le Vieux shuffled out to the back. He was wearing his usual rope-soled slippers. When he came back with the cheese he had a bottle in the other hand. 'You'll take a drink with us?' he enquired politely.

Hannah hesitated. She felt them watching her, waiting for her reply. It would be rude to refuse. She nodded. 'Thank you.'

Strange to know so much about him from her morning's reading. She looked round the room for signs of his dead wife, Marie. Nothing of a woman about the place. Everything clean but austere, the room functional, a space for living in the simplest possible way. The pig lying in her fresh straw enjoyed more luxury than these two ageing men.

Georges stood by the table, his eyes down. *Le Vieux* fetched three glasses from the sideboard and uncorked the bottle. The liquid he poured out was a dull, deep red. He passed her the fullest glass. 'Drink it. We make it ourselves. *A votre santé.*'

They lifted their glasses. Hannah's tongue recoiled from the drink. Thick and bitter tasting. She wanted to spit it out. A strange kind of wine, more like medicine. Some indefinable, herbal flavour. She put her head back and gulped it down, resisting the temptation to hold her nose. Georges was watching her sideways. There was sweat on his forehead as he smiled at her for the first time. His glasses magnified his eyes to such an extent it was hard to tell where they were looking. Through her? Past her? Like fishes swimming in a glass bowl. She took the cheese.

'I'll bring the money when I return the dish later on.'

'No hurry, no hurry.' The old man opened the door for her, so bent he seemed to be bowing. '*Bon appétit.*'

Marc was standing in front of her house looking at the white stones. 'Is this your doing?' he asked. 'I've been trying to decipher it. I took it to mean you'd gone out in the direction of the mountain.'

'I found them there. Someone had arranged them in a circle. I made a different pattern.'

He sniffed at the cheese. 'Smells good. My grandfather's a genius at goat cheese.'

'It's the first time I've been into his house.'

'Was Georges there?'

She nodded.

'He must be terrified of you. Did they give you something to drink?'

76

Hannah looked surprised. 'Yes, they did. A funny kind of red wine.'

'Tasting like cat's pee?'

She laughed. 'Well . . . rather. Very bitter.'

'You're all right, then. Nothing to worry about.'

'What do you mean?'

'You're safe. You can't do them any harm.'

'Harm? What d'you mean? I wouldn't want to.'

'They don't know that. Specially Georges. Dangerous foreign witch living next door. He thinks all women are witches. They have unknown powers. That's why they gave you the drink. A potion to make you harmless. Some foul herbal muck.'

'What's in it? Will it make me ill?'

'I shouldn't think so. Just wine and a herb infusion. Maybe a bit of pig's piss.' Marc started laughing at the expression on her face. He bent down and picked up the stones. 'Did you say these were arranged in some special way?'

'Yes. A circle with a line through it.'

'More of Georges' tricks. A magic man. Obsessed. He lives in a world of the supernatural, full of fears he has to ward off by means of symbols and rituals, poor old bugger. Helen could hardly believe he was my father's brother. My father was just the opposite, she said – rational, practical, very perceptive. A realist. Georges is all fantasy. When I was a child I was afraid of him. He was always doing strange things, walking round trees in a special way, burying bits of fur, talking to himself. He said terrible things would happen if he didn't. I was so frightened I used to hide on the roof. Helen tried to explain. She said it was a game he played to make himself happy. To keep away his fears. Gradually I stopped being frightened. He doesn't mean you any harm. Just trying to protect himself.'

Sarah came out of the house. 'There's some letters, Mama. The postman brought them. One's a telegram.'

Hannah opened it. From Philip. Sent from Libya three days before. 'Can't get away. Complications this end. Regrets. Writing. Love Philip.'

She read it out. Sarah was on the edge of tears. 'Oh dear, he won't need my beautiful map. I wish he was coming.'

'We'll take it back with us. He'll see it in London. I'm sure he'll like it.'

Marc was staring at her intently. 'It's from your husband?'

'Yes. He's . . . not coming here. I suppose there's too much work. He can't finish in time.'

She went in and sat at the kitchen table wondering, Am I glad? Am I sorry?

Marc had vanished from the doorway abruptly. She took out a knife and abstractedly began to nibble the goat cheese.

Thinking of Philip. How much he likes it. His pleasure in all the physical details of his life, clean shirts, hot coffee, the elegance of our sitting room in London that he designed – everything charcoal and white, no other colours except in the abstract picture on the wall where he allowed a flash of orange. The effect of the room is completely calculated, a controlled environment. The visual perfection of it takes people's breath away, as if they're walking into a painting.

I never use the room when I'm alone. It makes me an intruder. I keep the door shut. When Philip comes home it's nearly always the first thing he does. Go into his room. To sit there seems to restore some sense of balance in him. He breathes slowly as if he was meditating. I take him a drink. He sips it with slow, deliberate pleasure, his legs stretched out, head back against the velvet cushions, drinking in the reassurance of his own artistry.

Bi-Biche came into the kitchen and stood panting in the doorway. Sarah quickly filled a bowl of cold water for her. The dog slopped it noisily over the floor, water dripping from her bearded under-jaw.

'Shall I take her for a walk?' asked Sarah, looking for a distraction.

'Why not? Where's Harry?'

'He went to play with Claude on the old tractor down by the rubbish tip.'

'Why don't you go there too and pick some flowers on the way back?'

Sarah ran out, calling to the dog. Hannah got up and poured olive oil over the cheese. What was the herb that went with it? Perhaps she could find some growing on the hillside. Marc would know.

She walked down the alley and pushed open his front door. She had never been in before. The kitchen was on the right. No one there. Steps led up to the first floor, treads of red tiles set in a wooden frame,

he risers freshly whitewashed. So inviting, those cool steps leading
.o an area of darkness at the top where they curved round to a closed
door. She knocked softly. From inside she heard his voice call out,
Entrez!'

He has his back to her, bending over a work-bench in the middle of
the room as he taps something with a small hammer. That line of
white flesh again. Her body jerks, hooked like a fish on that thin,
white line. She shuts the door quietly, leaning against it, the room so
full of his presence – private, absorbed – it overwhelms her.

Music playing. Someone singing a French ballad, low-keyed.
Philip loves music. He plays records in his white room. We sit after
supper, the children asleep upstairs, and listen to the delicate gaiety
of Mozart. He loves him best of all. Philip's spirit dancing to
Mozart.

This singer's voice is slightly out of pitch as if it wasn't the manner
of the singing that counted so much as the words, the tenor of the
song. Am I trying to make a pun? That's why I came in here, obviously. Tugged by that thin white line. How extraordinary that we
should have to invent excuses even to ourselves. I thought I was on
my way to find a herb.

Marc looks sideways casually as he hammers. Seeing who it is he
straightens up and smiles slowly, a deliberate welcome. Hannah's
eyes are fixed on his –

> *Our eye-beams twisted, and did thread*
> *Our eyes upon one double string.*

The tug of the thread pulls her towards him, like a tight-rope walker
balancing over an enormous space. He stands there, pulling her forward with his smile. A rope of smile.

She puts out her hands and rests her finger-tips on his bare shoulders. Skin like brown silk. She leans forward and sniffs delicately as
if smelling a flower. A sweet, heady smell, smoky, a little of sweat. She
licks it. Slightly salt. Her hands slide up behind his neck and bend
his head towards hers. He's still smiling, as if it was an enormous and
delightful joke. As he bows his head to kiss her, he puts his arms
round her and presses her hips towards him. She can feel his penis
hard against her. Her hands reach down his back to the edge of his

79

shorts, pulling at the waist-band until they slip down to his feet. He moves one leg to step out of the entanglement. Leaning away from him she looks down. His penis stands straight out from his body like an animal with a life of its own. Unicorn rampant on a field of sable. Black curls reaching almost to his navel. She cups the swelling, pink tip against her palms. She can feel the blood pulsing through. Warm. Silkier, even, than the skin on his shoulders.

She moves slowly backwards, towards a couch at the side of the room, till she trips and they fall laughing onto the sheepskin cover. This time she wants to keep her eyes open, to savour the different textures of his body, his rough hair, his brown skin, his white skin, the expression on his face. Within a few moments she has lost herself, her eyes close and she wants only to come a thousand times, diffusing in the burst of fireworks exploding in her body like a million bright suns.

*

Marc had fallen asleep on his back, lapped by the sheepskin, his chest gleaming with moisture. Hannah leant on her elbow looking down at him.

For the first time in my life I haven't been afraid to show my sexual feeling openly. Philip doesn't like me to take the initiative, any more than he likes me looking at his penis. It turns him off. Marc's is soft now, floppy like another kind of creature, blind worm nuzzling against his inside leg. How beautiful it is. When I touch it with my lips the two skins are soft as each other. Lust is unfeminine. It's not included in the category feminine.

Hannah was obsessed with curiosity about the room. She wanted to read it privately, absorbing what it could tell her. She got up quietly and pulled on her dress, the tiled floor cool to her feet.

In the middle stood a jeweller's bench with a semi-circular piece cut out of the side for him to sit at. Below was suspended a wide leather pouch to catch any stones or bits of silver that fell from the piece he was working on. She walked slowly round like a cat, delighting in the room's atmosphere of concentration and repose, the craftsmanship of all the objects – both the tools and what he made with them.

There was a glass case at one end and displayed in it the most intricate miniature sculptures. Most were based on natural forms. A silver spider crouched on a web of fine-spun silver wire. A rectangular pendant that at first she took to be purely abstract reflected all the surface coruscations of a dry stone wall.

She almost tripped over a glass tank on the floor. Inside it two snakes were coiled in a bed of dried grasses. She crouched down to examine them more closely – a greeny-brown colour, gleaming and supple. Were they dead? She saw one eye glint for a second's flash of yellow, then still again. The movement started a shiver all down her back. Icy cold. Why should she be afraid? Probably they were harmless.

Marc was watching her quietly from the other side of the room. 'Aren't they beautiful? Georges taught me how to catch snakes.'

Hannah nodded and stood up. She did not want him to see her fear.

'I can keep my models in captivity as long as I need them. But it's hard work feeding them. Maybe I could get Harry to catch insects.'

'He mightn't know what to catch.'

'I'll show him. Where is he?'

'Playing on the old tractor. He won't do it, not if he knows their destiny.'

'Then I'll have to. This is the best time of day.' He pulled on his shorts. Then he put on a big black hat ready to go out into the midday sun. He paused by the staircase. 'Shut the door, I don't want any cats in here.'

She stood there thinking about another passage she had read that morning in Helen Grant's notes. From Caesar's *Conquest of Gaul*. She remembered struggling through set passages of it in Latin at school, weighed down with boredom, looking longingly through the mock-Gothic window at the sunlit grass outside. Nothing of what she read then remained with her. A meaningless exercise. But this morning's passage seemed suddenly relevant, about the people Caesar had found as he moved through Provence:

'The God they reverence most is Mercury. They have many images of him, and regard him as the inventor of all arts, the god who directs men upon their journeys.'

And Helen Grant's comment:

'Mercury was regarded as the god of luck and wealth, patron of travellers. He conducted the souls of the dead to the infernal regions. Generally shown as equipped with the caduceus, a rod entwined by two serpents, the petasus or broad-brimmed hat, and talaria or winged sandals.'

She had not seen wings on Marc's sandals, but the snakes and the broadbrimmed hat, those he had.

She heard a car draw up in the square outside. A moment later there were steps on the stairs and a voice calling, 'Marc?'

Hannah went to the doorway: 'He's gone out. I don't think he'll be long.'

A woman came up the stairs wearing an immaculate white trouser suit. Her thick, pale hair was gathered into a coil at the back of her neck, her face a creamy gold. She looked as if money had been massaged into every portion of her body, the indefinable air of the very rich, the glamour of gold. She glanced casually at Hannah, making her feel clumsy and disordered.

'I'll wait.' She sat down calmly in a blue canvas chair. Hannah went out, shutting the door behind her. Keep out the cats. Too late for this particular one.

In the square stood a white Mercedes coupé, the roof open. Hannah walked round it twice, slowly. On the front seat lay a green silk scarf. She wanted to tear it to pieces. She went into her own house to prepare some lunch. For the children. She could not eat.

Two hours later the car was still there. She looked at it from the kitchen window, unable to control her agitation.

'What right have I to be upset?' she thought. 'It's nothing to do with me.'

She filled a bucket and started to wash the kitchen floor on her hands and knees. Then she heard voices outside and the Mercedes engine starting up. A moment later Marc was in the doorway. She could feel her face sweating.

'Would you like to come down to the town later, to the café? I'm meeting a friend.'

Hannah looked up at him warily. 'A friend?' she asked. 'The same friend who was here just now?'

'You mean Chantal Daudet?' Marc smiled. 'She's a client. She came to collect a special commission she ordered after my last exhibition. She and her husband are on holiday nearby. He's rich. In plastics.'

Hannah blurted out uncontrollably, 'Do you sleep with your clients?'

Marc stiffened, his eyes cold. 'Does it matter if I sleep with my clients or don't sleep with my clients? It's of no importance.'

He went out. She remained kneeling by the bucket, her head bursting with humiliation and anger. Not at him but at herself. She scrubbed the floor so hard she broke a finger nail.

At five o'clock, to her surprise, Marc came back. He was wearing goggles again, like the time when she had first seen him, but now they were real motor cyclist's goggles. He handed her a leather jacket.

'Put this on. It's a windy ride. I've asked Elaine Pinet to keep an eye on your children.'

He had a powerful BSA that he used for going in and out of the town. The van he kept for journeys to Paris. She put on the jacket. It was too big. The sleeves reached over her hands. She zipped it up and climbed on behind, hugging him tightly round the waist. The engine roared noisily as the bike started off down the hill, banking round every corner like a motorised bird. She turned her head to rest her cheek against Marc's back, clinging to him with unexpected joy at the ride.

At the café Marc was greeted by a man wearing an Indian shirt, a gold ring in his right ear. His face burnt brown by the sun and his fashionable, drooping moustache made her think of Buffalo Bill. He looked at Hannah with interest as he shook her hand.

'Leo's a writer and photographer,' said Marc.

'What kind of writer?' Hannah asked, looking at him.

Leo shrugged. 'Fiction, pornography.' His accent was American, a Southerner's drawl.

'He's writing something for the catalogue of my October exhibition. A poetic monologue about the son of the soil of Provence, the welder of secret shapes, the prober into hidden forms . . .'

'Fiction, pornography,' interrupted Leo lightly. He and Marc began to laugh.

A few tables away a group of young hitch-hikers sat slumped in

83

their chairs, clothes and rucksacks scattered around them, the debris of their journey. Two of the rucksacks had Union Jacks sewn onto them and Hannah could hear English voices. A girl with her back to them was combing her long red hair as they passed a cigarette round. Each in turn took a deep puff and then handed it to his neighbour. Marc and Leo looked at them idly.

'Idiots,' said Leo. 'Where do they think they are?'

'What's wrong?' asked Hannah.

'The police are terrible just now,' said Marc. 'They're having a campaign against drugs, after that business in Marseille. Last week they arrested five students in the *boîte* down the street. I'd better warn them.'

He got up, and bent forward to talk quietly to one of the boys. The girl with red hair turned her head to hear what he was saying and Hannah saw with surprise who it was.

'Molly!'

The girl jumped up and came rushing over to Hannah, throwing her arms round her. Hannah was touched by her emotion.

'I was going to look for you,' said Molly. 'I got your address. I never thought I'd find you so easy.'

In this alien setting the young people looked extraordinarily English. The boys' hair was longer than any of the young men passing in the street, the girls' clothes far more bizarre. They looked disintegrating and vulnerable. Molly was wearing a long green skirt with a dirty white smock. Her face was pale.

'It's taken a week to get down here,' she said. 'Real rough. Two nights we slept in a field. I'm skint.'

Leo told them about a youth hostel outside the town where they could spend the night. The others were determined to hitch to the coast next day. But Molly was exhausted. She wanted to stay. Leo offered to pick her up in the morning from the hostel and bring her up to the village. He was clearly intrigued, whether for fictional or pornographic purposes Hannah could not tell.

*

It took Molly two days to recover. She slept for hours on the couch in the sitting-room, got up for small meals and cups of tea and gradually began to go for walks with the children. They brought her bunches of wild flowers and empty snail shells. They introduced her to every dog and cat in the district, delighted to have her there, half woman, half child, a link between their world and their mother's, moving easily from one to the other.

Hannah liked it too. She could spend more time with Marc. He took it for granted they would have coffee together every day after lunch, either on her terrace, or he would call her into his workshop from where they gravitated quite naturally to his balcony. Coffee began to have a special charge of meaning.

She felt more carefree than she had ever felt in her life before. Like a dolphin swimming towards another dolphin, dancing and playing in the waves, then swimming away again, unentangled by any net of commitment.

He seemed to prefer to see her in the afternoon. At least he rarely came into her room at night although she left the windows open. He was out a lot in the evening. She did not ask where. She had seen his recoil at any hint of questioning, the look of distaste. She pondered over what name to give the feeling she had for him. Could such a delicate exchange of courtesies as they shared be considered a kind of love?

Why is it so different with Marc? Because I don't know him? Because the familiarity that breeds the incest taboo hasn't had time to creep up on us? Anything can happen. No decencies to be observed. This is not someone I have to have breakfast with next morning.

When we're making love – for once the phrase seems to fit – I'm linked to Marc, and through him to a part of the outside world in a way that doesn't happen at any other time. The most complete imaginable means of expression. The small onlooker, isolated, detached, that usually nags away inside my head, disappears. I'm carried into another mode of consciousness, not that of separation but of completion, as if I was linked up to something that's always there if only I could reach it. A being beyond myself, a being that includes myself and Marc but so much more besides, a unity that could include everything.

When I try to recall the experience afterwards it's impossible. The old self is back again, questioning, analysing. Is it just sensual delight, that oceanic feeling, or something more – one of those small doorways to eternity?

Questions, always questions. I don't seem even now to be able to make a positive, definite statement about anything. The longer I live, the more uncertainty creeps up on me. I'm continually surprised in the staff room, at how sure people are of their opinions. They have views on everything. Jim Finnigan knows for certain there are more West Indians living on social security than any other ethnic group in Great Britain. He also knows, à propos of the same group, the male side of it, that their members when flaccid, may be, on the whole, rather longer than those of white British males but that once roused the white member is on average a quarter of an inch bigger in circumference. He establishes this important fact by the phrase 'It's been proved by medical research'. The first piece of information he offers, frequently, to the room at large. The second he saves to drop, privately, into the ears of female staff on an individual basis. He's dropped it in my ear twice. I've also heard the headmistress say in Assembly one morning, addressing the whole school on the subject of thieving in the cloakrooms, 'God is watching every single one of you.' I raised my eyes to look at her. Her thin face, red, slightly hairy, expressed no shade of doubt.

8

Molly's arrival had interrupted Hannah's nightly work on Helen Grant's notes.

Most evenings before she came Hannah had sat reading, taking books down to look up references, gradually disentangling the threads that linked her jottings together. And she began to see that what had intrigued the other woman was any clue of continuity. Nothing overt, no conclusions, but the pointers were there for someone else to follow. Would it be her job to piece these clues together, forming Helen Grant's juxtapositions into some readable whole? It would demand an involvement as great as hers had been. Was that why Marc had given her all these notes to sort through? A means of absorbing her in something at one remove from himself, linked, but not focussing on him. He was elusive. He did not like questions. The memory of her shame over his client's visit stung her.

Now, with Molly around, she felt bound to sit doing nothing as if she was there to entertain her. She was bad at it. She sensed Molly's growing boredom and restlessness, waiting for something to happen. She tried on all Hannah's clothes and asked if she had any pot, meandering on about her family, her determination to leave home as soon as she was earning enough money. She'd been doing modelling work in the evenings.

'What sort of modelling?'

'Photographic. A fellow in the office fixed it up for me. He belongs to a camera club. Dreary old sods they are but dead keen on their art work. That's what they call it.' She giggled.

'What do you have to do?'

'Just lie there in the nude. Lots of cushions and silk tassels. You know.'

Hannah stared at her. 'Don't you mind?'

'Why should I worry? The money's good. He said I might

go professional. He'd be my manager. Only I need a bit of experience.'

'Molly . . .' the counsellor, poking her bloody nose in, 'isn't there anything else you could do to make money, something a bit more . . . interesting?'

'Other ways are worse. Those old farts don't touch you, only look. Where's the harm?'

The society of voyeurs, the eye pressed against the aperture like a keyhole. Click. Art work. No involvement. Just an eye framed against a naked body. She could not think of any alternative to offer that would mean anything to Molly. She was no longer the pale girl in the doorway of the schoolroom. Events had intervened. Hannah had played her own part in that. Her scruples would be better directed towards herself.

Molly looked out of the window. 'There's that Leo.'

He was parking his Renault 4 in the square. They heard his voice calling to Marc and a few moments later Leo almost fell into the kitchen.

'Holy shit, what's this fucking snake doing here?' He pointed to the doorstep. Molly screamed, jumping onto a chair with her long skirt hobbled round her ankles. Marc said, 'It's dead.' He bent to pick it up. '*Merde!* It's one of mine. It's been missing since yesterday. I thought it was loose in the room somewhere.' He examined it carefully. 'It's neck's broken. Georges. He must have got into my room while I was out. Cunning old devil. Why the hell does he have to take my snake, couldn't he have caught his own?'

'Perhaps,' Hannah shivered, 'it . . . had to be yours.'

'A dead snake is supposed to be good luck. It wards off evil.' He looked at her. 'It's outside your door, Hannah. It must be meant for you.' His voice was teasing. 'To protect him against you, do you think, or Molly?' He walked across the square and threw the snake over the wall. 'Leo says there's a *fête* at Saint Jacques. Do you want to come?'

It was the first time Marc had asked her to come out at night. Hannah longed to go. 'What about the children?'

'Bring them too.'

Molly jumped down. 'I'm coming!'

Hannah ran upstairs. The children had only just got into bed. Their excitement equalled Molly's.

All the streets into Saint Jacques are cordonned off so they have to park on the outskirts. A brass band draws them towards the centre, distant at first but growing louder and louder as they get near, music reverberating off the stone walls surrounding the square, a cannonade of trumpets. The band is drawn up as if on parade. In the very front Hannah recognises the postman who brings the letters up to the village every day at ten o'clock. His stout body is squeezed into a white uniform like a naval captain in the tropics, hung with loops of gold braid, a peaked and braided cap on his head, as he blows, his red cheeks distended to bursting, into a tuba. Beside him a small boy in a miniature replica of the same uniform marches up and down on the spot.

In a side street Claude's mother, the school teacher, is lining up children to lead the procession. Each one carries a paper lantern on the end of a pole, lit from inside by torch bulbs so the narrow street is a Milky Way of coloured lights. The first piece of music comes to an end. The children prance with steps as light and bobbing as their lanterns to the front of the band. The postman holds up his hand, signals, and with a blast of brass the music begins again.

Now the whole band begins to march slowly forward round the square, the children leading, down the main street, circling the church at the bottom and then back again. Hordes of young people follow at the side of the band. Harry disappears, caught up in the excitement. For a moment Hannah loses sight of him, then, as the band turns, she sees his blond head, fairer than the others, at the back. The musicians stand to attention, blow a final chord, and then disperse into the crowd, turning themselves in a matter of moments from performers into spectators of the next event.

On a raised wooden dais a pop group is unpacking instruments. A man in a glittering, satin tunic props a sign in front of the microphone: *Les Sauvages*. The electric guitarist plays a few notes to test the wiring. Suddenly they begin. Not the natural orgy of brass but a frantic sound amplified into distortion by the loudspeakers suspended from the balconies of houses round the square. A space clears in front of them, the older people pressing back against the walls while the younger ones start to dance, jerking their arms like languid marionettes. Two young men on Hannah's left are staring at her. Surely they can't be going to ask . . . No, of course not. It's Molly.

'*Vous dansez, Mademoiselle?*'

Molly, as cool as the rest, begins to manipulate her body rhythmically. Her eyes stare, seemingly into vacancy, over the young man's head. The young man, shoulders hunched, looks down at the ground.

After three numbers the music stops. The speaker comes forward and announces a sequence of Latin American rhythms. The young people dissolve into the background, the older ones step forward. Now it is their turn to propel each other round and round the square. Hannah sees the postman again, clasping a woman in brilliant green. Suddenly Monsieur Terrain's eldest son is standing in front of her. She has only ever seen him behind the wheel of a tractor. He bows, immaculately clean in a blue suit. Hannah looks sideways at Marc. He is laughing, but silently, his black eyes shining. You bugger, she thinks, superior bugger.

Awkwardly she begins to rumba. Years since she has done so. Monsieur Terrain holds her at a precise distance. She can feel the sweat from his hand through the thin cotton of her shirt. An enormous hand, steering her heavily, like a tractor. Over his shoulder she sees Marc, Leo and Molly standing together, laughing. Marc bends down to hear something Molly is saying and puts his arm round her shoulder. Her face turns to smile up at him. Hannah's whole body jerks as if someone had shot her. She stumbles. Monsieur Terrain steadies her with an apologetic '*Pardon*' as if it was his fault. He turns her back to the onlookers. Out of sight the image still transfixes her – Molly smiling at Marc, his bent, careful head.

She is dancing just below the musicians. One of the satin-shirted players shakes his maracas at her invitingly. The shock she feels comes not only from the knowledge that, of course, Marc finds Molly attractive, but, even more, from her own reaction. That she should respond in such a mechanical, uncontrollable way. Totally unexpected. Is it because she was caught unawares? She braces herself for a further exposure as Monsieur Terrain steers her round again. They have disappeared. Oh God. She strains from one side of his head to the other, trying to get a clear view. Could they have gone off altogether and left her at the mercy of Monsieur Terrain for the whole evening? Mightn't Marc think that rather funny? She searches hopelessly among the spectators. Not a sign. Then, at the edge of the dancers, she sees Sarah waving to her. The number ends. Monsieur Terrain unpeels his hand like a piece of Sellotape. He bows again, *Merci, Madame.'*

She finds herself bowing in return, as correct and formal as he is. He takes out a clean white handkerchief and mops his forehead, shining with sweat. She hurries over to Sarah. 'Where are the others? Where's Marc?'

'In the café. They told me to bring you.'

They are drinking *marc*, a drink Hannah likes especially. Except for Molly. She and the children have Pepsis. Molly smiles at her with open affection. Hannah tries to smile back, ashamed. Anxieties that belong to another time, another place, other people. Looking in through a lighted window at her mother bending down behind her step-father's chair to lay her cheek against his head. He looks up and they kiss each other silently. Hannah, standing in the garden, feels a sudden sense of exclusion. They have forgotten her. They will go away and leave her behind. They did go away, and she stayed with her grandmother whom she grew to love. Her grandmother was alone and so she never excluded her except, later on, by dying.

Marc smiles ironically. 'Enjoy yourself?'

She could not imagine him dancing the rumba or, come to that, dancing at all. An indignity he would not readily submit to.

Marc's half-way in age between me and Molly, thirty-five, twenty-eight, sixteen, and yet in his tastes, his style of life, nearer to Molly than me. No one pitches themselves forward after the age of eighteen. Most look yearningly behind. Is that why I'm so drawn to him? I know no one of his age in London. There's Nick Gates at school but I hardly know him. I saw him once in the park, carrying a small boy on his shoulders. The man with him was pushing a pram. There was a girl too, laughing. I wondered if she was his wife. I was on my own with the children as usual. I looked at them longingly. Men just as concerned with children as women.

Philip never pushed the pram. He never had time. Why has he made the divisions so absolute – what he does, what I do. I must have pushed it for a hundred miles. It wouldn't fit in with his idea of himself. Father of the household, breadwinner, dominator.

He likes showing Harry how to do things. If Harry argues or lose
interest he gets angry. Spoiling his role. He's scheduled a time abou
Seven to seven-thirty. Being a father. All part of his obsession for it
time. It mustn't be wasted. A tick-tock, clock-watching kind of man

Back punctually at seven. I'm supposed to have a snack ready. Iced
beer in the fridge, the table laid for supper. My role as wife. Harry
and Sarah are supposed to run eagerly to welcome him. Sometimes
they're watching the television. He has to prise them away, protest
ing. They don't play their roles so readily. Is it the pressures at work
that have made him so sensitive to anything threatening at home? He
demands order, predictability. A game I must play of obeisance to
the person who won't go away and leave me, rituals of dependence
that have distanced me more and more from the child in the garden
looking in through the lighted window.

At the next table Madame Corneille was sitting with a dark-haired
woman of about thirty, very good-looking. As Hannah looked up she
caught her eye and immediately came over. Had she forgotten the
jar? It seemed so. It was clearly Molly she was interested in. Hannah
introduced them. Madame Corneille bowed as formally as the younger
Monsieur Terrain. Hannah felt sure she would have liked to ask
Molly to dance, if only such a thing were possible. In the old
fashioned style. A foxtrot. Tea for two. She was wearing a grey
velvet suit. She must know how well grey suited her.

'English visitors are always welcome at my house. Perhaps Madame
Straight will bring you one day?'

Molly was pleased. She liked attention. Madame Corneille shook
hands all round and went back to her own table. The woman with
her, Leo said, was a well-known maker of feminist films. Molly
looked attentive. Perhaps she could get her a screen test? Leo
shrugged, giving Molly a sardonic look. Madame Corneille had a lot
of influential friends. Molly looked across at the other table, cat's
eyes smiling round the corner of her face. Something in the quality of
her smile gave Hannah the shivers. Leo, absorbed in Molly's every
physical gesture as if he was trying to commit them to memory, asked
her to dance.

Hannah, watching them, felt as if she was on a stage set. An arena
for public happenings. The square at Saint Jacques was almost too

retty, houses colour-washed in shades of ochre and pink. People eant over their balconies, watching the show, both part of it and part from it, neighbours performing for each other, seeing and being een. She tried to imagine such a scene in Paddington or Islington. Both of them once had village greens. Impossible. All one way streets, hrough-ways, container lorries thundering by, designed for traffic o maraud across, not as places to celebrate in. And the people who odged there only momentary inhabitants. Molly said she had moved our times in the last six years. Temporary accommodation, from one ecrepitude to another.

Leo came back to the table while Molly went on dancing. He egan to talk about what was going to happen to Saint Jacques. He ad been to Avignon to look at the plans. They were proposing to urn the whole area into a vast regional play park – mini-golf and so n. Below the old fortified village, little concrete villas were to be uilt with a supermarket in the field where the wild jonquils flowered n spring. Leo's small house looked out over this field. He said to Marc, 'It'll be your turn next.'

'Was there anything in the plan about it?'

'Stage two. The second phase.'

Hannah burst out, 'But lots of houses in Marc's village are empty. Nobody lives in them.'

Marc said with a shrug, 'Only because most of them belong to Elaine Pinet and her sister. Their father owned half the village. But hey've quarrelled. They can't agree about anything. So that means hey haven't sold them yet. It's only a question of time. If the price vas big enough they'd sell.'

'What about Monsieur Terrain. He owns most of the land. Would e?'

'His sons might. They're only interested in money. They want vives. Why do you think none of them are married? Because Papa von't give them their share and let them get out. He needs their abour. Girls won't marry farmers any more. Too much hard work. Especially if it means living with the in-laws. So they can't get anyone o have them. Once the old man's dead it'll be different. They'll plit things up between them, sell off half the land for building lots.'

'Doesn't the lavender make money?'

'Some. At the moment. But it won't last. The chemists have discovered a way of synthesising the scent. It'll be cheaper. They won' need flowers.'

'What about the rams' glanders?' said Hannah.

'What's that?' asked Leo hopefully, 'It sounds pretty obscene.'

'Lavender oil is a cure for it, and for nerves and hysterics and falling eyelashes. Will chemical lavender do that too?'

Marc took her hand, laughing. 'Did you get that from Helen's notes?'

She nodded. Leo said gloomily, staring in front of him, 'Don't worry. They'll grow lavender all right. A small field easily seen by passing tourists. Then they'll buy the chemical stuff in bulk and syphon it off into tiny bottles, pretty little labels, "Lavender from Provence", cures . . . what did you say? Glanders?'

Hannah nodded again.

'The poor creeps will think it's an aphrodisiac. Sell like anything, fast as they can package it up.'

Hannah, laughing, said, 'They'll be using the wrong stuff. What you need for that is the fat from the intestines of a strong, male, wild boar.'

Leo stared at her. 'That from Marc's aunt too?'

'Yes.'

He put his hand on Marc's shoulder. 'Marc, she's on to a fortune. We'd better set up in business.'

Hannah looked from one to the other, asking, 'Isn't there anything you can do about it?'

'Impotence?' said Leo gravely. 'Not usually. It's a serious matter.'

'The plan for the regional park. Can't you stop it?'

'How?' He stroked his moustache. 'Most people are crazy for it, wouldn't you say Marc?'

Marc nodded. 'A lot of them.'

'Marc and I are privileged. We live here. We earn our bread. The two things aren't synonymous. We don't even stay here all the time.' He waved his hand at the dancers. 'Most of these guys depend on the place. They'll be only too glad to sell crap to the visitors. They'll start cafés, let out rooms, open pizzerias. Visitors will descend like flies on a shit house, a far richer crop than all their cherries. Clean, asy work, battening on tourists, only corrupting. Very corrupting to he soul. Look what's happened on the coast. You can't set foot on a centimetre without money. People look at you not as another human being but a walking cash box, calculating how much they can shake out of you before you pass on your way.'

The next in the long line of invaders who'd come to Provence, thought Hannah. She had a sudden fear that the changes would be more invidious, faster and more destructive than all the barbarities that had gone before. The end of an era. A giant leap from the pre-industrial to the post-industrial. And not just here. The whole of the Mediterranean, Italy, Spain, North Africa, all one vast leisure park, their inhabitants a new race of servants, waiting on the pleasures of he rich. Playground attendants. Was this what Helen Grant had foreseen? Was it this that had given the impetus to all her note-taking, digging into the past to find the links that bound it to the present before all continuity was lost?

Harry was tugging at her arm. 'Mama, come and see something, please come.'

A man had set up a hoopla game. People were trying to throw wooden hoops over the head of a live duck swimming in agitation to and fro across the *bassin* of the fountain. Suddenly it struggled to take flight, beating its wings frantically against the water. It rose a few inches into the air then fell back with a splash because one leg was tethered to a post. The onlookers shouted with amusement. Tears were running down Harry's cheeks. Hannah had never seen him cry silently before. She pushed her way back to the café.

'It's late. I think I'll take the children back. Molly can stay with you, can't she?'

They walked away from the square, music following them all the way to the car. The children slumped drowsily in the back as Hannah drove up the hill. In the gleam of the headlights a silver-brown shape leapt across the road.

'What's that?' Harry was instantly alert.

Hannah slowed down as a second one went bounding after the first. 'Foxes, out hunting.'

She drove slowly on. Harry had forgotten the duck. She heard him murmuring quietly, a note of wonder in his voice, 'My first fox. Two first foxes.'

95

She fell asleep as soon as she got into bed. Some time later she wa woken by the noise of Leo's car radio blaring through the open roc of his car. She heard Marc's laughter and Molly's, then the car drov off again. She listened for the sound of her own front door. She di not hear it.

She sat straight up in bed, jealousy exploding like a fire bomb. Sh imagined their heads together, Marc's neck bent like a deer croppin the grass. She wanted to scream out loud. Her mouth opened. Th muscles in her neck clenched. Then, abruptly, she fell back onto th pillow, fighting to get control.

Tiger, get out of my head. I don't want you in my cage with you foul green eyes glowing obscenely in the dark. Your animal smell smothering me. I can't breathe. Sheathe up your cat's claws and pac away from me. And don't leave any crap lying around to stink th place out after you've gone. Tiger, get out.

The last three words she shouted out loud, a shrill strangulate noise. She got out of bed and walked up and down the room, si paces and turn, six paces and turn, like the tiger she was trying t exorcise.

She had never known jealousy before, such degradation. To b obsessed with the physical image of two people, locked togethei excluding her. Was that the clue? The child in the garden had know exclusion, but the remembered emotion was nothing like this, nc violent, obsessive. More a sense of desolation, the outsider lookin in on something unattainable.

Out on the balcony the wind was getting up, blowing strongly fror the north west. *Mistral*. She went to the parapet and stood listening

No sound from Marc's house, just the wind funnelling up th alley. Then, faintly, she heard music. The studio window must b shut. The soft, nostalgic voice of Leonard Cohen . . . *but tonight wi be fine, will be fine, but toniiiiight will be fine*.

That tape, he's played it to me so many times.

Why do we need to idealise the person we love? Marc's a shit. B any normal standards he's a shit. Normal standards? Only the con ventions of respectable social behaviour, the business of considerin the feelings of other people. He doesn't consider them. He follows hi

wn feelings of the moment. No compromise. This gives him a sort
f integrity that I even find myself admiring and so I come round,
gain, do I, to a need to idealise?

Could I live like that? I don't know how. For so many years I've
ipped into something almost completely the opposite. Love starts it
ff, the desire to do nothing that might displease the other person, to
e what they want you to be.

When I married Philip I felt nothing but gratitude. For three years
d been caught in a relationship in which I was swallowed whole and
hen spat out again. A small, congealed mass. An owl pellet. I cut one
pen once and found inside it the perfect skeleton of a mouse. No-
hing else left, just a thin skeleton of bone.

I was the man's research assistant, the Professor of Social Adminis-
ation. He employed me for my mind, then he went on to my emo-
ons, finally my body. Once he'd exhausted all the possibilities he
ad no further use for me. The book was finished, that was his only
oncern, my contribution acknowledged briefly in the foreword; 'I
ould like, too, to thank my research assistant Hannah Calvert, whose
evotion to the project has been a continual encouragement.'

He threw me away like a worn-out glove. Philip picked me up out
f the rubbish bin; to be precise the graduate common room. Philip
dmired my ex-boss. He attended one of his seminars. I think that
ust have been part of my attraction. The Professor's girl. When I
ll he was there to catch me.

Without him I would have disintegrated. I got to depend on him
ompletely. He took me out to meals, came with me to buy new
othes. He was more interested in them than I was. He wanted me
o be decorative. He made all the decisions. When he suggested we
hould get married it never occurred to me not to. I liked the idea. A
ife.

So that's how it all began, with gratitude that anyone could be so
nd, that I was, unaccountably, wanted. He made me feel safe. I
ied to please him. I gave up the violin because he couldn't stand me
ractising.

We were happy, playing at house. I entertained his friends. We
greed the most important thing was his career. He began to be suc-
essful. We played at mothers and fathers. Naturally I gave up my

97

job to look after the baby. And so the construction, the web – wha
ever you like to call it – was complete. What Philip requires is cor
plete dependability. He needs the security just as much as I did. I
picked me out at my most vulnerable just for that. Knots of oblig
tion.

I'm thinking about it very clear-headedly, very precisely on tl
windy balcony with the *mistral* blowing up the alley, and I'm begi
ning to hate him. Is it Philip who turned me into this zombie? I'
afraid to be anything else.

It all seemed so rational. Small children need routine. It mak
looking after them easier. Now I begin to see that it's Philip's way
controlling us. It's Philip who needs the routine. Strategies for su
vival. We pick them according to our most urgent need. Philip
strategies for survival. He enmeshed me with them.

Marc's is just another technique. He wants to live alone, to pr
serve himself from the excursions of other people into his soul.
think it's a kind of claustrophobia he suffers from. He needs a spa
all round him. If anyone gets too close he can't breathe. He war
affection only on his terms. His strategy for survival. I think I may
needing a new strategy myself.

Hannah was blown in from the balcony, shutting the windov
behind her. She lay down on the bed. For the moment the tig
seemed to have gone, shut like the wind outside the balcony window
There was not just one wind but two or three, blowing from differe
directions, in gusts, making the guttering clatter outside the windo
She thought it would come adrift. The noise was irregular, whi
made it worse, frantic, as if something was clamouring to get in.
tormented night.

She woke up exhausted, but the noise had gone. She thought fo
moment she might have dreamt it but then she saw, outside on tl
balcony, a pot of geraniums overturned, the earth spilling onto tl
tiled floor, the flowers broken.

9

Hannah was reluctant to open the sitting-room door. In case Molly was not there. She sat sipping coffee in the empty kitchen. Sarah came downstairs sleepily rubbing her eyes after her late night and sat down to her bowl of hot chocolate. 'Mama, it's Saturday. You promised to take us down to the market.'

'All right.'

'Where's Molly?'

'I'm . . . not sure. Maybe she's still asleep. Wait, Sarah . . .'

It was too late. Sarah was already opening the sitting-room door. Hannah, almost against her will, found herself standing behind her in the doorway.

Molly lay on her back, her head turned to one side, red hair tangled round her peaceful face. Sarah whispered, with awe, 'Isn't she beautiful?'

Hannah answered slowly, her voice half-choked, 'Mm. She is.'

'Why do people look more beautiful when they're asleep?'

'Perhaps because they're not protecting themselves.' Looking down at Molly's vulnerable body, covered only with a sheet, Hannah could feel nothing but a curious, bitter tenderness. It came without her wishing. She suddenly remembered their first meeting – Molly on the medical couch in her room, the long fingers that now lay in stillness on the white sheet working over and over the blanket. And now it was she, Hannah, wanting to make some kind of appeal to the sleeping girl, an appeal that could hardly be spoken.

'We must wake her up. Molly wants to come,' said Sarah.

'I'll make her some tea, then you can.'

On market day the centre of the town on the main road below Saint Jacques is closed to traffic. Stalls fill every narrow street, piled high with vegetables, fruit, infinite variety of cheeses and pâtés, bowls

99

of different coloured olives, bunches of dried herbs. Confronted with such a dream of *gourmandise* Hannah could not make up her mind what to buy but hovered uncertainly in front of the cheeses requesting small snippets of the most enticing. She also tasted all the olives and decided on green ones slightly crushed and smothered with herbs and garlic. She was so involved in choosing that she did not at first notice Marc standing a few yards away at the fish stall, smiling at her. He looked pleased. With what? With seeing her? With Molly? With himself? She felt herself blushing. A relationship in which there was so much uncertainty – so little continuity. She could take nothing for granted. A kind of obstacle race in which the obstacles were her own expectations. Each day a new beginning.

He waved a bag at her, calling out, 'Something special. Come and eat them when you get back.' Then he turned away into the baker's shop.

Everyone in the village comes down to the market – the focal point of their week, winter and summer, as it has been for hundreds of years. Madame Pinet gets out her old Citroen, black and low-slung, a thirties' model, the kind that Maigret might drive in an old film. Her husband, departing to the cemetery to join the rest of *La Famille Pinet*, left her this reminder of his once tangible presence, solid, respectable, a little like a hearse. Beside her sits *Le Vieux*, behind her Georges with their baskets beside him on the back seat. They stand with other small-holders at the edge of the pavement outside one of the busiest cafés in the square, displaying their goat cheeses, melons, a few figs and bunches of herbs. Hannah bought a melon and four figs for the sheer pleasure of greeting them in this different setting, of seeing Henri Bonnieux's brown face fold into his Punchinello smile and shaking his hard, dry hand.

Harry was disturbed by the caged birds nearby.

'They're only birds,' said Molly, looking at Harry as though he was daft. 'What you on about?' She took them off to the section that sold clothes, trying on jeans' jackets with as much laughter and quick repartee with the fellow behind the stall as if she were back in Chapel Street market. She understood little he said – he understood nothing she said – but the tone of voice was familiar. Molly had no intention of buying anything – she just liked trying things on.

'Isn't Spain very near here?'

Hannah looked startled. Near? What could Molly mean? Two days hard driving, was that near? She had an extraordinary innocence, or was it just ignorance? Whatever it was, it was refreshing. She knew nothing, except what she had experienced herself, and she was ready for all new ventures, swimming towards them with a half-smile on her lips.

It was prawns Marc had bought in the market. He put them on the table in a green glazed bowl. Hannah leant forward.

'Mmm. Prawns.'

Molly looked at them silently, expectantly, then she murmured, 'I've never tasted prawns. Mam said they're dirty. She wouldn't let us.' She picked one up and bit into the tail. Then she spat it out. 'Tastes like toe nails.'

Marc banged his fist on the table and shouted with laughter. Molly looked across at Hannah who was expertly splitting a prawn down its belly and levering out the flesh. She passed it to Molly.

This time she hesitated a moment then bit delicately. 'It's good. Tastes like the sea.'

'So you've tasted the sea at least?' said Marc. He couldn't stop laughing. Molly smiled at him, fully this time, putting out the tip of her tongue as pink as a prawn.

'Give us another, then.'

'What we need,' said Hannah, 'is a bottle of cold Chablis.'

'There's only red and it's anything but cold.' Marc got up to go to the cupboard.

'It's all right,' said Hannah, 'I've got some in the fridge.'

She went out into the sun. After the cool twilight of Marc's green-tiled kitchen she was dazzled. She put up her arm to shade her eyes and nearly bumped into Sarah.

'Are you coming for lunch, Mama? I'm making some salad.'

She was shaking the lettuce energetically in a wire basket. Cool drops of water showered Hannah's feet.

'Don't wait for me. We're eating prawns.'

Sarah made a face. 'Ooogh!'

'I'm just getting some wine for Marc. I'll see you later.'

She took two bottles. After the prawns Marc offered them tomato

salad sprinkled with fresh basil and a ripe, pungent cheese. Molly, t
her own surprise, seemed to enjoy that too. They sat back in the
chairs with a great feeling of well-being, smiling foolishly at eac
other. Molly's smile stretched into an enormous yawn.

'Come on,' Marc pushed his chair back, 'We'll have a siesta on th
terrace.'

Hannah found it difficult to balance when she stood up. Sh
noticed Molly, too, swayed as she walked.

They climbed the stairs and went onto the flat roof where tw
mattresses were already laid out.

'Make yourselves comfortable.'

He shut the door behind him and locked it. A familiar gestur
Hannah felt a moment's unease and then her drowsiness overcam
her and she stretched out in the sun. It was almost directly overhea
a palpable presence like a warm tongue licking her arms. Moll
flopped onto her belly and Marc slid between them turning to Har
nah with his arm over her chest and his face in the curve of her nec
She could feel his mouth nuzzling her skin. She was almost aslee
when his hand turned her head towards him and he started kissing h
face. Half-conscious, her tongue met his in a salty exchange. The
both smelt of prawns.

'We'll get too hot with these things on.'

Marc knelt to strip off his T shirt. He pulled Hannah's cotto
trousers off and she unbuttoned her thin blouse, half sitting up. Eve
the effort of doing that in the overwhelming sun was too much. Sl
collapsed back onto the mattress. Her eyes closed.

When she opened them again she saw Molly had taken all h
clothes off. Her body was completely bare to the sun, extraordinari
white and soft looking, as if it had never been exposed before. A ne
experience – never tasted sun?

Suddenly Hannah caught her breath. Marc's hand was creepir
over Molly's luminous skin as he said, 'Red pubic hair. What a rarity

His fingers twined themselves into the rough, red curls, pulli
them straight and letting them spring back again. Molly looked sid
ways at Hannah with her half smile. Hannah closed her eyes.
moment later she felt a touch on her foot, gentle strokes massaging
up and down. Her skin prickled with shivers of pleasure. She open
one eye and immediately stiffened. What was happening? Her bod

onging for Marc's, was confused. Surely it wasn't his foot touching
er. Or was it? She raised her head slightly and saw that Molly had
tretched one leg across to reach her foot. Molly's toes stroking
er skin. She saw Marc's hand move upwards to knead Molly's
ale belly then suddenly he lifted a handful of flesh and squeezed it
ightly.

'You're flabby, girl, getting fat. Better watch it. Look at Hannah,
wice your age and smooth as a seal.'

His other hand was stroking Hannah, this thumb pressing into her
roin. She jumped up in fury.

'That's nothing to do with it. Nothing to do with anything. Is this
meat market?'

She was nauseated, as if she might be sick at any moment. Snatch-
ng up her trousers she swayed and almost fell, dizzy from the sudden
novement. The door latch grazed her finger as she struggled with the
ey then, wrenching the door open, she rushed out of his house,
lripping blood from her torn finger onto the stairs.

No one in her own kitchen. She went straight upstairs and fell onto
he bed with her face in the pillow, her heart pumping like a long-
listance runner, her chest constricted and painful and yet still, in the
entre of her belly, an urgent desire to make love. She put her hand
lown and clenched it between her thighs, pressing them together in a
imulated rhythm. Sometimes in her sleep, dreaming of making love,
uch movement could bring her to an unexpected point of pleasure.
She would half wake on a surge of feeling and then slide back into
leep. Now it was hopeless. Nothing but an irritation that only in-
reased the tension and her self-disgust. She let out her breath with a
reat sob and began to cry, her body shuddering with groans as if it
vas acting a part that had nothing to do with her. An exaggerated
erformance.

Sarah was sitting on her bed, saying urgently, 'Mama. Wake up. I
nust tell you something.'

She shook her mother by the shoulder. Hannah's thick hair com-
letely hid her face. Sarah pulled it aside and stroked her cheek. It
vas damp and hot.

'Mama, wake up. I'm terribly worried about Bi-Biche.'

Hannah rolled onto her back and opened her eyes. Her head throbbed.

'There's something the matter with Bi-Biche. I think she's hurt.'

She struggled to focus on Sarah's small, excited face. 'Mmm?'

'There's blood on the floor.'

'Has she cut herself?'

'No. I looked at all her paws and there's nothing wrong. Then found out. It's her bottom. She's bleeding from her bottom.'

Hannah smiled and took Sarah's hand in hers, squeezing it gently. 'That's nothing to worry about. She must be on heat.'

'Yes. She's hot. She's panting a lot.'

Hannah laughed. 'Not that kind of heat. It means when the blood comes down – to make puppies. Like women have every month, only dogs don't have it so often.'

Sarah's face was alive with interest. 'Does it hurt her?'

'No, of course not. No more than it hurts us.'

'Does it hurt us?'

'Not usually. Perhaps for the first few hours. Some people get a kind of cramp in their stomach.'

'Will you come and see?'

'In a moment.' Her eyes closed. 'Let me wake up first.'

'Will you come if I make a cup of tea?'

'Mmm.' She sank back into sleep, till the rattle of a tea cup, very near, forced her eyes open again. The cup was level with her nose. 'Careful. It'll spill.'

The cup was withdrawn a few inches. 'Sit up, Mama. You can't drink lying down.'

She pushed herself half upright against the pillows.

'Why are you so sleepy?'

'Too much wine.'

'Are you getting alcoholic?'

She shook her head, smiling.

'You look awful. Like an old tramp.'

'Oh God. Do I? I'm sorry.'

The tea revived her enough to go downstairs.

The dog, her fur dusty, lay panting on the floor. Smears of blood

104

on the tiles. Harry was cradling her head in his lap and stroking her ears. 'Bi-Biche. Poor Bi-Biche.'

'How do you know if a dog has cramp?' asked Sarah. She was crouched on the floor, her face turned sideways to stare into the dog's eyes. Bi-Biche thumped her tail, too exhausted to get up.

'I don't think dogs get cramp,' Hannah said, putting down a dish of milk. 'Bi-Biche,' she called, 'are you thirsty?'

The dog jumped up instantly and drank.

'That big dog from the café at Saint Jacques was trying to come in,' said Harry. 'I shut the door. I'm scared of him.'

'I don't think he'll hurt you. It's Bi-Biche he's after.'

She mopped up the floor and put down an old piece of matting. 'There. She can lie on that. Don't let her on your beds.'

For the rest of the day there was continual activity outside the house. The dogs from all the neighbouring villages, as well as the local ones, gathered in the square. The big dog from Saint Jacques kept them easily at bay. When Bi-Biche was in the house he guarded the front door. When she came out he kept close by and mated her vigorously more than once. He was almost too big. Bi-Biche looked back at him dolefully, sagging under the weight, and sometimes frustrated his attempts by lying down in the middle.

On Sunday Hannah came down late to breakfast to find Molly's things gone and a scrawled note on the table: 'Thanks for the bed. See you around.' She must have come in during the night to collect her few belongings. Where was she?

Hannah could only presume she had gone to stay with Marc. The idea tormented her. She tried to keep her imagination in check by busying herself with the children, taking them out, going swimming, walking on the mountain.

Each time she went in or out of the house Georges seemed to be lurking by the barn door. Whenever he saw her he smiled in a twisted, odd fashion, more like a grimace, his right hand held open in front of him, half extended, as if waiting for her to shake it. He made her uneasy. She waved her hand gaily and tried to smile back in another grimace.

The frenzy of the dogs compounded her misery. After nearly twenty-four hours of continual attendance the big dog went away, presumably to get some food. Immediately there was intense competition to take his place. Madame Corneille's little Fox, excited beyond measure but too small for Bi-Biche, clung desperately to her hind leg and snapped and snarled at all comers. There were several fights. Berger, the sheep dog from the Terrain's farm, got Fox by the neck and flung him contemptuously away. Then he and Bi-Biche ran off up the path to the mountains. Old friends.

Late that night there was howling, a sound of desolation, beside the fountain. It went on and on.

'What's that?' Harry looked anxious. 'Is it a wolf? Are you sure there aren't wolves here, Mama?'

He had seen the old dog collar armoured with metal spikes that Madame Pinet kept hanging behind the bar. It was fifty years old. Her father-in-law's sheep dog had worn it, she said, to protect his neck against the wolves.

'It's the big black dog back again,' said Hannah, looking out of the window.

'What's wrong with him? Why is he crying?'

'He's in love. His lover has gone off with someone else.'

Claude's mother came out of her doorway with a bucket. She dipped it in the fountain and flung water all over the dog, shouting abuse as he dashed dripping into the shadows.

'That'll teach you to come poking your dirty nose into this village. Get back to your rubbish dump down the hill. *Salaud!*'

She clanged the bucket sharply against the stones and went back inside.

Once the children had gone to bed Hannah sat down to the notebooks and tried to focus her attention on them. Something caught her eye, the heading 'Folk medicine', and under it a list of recipes:

'For a sty put a cut clove of garlic near the eye.'

'Leeches – keep them in glass bottles filled with water. You can use the same leeches over and over again. When they are full of blood they drop off and then you must milk the blood out, wash them and put them back in water. Or you can give them wine to make them sick.'

'A love potion. If a girl wants the man she loves to fall under her spell she should bake him a cake and stir into it seventeen drops of her menstrual blood. Once he eats it he will fall in love with her.'

The words leapt out at her from the page. When's my next period? I had one the week before I came here so I won't have another until just before the end of the holidays.

She began to walk up and down in agitation. Could I really do it? If it worked, if I was sure it would work, I might. What am I trying to do? Degrade Marc to the pitiable state I'm in? What I love about him is that he's free, that he doesn't need all the little props most people find essential. And yet some other part of me wants to drag him down, to possess him.

The idea of possession. Where does it come from in the human psyche? Such a hopeless one. Remember Petrarch writing letters from Vaucluse not far from here. Helen Grant quotes him again and again, the greatest poet who ever lived in Provence, she says, who withdrew himself for purposes of self discovery. Unsuccessful as a lover.

Hannah read again Petrarch's letter to Stefano Colonna that Helen Grant had copied down. April 1352.

Do you then, finding in the whole world no place that offers quietness and solace, enter into your own room and into yourself: keep vigil with yourself, walk with yourself, stand still with yourself. Nor think that you are alone if you are with yourself: if you are not with yourself you would be alone even in the midst of a throng . . . You may learn that nothing that is not of the soul can make you either happy or miserable; that all things that are your own are within you; that nothing that is not your own can be given you, and nothing that is your own can be taken away.'

The words calmed her as she read them aloud slowly, like an incantation. She was not entirely able to understand them.

Perhaps Marc is trying to teach me something. Or is he deliberately teaching? No. That would be too didactic, not in his character. Perhaps I'm just learning, by myself. That he isn't interested in anything exclusive. We're free to explore any relationship we want. He may not even have thought about it. Just being himself.

He exists. Like the tree growing in the field behind the church. If you bump up against it you begin to find out what it's like. The bark is abrasive to the touch. Leaves of a certain shape and tint of green. They stretch themselves out to the sun, feeding the trunk by a cunning mutation of light.

Consider the branches. If you dislike their shape you can only chop them off. But if you trim it too severely the tree will die. It won't be able to survive.

Philip has reduced me to the minimum number of branches for survival. A very weakened tree, somewhat deformed in shape. I thought I was beginning to grow in a new direction but the first rough wind has made me only too aware of my own deformity. Perhaps one of the greatest crimes you can commit against another person is to try to control them, to drag them into the circle of your own limitations, imposing a deformity that will fit your own. Is that what I want to do to Marc?

It was very unpleasant, this recognition of her own deformity. She tried to envisage it in corporeal terms, to find a physical manifestation. She took a cushion and stuffed it into the back of her shirt. Hunch back. Bowing her shoulders to keep the cushion in place she paced round the room, her neck thrust forwardly like a tortoise carrying its heavy shell. Next she took the shoe off her left foot and put both on her right, one inside the other, to give the illusion of a club foot. She dragged her right foot heavily to one side. Then, throwing off both shoes, she began to walk like a spastic, jerking her legs out and shaking her head, each step a convulsion. Quite suddenly she stopped. She was standing by the light switch. She turned it off and closed her eyes. Blind. Instinctively she put out her arms, her footsteps slow and tentative. She was feeling her way in a room not altogether familiar, afraid of stumbling in the dark, and she became aware that her hands were like sensitive antennae, all her energy concentrated into the tips of her fingers. She was using them in an entirely new way.

As she moved slowly forward, exploring the objects in her path, her sadness and sense of oppression began to lighten. She became absorbed in the discovery that her own bodily awareness could actually begin to change. For the first time she began to feel a little bit hopeful. If you were able to recognise your own deformity could it, in some way, form a starting point?

Still with her eyes shut, she progressed through the kitchen towards the stairs and climbed them slowly, one at a time, hands gliding over the rough walls, a world of tactile curves and coruscations entirely new to her. She undressed in the dark and lay down peacefully on the bed.

She had the words permanently in her mind now. Nothing that is not your own can be given you, and nothing that is your own can be taken away.

10

Next morning Bi-Biche was back. She and Berger played round the fountain, grappling with their front paws together, like puppies. Then they lay down in the shade side by side to sleep.

'She likes him best,' said Sarah. 'I think she loves him.'

Unexpectedly, and rattling as if to reflect the emotions of its owner, a grey car drew up in the square. Madame Corneille. She jumped out and looked round angrily. The only person in sight was Hannah.

'Madame, my little Fox has been massacred – terrible, his neck. I have been to the *vétérinaire* and pay much money. He has stitches, poor darling. Your young friend, Molly, tells me he was seen in the village yesterday. Do you know anything?'

Hannah stared at her. Molly? What had Molly got to do with it? She felt a veiled accusation in Madame Corneille's questioning. When she was angry her silky grey hair flew around her head like the wings of a bird whirring in distress. Then as she calmed down it settled on her neck, each feather in place.

At that moment Fox's nervous face appeared at the car window and he saw his assailant sleeping in the shade. He exploded in a frenzy of barking, hurling himself at the glass.

'Fox! What's the matter with you?'

Madame Corneille had started back to the car when the big dog from Saint Jacques came bounding up the street growling deep in his throat. In a second Berger disappeared up the path. Harry darted away in the other direction.

The big dog went up to Bi-Biche and started licking her solicitously. She lay there, a look of resignation on her face.

'What makes that dog from the café here?' Madame Corneille strode over to inspect them more closely. 'That bitch – *en chaleur*. She makes all this trouble. Whose bitch is she?'

Hannah hesitated and shrugged. 'A . . . a stray.'

Sarah came out of the house with a dish of spaghetti for Bi-Biche. She called to her tenderly. 'Bi-Biche, come and have your lunch darling. Lovely noodles.' She put the dish down and patted the dog's back. Little dust clouds flew out at each pat.

'A stray? Why is your daughter feeding her?'

Sarah looked round, startled. Hannah said quickly, 'She likes her, Madame Corneille. She's very fond of dogs.'

Madame Corneille's face twisted with disgust. 'Fond of dogs! A bitch like this can make infection round the whole *quartier*. The only solution is to take it to the *vétérinaire* to be destroyed. Disgusting, to let it go around in that condition.'

Sarah's face was getting redder and redder as she stared at Madame Corneille. Now she rushed between her and Bi-Biche and shouted, 'She's not in a condition. She's on hot. She can't help it. It's nature makes the blood come down. It happens to women too, you know. Hasn't it happened to you?'

Madame Corneille stood there in amazement. For once someone had spoken as forcefully as she did herself.

At that moment Harry came running into the square pulling Marc by the hand. He must have been working. He was wearing his special goggles. He said impatiently, 'What's the matter?'

Madame Corneille looked at him coldly. 'This bitch is causing much trouble. My Fox has been very badly bitten.'

Sarah rushed up to Marc and took his other hand in both hers. 'Marc, oh Marc, she wants Bi-Biche to be killed because she doesn't belong to anyone.'

'I beg your pardon, Madame Corneille.' Marc's goggles made him look sinister, almost threatening. His voice was quiet. 'This dog is not a stray.'

Madame Corneille stared at him.

'Bi-Biche.' Marc let go of Harry's hand and snapped his fingers. 'Come here.'

The dog sidled towards him wiggling her tail, then lay down at his feet and rolled onto her back displaying her belly expectantly. Marc sometimes delighted her by scratching it with his bare toes. He did so now.

'She's my dog, Madame Corneille. Any complaints?'

Madame Corneille's face was white. 'If she is your dog, Monsieur, as you say, perhaps you will keep her under control.'

'Under control? I don't think I understand. She's a very friendly, well-behaved dog.'

'She should be shut up.'

Marc's eyes were shining. 'But to keep her shut up, Madame, would be to deprive both her and the dogs of the neighbourhood of a very enjoyable experience. She has what you might call a social function to perform. Any bitch has a right to fulfilment. Aren't you in favour of Female Liberation, Madame Corneille? I would have thought that you of all people . . .'

Madame Corneille's car door slammed and the *Deux Chevaux* spluttered out of the square. Sarah put both arms round Marc's neck and squeezed him tightly.

'Thank you, Marc. Is she really yours?'

'Why not? As long as you look after her.'

'Oh, I will. Don't worry, I will.'

'Harry came to get me. He said the landlord was needed.'

Hannah had not seen him for almost two days. It surprised her how easy it was to avoid someone in so small a village. She raised her eyes as far as his shoulders and murmured, 'Harry was right. Madame Corneille has a curious effect on me – like a stoat with a rabbit. I get . . . paralysed.'

'I'm in the middle of something. See you.'

Exit Marc, an arm round the shoulder of each child.

Like a fourteen-year-old school-girl, unable to meet his eye. Waiting to see what his reaction will be. I'm trying to get some idea of his feelings about me in order to decide on my own behaviour.

Good God! Don't you see what you're doing? You're manoeuvring yourself into being controlled by him even though he has no interest in doing it. Waiting for his cue, just as you wait for Philip's, passively, as if you had no autonomy. Trying to push the responsibility over to someone else. The habit of a lifetime, how hard it is to change it.

For the first time she wondered if what she had embarked on would hurt Philip. At the thought of it her mind bolted like a horse shying at hidden danger. Her strategy for so many years had been to avoid anything that would hurt him. The desire for approval. The habit of a lifetime. She murmured slowly, out loud.

'Philip is not here. He chose not to be here.'

The children came back. She asked Sarah, 'Is Molly there?'

'No, I didn't see her. Where do you think she's gone, Mama?'

Sarah was puzzled by Molly's sudden departure. She was not used to people disappearing.

Claude and his mother came out of their house carrying swimming things. Claude pointed at Harry. 'You and Sarah, you swim? You come?'

His mother nodded encouragingly. Claude was learning English at school and she wanted him to practise. Harry, obligingly, had adopted a kind of pidgin English with Claude, modelling himself on his favourite film character, Tarzan, with Claude cast in the role of a friendly monkey. Now he tapped himself on the chest.

'Me come. Me fetch costume.'

He let out Tarzan's famous animal screech and darted into the house. Hannah could not help laughing. Sarah looked at her scornfully. 'Don't laugh. It makes him worse. Can we go?'

Hannah nodded.

'You won't mind being alone?'

Hannah hugged her. 'Of course not. Have a lovely time.'

They drove off.

Hannah went back into the sitting-room and sat down at the table. Through the window she could see Georges coming down the road with a basket of melons. A car passed him coming into the square, radio blaring. Leo's. Georges cringed to one side. In the front seat sat Molly. She was laughing, her hair blowing in the breeze.

They jumped out and began to unload things – two cameras, a tripod, what looked like photographic lights on long stands. Georges had hidden himself behind the stone wall that bordered the road, clutching his basket of melons. He peered surreptitiously over the top. Leo and Molly carried the equipment down the alley to Marc's house and disappeared inside.

Georges climbed over the wall and moved towards the car, looking all round to make sure no one was watching. A curious, flat-footed walk like a penguin. He walked round the car warily as if it was some dangerous animal. Then he put down his basket, and leant through the open window.

He seemed to be searching with his hands over the back of the passenger seat. He must have found what he wanted because he stood up again, holding something in front of him, invisible to Hannah at that distance. What could it be? One of Molly's hairs? He picked up his basket, hurried towards his own house and went inside.

About five minutes later he came out again, carrying a small bottle. He walked three times round the car, muttering to himself, then leaned over the open roof and carefully sprinkled some drops of liquid onto the seat.

What the hell is he doing? Trying to protect himself against Molly? But why did he put the dead snake outside my door, not his own? Hannah suddenly wondered if the snake had been to protect her. She wished Marc had not thrown it away.

The postman was crossing the square. Georges sidled away. Characters walk on, characters walk off. I could sit here all day recording their exits and entrances. He knocked and handed her a letter with a Libyan stamp. The Roman messenger with news from the battlefield.

Dearest Hannah,

Hellish hot here. My skin's all flaking off. I've used up a whole tube of Nivea. It's even too hot for me. (You won't believe that.) This is the most extraordinary country. Totally puritanical. Gaddafi is a kind of Moral Rearmament figure. The worst thing is no drink. I've exhausted the supply of whisky I hid in the shampoo bottles.

I hope you weren't too disappointed by my telegram. I'm sorry the work has dragged on so long. My colleague this end is in a very tricky situation. Political. I'm afraid if I don't stay to see things through with him the whole contract may come unstuck. Please explain to the children why I can't join you and tell them how much I'm looking forward to seeing you all again.

I've decided I like the desert. All that pale sand. It makes me feel like a painter looking at a blank canvas. (You know I always wanted to be a painter.) I was walking around with the Planning Minister and we began to talk about building a city all of stainless, incorruptible steel. Isn't it a fantastic idea? You can see Gaddafi's influence! Something that would last thousands of years, exactly as the designer imagined it.

I should be back in London very soon after you get back. Do bring me one of those delicious goat cheeses. Hope you're not getting too fat. The food here's so lousy I've lost a bit of weight. I'm getting rather sick of hotel life and looking forward to some of your home comforts. Darling Hannah, have I told you lately what a wonderful wife you are? None of this would be possible without your support. You don't say much in your letter about people. Have you met any you like? I do hope so. Give the children a big kiss and tell them I've got some presents. I think of you all every day,

Ever your loving,   P

Philip worries about getting fat. He weighs himself every day and refuses to eat bread or potatoes, and so on. He can't, he says, give up drink. He watches my waistline too. There's a calorie chart on the kitchen wall. I know it by heart. Since we've been here we've had *pommes frites* every day. Sarah and Harry's favourite food. French potatoes are delicious. Have I got fatter? It doesn't show so much when you're brown. I'm thinner than Molly at any rate, a good deal. Would Marc mind if I got fat? I don't think he would, somehow. His client was nicely rounded, a golden goose.

Hannah put the letter back in its envelope. The messages it brought were not for her. At least they elicited no response. They seemed to be written to someone else. She looked at the envelope. 'Mrs Philip Straight.' How crudely symbolic of her own loss of identity. The wife who exists only as a prefix to her husband's name. With sudden anger she crumpled the letter up, and threw it into the wastepaper basket.

She sat staring at the notebooks, wondering which to open next, but her curiosity was focussed on what was happening in Marc's studio. What were they doing? If she wanted to know she would have to go and find out. They had not, after all, rejected her. She had run away. If she wanted their company they would expect her to come and find it. Her grandmother's voice: 'Don't help yourself, Hannah. Wait till you're asked.' The habit of a lifetime. You could wait forever.

She got up and forced herself to walk down the alley to Marc's door. It was shut. She opened it and ran up the stairs to push open the door at the top.

Spotlights all directed at the couch. Molly lying there naked, her head thrown back against a cushion, arms stretched wide, legs splayed over the edge. Between her legs Marc kneels, resting his cheek against her crotch. His hands reach up towards her breasts. Molly's eyes are shut, an expression of cat-like pleasure on her face. Did I look like that last week? Leo is standing behind the camera.

'Sweet Jesus, don't any of you guys move.'

He clicks the shutter.

Hannah turns and runs down the stairs, up the alley and into her own front door. She leans against it, shaking from head to foot. There is nowhere to go, nowhere to get away from that spotlit picture hanging in her mind. She bangs her head against the door violently to drive the image out. It hurts so much she has to stop. She goes over to the sink and vomit pours out of her mouth of its own accord, her stomach heaving and retching until it is empty. She runs the cold tap and washes her face over and over again to rinse away the nausea.

The door opens behind her. Steps on the tiled floor. Two hands slide gently over her shoulders and press her head back against warm, hard flesh. She knows the smell.

'Hannah . . . Hannah, what is it?'

She says nothing.

He turns her round to face him, limp as a drunkard, holding her face in both his hands. 'Hannah, beautiful Hannah, you're shocked!'

His face is concerned but also half laughing. It enrages her. She punches him hard in the shoulder, shouting, 'Molly's only sixteen!'

Now he is openly laughing. 'Is it moral outrage?'

She bursts into tears. He leads her into the sitting-room and pushes her down onto the couch, sitting with his arm round her shoulders. 'Is it Molly you're worried about or yourself?'

She shakes her head, angrily wiping the tears away with the back of her hand. 'I don't know.'

'Molly can look after herself.'

'What were you doing? What in God's name were you doing?'

'Leo wants some photographs for his new book. A collection of poems and pictures. Molly told us about being a model and Leo wanted to try something. We did a few the other night after the *fête*, at Leo's place. Molly's good. Her face is like blotting paper – it can take on any expression you want. She makes love to the camera.'

'And you?'

'A man's only incidental. A woman would do just as well. Didn't you sense that on the balcony? What matters is that someone should be watching.'

Hannah stared at him.

'Don't look so upset, Hannah. You don't have to make a moral judgement. That doesn't come into it. Molly's a freak. She's ... amoral. A kind of holy innocent, waiting for things to happen.'

Did he think that excused everything? The abortion. Molly letting things happen. Another strategy for survival, letting other people take the responsibility, someone else the fall guy. On abortion it was fine. On pornographic photographs it's Leo and ... Marc.

'Why are you involved?'

'I'm not, in any way that matters. Just helping Leo. He couldn't think of anyone else to provide the erotic element. Haven't you noticed I'm erotic?'

Hannah drew back her hand to hit him but he caught her by the wrist. She said fiercely, 'I've noticed you're a shit.'

'Thank God for that. I was afraid you hadn't.' He was laughing more than ever. Then he went on, 'If the pictures work out Leo will be able to get Molly plenty of money from his publisher. And he's lining something else up for her.'

'What?'

'After you left the *fête* on Friday, La Corneille and her friend came over. Leo knows the other woman quite well. He's worked with her on a scenario. At the moment she's preparing for a film on the Pre-Raphaelites. She's very interested in Molly. She thinks she'd be right for one of the women. Rossetti's wife, I think she said.'

'Eleanor Siddal.'

'That's it.'

'That's strange, I thought of Rossetti the first time I saw Molly.'

'Leo took her to La Corneille's place yesterday. He'll act as her agent, make sure she gets the right kind of contract, all that crap.'

'But Molly hardly speaks French. Only what she learnt at school.'

'La Corneille wants her to stay with her for a month to coach her for the film. There's not much speaking in her part.'

'But what will happen to Molly? Madame Corneille will eat her alive. You said her garden was littered with the bones of . . .'

'Not Molly. She likes the attention. Something new for her. La Corneille's eating out of her hand. She's never met anything like Molly before.'

'But it's horrible Marc, it's corrupting, it's . . .'

'Cool it, Hannah. All Molly wants is to get out of that rat-hole she lives in in London. What other chance has she got? Nothing to offer except her face.'

Hannah said quietly, 'I thought since she left here she was staying with you.'

'Maybe she had the same idea. She brought her things round but I took her straight down to Leo's. I can't have anyone living with me. It would interfere with my work. I'm not interested in being anybody's Daddy. Leo is.'

Hannah could hardly disguise her relief. Marc put his hand on her cheek and stroked the corner of her mouth with his thumb as he said, 'There's only one reason Molly came after me. Because of you. It makes me interesting.'

Hannah looked puzzled. He went on, 'I thought there might be something . . . between you. Molly turning up like that. I know so little about you, Hannah. You're very mysterious to me.'

Mysterious? Hannah looked at him in amazement. She felt totally transparent.

'I suppose that's why I took you both out on the balcony. I thought I might find out something.'

'You mean you engineered it?' She was humiliated.

'Of course not. It just . . . happened like that. But I did learn something.'

'That I don't go for group sex?'

'That you're afraid, afraid of uncertain situations. You don't like not knowing what's going to happen. You run away like you did just now.'

He spoke without any hint of condemnation, offering her an interesting piece of information. She felt very small, shrinking inside herself.

'I'm too old, Marc. I'm conditioned by the way I've been living for so many years. I can't . . . disentangle things. Sex, love, thinking, feeling – they're all mixed up. For me sex is something very personal and . . . well, private.'

Marc put his arms round her and held her close to him, biting her ear. 'You're wonderful, Hannah. I like you just the way you are.'

To be called wonderful twice in one day? By two different people? Did either of them know what she was like, was there anyone to know?

'Marc . . .' She spoke hesitantly. 'That could never be . . . enough for you, could it? A commitment to one person?'

'The last thing I want is to know what's going to happen. I like things . . . unexpected. I want to explore all the possibilities. That's very important for me, the . . . silent language of the body.'

Hannah was struggling with herself. Even stronger, she realised, than the desire to possess the other person was the desire to be possessed. Was she ready to do anything more than exchange one serfdom for another?

Marc pulled a letter out of his pocket. 'I had a letter from Janine this morning.'

'Your half-sister?'

'She's in the Alps. She wants me to meet her for a few days' walking. It's something we always used to do together, but I've been too busy this year. Have you ever been to the Alps?'

Hannah shook her head. She wanted to cry out, 'Don't go!'

Marc looked at her speculatively. 'I wondered if you'd like to come. What do you think?'

'Would she mind?' She could not hide her delight.

'Of course not. I want you to meet her. And Harry and Sarah would like it, I think.'

Hannah put her arms round his neck.

'I take back what I said about you being a shit.'

'Don't say that.' His face was serious. 'I don't want to have to prove it.'

'A part-time shit.'

'We'll go tomorrow.' He smacked her hard on the bottom and went out.

Hannah washed her face under the cold tap again. She felt lightheaded. A little earlier she had wanted to destroy herself. Now she was flying over the tops of the trees, gliding through the air like one of those birds round the church. Was she going crazy?

Towards evening there was a knock. Molly came running in carrying flowers, like a child wanting to be forgiven. Sarah hugged her Molly looked shyly at Hannah over Sarah's head. 'I'm not going back to London.'

'Marc told me.'

'I'm going to be in a film.'

Sarah was beside herself with excitement. 'In a film? Molly, will you be a film star, will you have pots and pots of money?'

Molly smiled. 'I dunno. It's a chance, isn't it?'

Hannah stood stiffly by the stove where she was cooking rice. Just the sight of Molly revived her feeling of nausea. Molly was waiting for her to speak. She said slowly, 'If it's what you want, I suppose so.'

'What's wrong with it, then?' She sounded defiant.

'I don't know . . . Do you think you'll be all right? All those funny people . . .'

'They're no funnier than what I meet in London. That Leo, he's a nice guy, isn't he?'

Hannah suddenly wondered, looking at Molly's beautiful, expectant face, if she was jealous that Molly had replaced her own influence so quickly with someone else's. Jealous of Leo? Of Madame Corneille?

'I don't know, Molly. I don't know much about him.'

'If I don't take this chance while I've got it I may never have another.' For a moment she looked desperate. 'I can't go back That drunken old pig, bashing us all the time. I never want to go back.'

'What about your mother?'

'I'll write to her. Maybe I can send her some money later, when I get some. I thought, if you . . . if you . . .'

Hannah waited.

'Could you go and see her, tell her I'm all right.'

Hannah said warily, 'How will I know you are? What can I say to her?'

'You'll think of something, won't you?'

Molly smiled, her cat's tongue showing a pink tip. It was impossible not to smile back.

> *The blessed Damozel leaned out*
> *From the gold bar of Heaven;*
> *Her eyes were deeper than the depth*
> *Of waters stilled at even;*
> *She had three lilies in her hand,*
> *And the stars in her hair were seven.*

II

Janine met them at the hostel at the head of the valley leading into the lower slopes of the Alps. She was in the bar. When Marc kissed her she clung to him a moment, resting her head in the curve of his neck.

'It's a long time since we walked together, Marc.'

'I hope my legs can still do it.'

She pushed him away, laughing, to inspect him.

'You've got fatter.'

'Success. A bit of success is very coarsening.'

'I've just done a week's climbing with some university friends. It took me three days to get over the stiffness.'

'Hannah's never been in the Alps. She's curious.'

Janine turned and shook hands with Hannah. She looked dubiously at her feet. Beach shoes.

'They're my most comfortable pair. I'm afraid of getting blisters,' said Hannah awkwardly.

'Oh, well. There's no real climbing involved. I expect you'll be all right. Shall we have a last pastis? There won't be anything much at the hut.'

Her intention was for them to spend the night high up at a mountain rest house. You could walk for days like that, from one hut to another.

They took very little with them. Hannah stuffed their tooth brushes, a comb and towel into the pocket of her jacket. Marc tied a huge sweater round his shoulders. Janine had a canvas satchel slung on her back with biscuits and chocolate in it.

The path started to climb immediately. Looking up they could see the narrow track they were to follow winding between the rough grass and rocks. They stood aside for a family of four walkers on the downward journey, the father carrying the smallest child on his shoulders, their mouths stained purple.

'Myrtles,' said Janine. 'The bushes are higher up.'

She has the grace of a mountain deer as she walks ahead, turning her head delicately to get her bearings where the path forks. Her hair curls close to her head, round her ears, on the nape, dark like Marc's but softer. She's very thin and yet resilient, a controlled energy in her step that I envy, thought Hannah.

The children kept up easily and sometimes darted ahead, but her own legs ached with the effort of climbing.

Marc noticed her flushed face and patted a flat piece of rock beside him.

'Shall we rest a moment?'

She sat down gratefully. Around them among yellow and white flowers and one blue one like a bell, hovered small brown butterflies. Already the hostel looked far away below them. Harry picked out Marc's van, tiny in the car park. Down the gorges on all sides of them came the sounds of softly rushing water. On their left the path crossed over one of these streams marked with stepping stones round which the water splashed and foamed restlessly. Janine and Marc hoisted the children across.

'I think you'd better take your shoes off. Boots are tough but I don't think your shoes will stand up to a wetting.'

Janine spoke kindly. She was not trying to put her down. Even so Hannah felt foolish as she took off her shoes and hopped, bare-footed, over the stones. One foot slipped ankle deep into the water. It was freezing. Her foot ached with the sudden shock of cold and she leapt for the bank. Then she bent down and cupped her hand in the water to drink. Deliciously pure. She held it in her mouth for a moment, savouring it, then, with a sudden cry of pain, swallowed it quickly. One of her back teeth, with an old stopping, had reacted violently. She rubbed the gum quickly and put on her shoes and socks to follow Janine.

Half way up the mountain, snow was packed tightly into a gorge whose deep cleft was always in shadow. The force of the water from the melting glaciers above had cut a way through, below the frozen snow, so that a white bridge of ice had formed above the stream which suddenly plunged down a steep drop of rocks in a curtain of spray. As they came nearer the sound of the waterfall grew louder and louder. The path ended abruptly where the snow started.

'Where do we go now?' asked Hannah.

'We cross the gorge here where it's marked with those sticks, and then follow the red arrow on the other side.'

'Is the snow solid?'

Janine smiled reassuringly.

'It's never melted through this year. It's a nervi, packed hard as ice. You just walk across.'

It looked perfectly possible. The width of the snow was about seventy yards from one side of the gorge to the other. Janine started across holding Sarah's hand. She walked slightly sideways, digging her boots into the dirty, white surface at each step. Hannah began to follow. She placed her feet exactly where Janine's had been, fitting her heels into the dents. Good King Wenceslas. Suddenly one foot slipped, her other leg shot from under her, and she felt herself sliding uncontrollably downwards.

'Fall flat. Get flat on the ground.'

Marc's shout, urgent and angry, forced her to try to do as he said. She hit the ice with a thud and scrabbled at its harsh surface with her fingers.

'Try to get a grip and keep where you are.'

She bent one leg to make the angle of her body less precipitous and dug with her finger nails. The surface was freezing. Sideways she could see Marc picking his way slowly towards her. He rammed each heel in with a thud and tested its security before taking the next step. Janine had turned and was coming back, but much higher up.

Hannah realised she must have slipped a long way. She turned her head to look down. The snowy surface sloped steeply towards the edge where she could hear water gushing out from below. The wind blew some of the spray back at her. She shut her eyes, clenched in a trap of terror as she fought back the desire to scream. If she could not keep control she would start sliding again. Her hands ached with cold. Suddenly she remembered the moments before Harry's birth, the same overpowering urge to scream, her terror of losing control while the midwife's voice insistently, quietly, repeated, 'Keep calm, keep calm. Remember your breathing, get control of your breathing.' She seemed to be holding her breath in a hard ball inside her chest. Slowly she let it out and as slowly drew it in again. Breathing. Concentrate on your breathing.

Marc, a few feet away, leant towards her with his hand out, his face anxious and frowning, his scarlet sweater falling over one shoulder. See if you can reach me. Lift up one hand carefully. Keep holding on with the other.'

She dug her left hand harder than ever into the gritty surface of the snow and raised her right hand towards Marc. He gripped it strongly. His hand felt extraordinarily warm. The contrast of flesh and snow.

'Now get on your knees and try to stand up.'

Her legs were cramped from the strain of lying there. She found it painful to move them.

'Don't jerk,' he shouted. 'Slow as you can.'

Little by little, she pulled herself up. Marc swayed slightly as he took the weight but kept his balance. Her legs were shaking uncontrollably. Looking up she could see Janine above them leaning against one of the sticks that marked the way across, a child at each side.

'Can you go on?'

Marc's voice was anxious, his upper lip covered in sweat. Staring at the drops of sweat she forced herself not to look behind and nodded. She could not speak.

'I'll go first. Hold my hand tightly and put your feet in my marks. We'll go very slowly.' They climbed, sideways, as far as Janine. As soon as they got to her she reached out and took Hannah's other hand. The children were holding firmly to the marking stick, their eyes huge with strain.

'Get behind her, Janine,' said Marc. 'She can keep her balance between us. Harry, go in front of me where I can keep an eye on you. Sarah, you follow Janine.'

Slowly, what seemed an agony of time to Hannah, they crept in procession across the icy surface. As they reached the grass on the other side Marc ran the last few steps and threw himself down on a rock, laughing and laughing.

'That's fine. You made it all right. Thank God.'

He pulled Hannah down and kissed her roughly on the cheek, hugging her to him then suddenly squeezing her shoulder so hard she cried out.

'Crazy cow,' he shouted, 'that's what you are, a crazy cow.'

Her limbs were trembling. Harry clung to her arm anxiously. Janine opened her canvas satchel and took out a small flask.

'Have some cognac.'

Hannah still could not speak. She took the flask and gulped down some brandy. Too much. It choked her. She began to cough and then her coughing turned to laughter and she and Marc leant against each other laughing and drinking alternately, exhausted. Harry and Sarah ate chocolate, staring from one to the other.

'What do we do now?' asked Marc. 'Can you go on? The hut's up there.'

He pointed above him. Perched on a flat crag, Hannah could see a wooden hut like a doll's house, a flag fluttering beside it, no visible way of reaching it.

'How do we get there?' she asked. 'Do we have to climb? I can't see a path.'

'It's there,' Janine said quietly. 'It zigzags between the rocks, that's why you can't see it. It's not a difficult climb.'

Below them was an almost sheer drop. To the side the frozen nervi.

'Do you want to go back?' asked Marc.

Hannah looked at the dirty surface of the nervi with horror.

'Would I have to cross . . . that again?'

Marc nodded.

'There's no other way.'

She began to shake.

'I couldn't. Not without a rope or some proper shoes.'

She looked down at the drop below them, giddy with fear.

'I didn't . . . I didn't know I minded heights.'

She felt ashamed of a weakness she had not even been aware of before. She was afraid of infecting Harry and Sarah with it. Like being afraid of snakes. Such things were catching. Marc put his arm round her shoulder.

'We'll go on, then. We're more than half way. You can walk between us.'

The path was only wide enough for them to move in single file. Janine led the way, her feet sure and agile on the stony surface. There were clumps of myrtle bushes on each side and she stopped to feast on the purple berries, gathering a handful at a time before stuffing them into her mouth. Hannah copied her, crushing the sweet juice against her tongue. The children ate one berry at a time, too impatient

126

o gather a handful, their fingers darting round the shiny leaves. Hannah's pleasure in this new taste dissolved some of her fear and she turned to look at Marc behind her, his smile stained dark red with juice.

They were startled by a high-pitched scream echoing down from somewhere above them. A brown animal like a large cat dashed away across the rocks.

'What's that?' Harry asked with excitement.

'A marmot. Plenty of them up here.'

Hannah began to look upwards with more interest, hoping there might be another, when unexpectedly round a corner she saw the hut perched on its promontory of rock, just ahead.

'How on earth did they get it here?' she asked.

'Helicopter. The bits are prefabricated. They fly them up and put them together on the site.'

They sat down on the edge of the promontory to get their breath. It was growing dusk. The sun had already disappeared behind the mountains but the sky was still stained a dark pink, like blood diffusing in water, strands of colour drifting further and further apart, fading into the darker grey. The sense of space, the stillness, were exhilarating but also, somehow, oppressive. Although they had climbed quite high they were still encircled by the dark peaks above them, inhuman presences. She decided she did not like mountains on this scale, except at a distance. Close up they were overpowering. The mountain, as she had thought of it, behind the village was not really a mountain at all in these terms. It was on a human scale. These massive forms were something quite other.

Sitting still they began to feel the cold and Janine led them up the wooden staircase into the hut. Inside it was like a ship's cabin. A young man shook them by the hand. The guardian of the hut. He remembered Janine from a previous visit. He was a student, working here in his vacation. He had to bring up the food once a week on his back.

There were only two other visitors – middle-aged, women school-teachers spending a week in the mountains climbing from hut to hut. Serious walkers. They asked to be roused at six so they could be sure of an early start. The student cooked a surprisingly good supper of soup and spaghetti. When the children fell half asleep over it Janine put them to bed in the end compartment of the hut.

There was a record player on one of the tables. Most evenings, said the student, he played music. His only entertainment. He put on some recent pop, the singer's voice effeminate, slightly hysterical, the base chords repeating over and over again monotonously. The teachers exchanged glances. This was not what they had climbed a mountain for. When it ended one of them asked politely, 'Have you . . . anything else? Some classical music?' He shook his head, leafing through the record sleeves, then pulled out one that seemed more hopeful.

'How about this, vintage jazz, Louis Armstrong?'

The trumpet speaks sweetly out of the machine – a different style, a different age, a more intricate rhythm. Marc and Janine look at each other, their eyes shining. They move towards the only open space in the room. Casually they start to dance. Old style jive. Their right hands touch for a moment across their bodies as they propel each other away in a half turn, then back again, their gestures perfectly co-ordinated in an effortless harmony of physical understanding. Hannah has never seen such dancing, fireflies on a summer evening, as they respond to every throb of the trumpet's song. Sound reflected in movement. Their dark heads move together and apart again, their eyes holding each other's, mouths smiling, half open.

As she watches them Hannah knows now why Marc has always given her this sense of self-sufficiency. His commitment is already made. Unquestioning, total love for his half-sister. Dancing, they are two halves of one person, so complete is their absorption in one another. She could never meet him at this level. He is not available. It must be the reason why he asks so little, slipping lightly through the mesh of any attachment. Mercury, the other name for quicksilver. Now she can see his winged sandals.

The music ended. The school teachers clapped their hands in appreciation. Marc and Janine came back to sit each side of Hannah. One of the teachers bent forward. 'Where did you learn to dance like that? It reminds me of when I was young.'

Marc laughed and took a long drink of water. 'There was a girl staying in our village one summer when I was about thirteen. She taught me. I showed Janine. That summer we danced every evening to our mother's records.'

Janine looked at him, her smile enigmatic. Hannah felt as if she was sprawled once more back on the icy nervi, falling.

Marc put his hand over hers. 'What's wrong? You're trembling.'

'I don't know.' Her voice, even to her own ears, sounded distant.

Marc rubbed her hands in both of his. 'My God, you're freezing, Hannah. You must be tired as hell after that trouble on the way up. We should all be in bed. Janine,' he stood up, 'you'd better show her where to go.'

Men and women were divided into two separate compartments, a partition in between, crammed with communal bunks, three tiers, one on top of another. Hannah climbed up to the top bunk beside the sleeping bodies of the children. Janine took the middle and the two teachers the bottom. They muttered '*Bonne nuit*' and almost immediately Hannah could hear a slow, rhythmical snore coming from, below. She unfolded a blanket and wrapped it round herself, putting another under her head as a pillow. It smelt overpoweringly of stale sweat. Curling up like a child with her hands pressed against her cheek she fell into the sleep of exhaustion.

*

The window of the bunk room was high up, uncurtained. Hannah was woken by Harry's excited whisper. 'We're on top of the world. We're going to fall off.' He turned to see her smiling at him. 'Come and look.'

The children were squeezed together at the end of the bunk, staring out at the unnerving space the other side of the glass. Hannah wriggled up beside them. The shapes of the mountains were almost invisible behind swirling clouds of mist.

'What's the time?' Hannah asked Sarah. Like her father she always wore a watch.

'Seven o'clock.'

Sarah swivelled round and sat up, bending her head to avoid the roof of the hut. 'Harry's disgusting. He was watching those two ladies dress.'

'They didn't know I was watching.'

Hannah looked quickly over the edge of the bunk with embarrassment.

'It's all right,' said Sarah. 'They've gone now.'

'Do you know,' said Harry, no longer whispering and glancing sideways at his mother, 'one of them was wearing four layers of kind of underwear. First she had a vest, one of those long woolly ones then a T shirt thing, then a shirt and then a proper jersey.'

'Three layers of underwear,' Sarah interrupted. 'One was overwear.'

'She must be boiling,' said Harry, 'she had a layer of fat as well.'

Janine appeared in the doorway. 'There's coffee if you'd like some.'

At the table all Hannah's anxiety came pressing in on her. She would have to face the journey down. No helicopter to winch her of in a magical air-lift. Marc's face was crinkled with sleep. He put four spoonfuls of sugar into his bowl of coffee then dipped a *biscotte* into it Bits floated off into the milky liquid. Harry, watching him closely, did the same. How odd, thought Hannah, I've never seen Marc at break fast, a tiny network of unfamiliar ritual. The back of his hands are covered with fine, black hair, even his fingers. First the sugar, then the *biscotte*, probably since he was three years old, leading himself un obtrusively into the day. He doesn't even notice me watching him hardly awake. If I saw these same movements every day would they still delight me? It's the sense of the other. Everything he does has a fresh vibration for me.

'Marc, is there another way down?'

He looked up. 'Another way?'

'Do we have to go back by the nervi?'

Janine, sensing the tension behind her question, intervened, 'I'm not sure. There may be a different path. I'll ask Jean-Paul.'

She went into the kitchen. Marc looked at Hannah for the first time fully and smiled at her. That's nice. He's not cross with me for being afraid. With Philip I always feel I have to disguise my frailties as if they were an intrusion on his time, something he shouldn't have to bother with. He is competent, so I should be. So much of myself is censored, the weaknesses papered over as if they didn't exist. I've learnt to economise with the demands I make on him, even on my self. I should have known I would be afraid of the mountain. Janine came back smiling.

'Yes, there's another way down.'

'Is it difficult?' Hannah rushed in with her question. It might be worse than the nervi. Janine shook her head.

'He says not. Steep in one or two places but no gorges. I'm sure it'll be all right.'

Hannah let out a great sigh. 'I think I'll have some more coffee.' Smiling at Harry, she took a *biscotte* and dipped it in as he had, copying Marc. Absorbing the beloved. Imprinting his movements onto her own.

They cleaned their teeth in the ice-cold trickle of water that ran behind the hut. Janine said quietly, 'Look behind us. Move gently.' On a rock about sixty yards away, two marmots were crouched steadily watching them. Harry jerked his head too quickly and with a sudden scream they jumped away and began to climb the rocks behind. He ran after them whistling entreatingly but the rock face soon defeated his efforts to climb it. The sun, at a sharp angle to their right, was rapidly dispelling the mist and, as Harry turned, a shaft of light shone directly onto his form against the rock, transforming his hair into a silhouette of gold. He crouched down pretending to be a marmot and with short, delighted screams bounded towards them. At that moment such intensity of feeling came over Hannah it was as if she was the sun herself shining towards him.

They started down the mountain. In some ways it was worse. Whereas before Hannah had been able to keep her eyes on the path as it led upwards, now, in looking at the track she was following, her vision inevitably included the sheer drop beyond. The downward gradient made it harder not to stumble. Harry rushed ahead calling to Sarah, 'Race you to the bottom.'

'Harry, be careful, don't go too fast.'

The note of panic in her voice made Marc put his hand on her arm and say quietly, 'Don't fuss. You'll only make them nervous.' Then louder to Harry, 'You mustn't run down a mountain, Harry. You can run up but never down. How many different kinds of flowers can you find?'

It was a brilliant suggestion for slowing him down. Harry immediately began searching the foliage at the side of the path. Mountain flowers are more delicate than their counterparts in the valley, as if the difficulties of survival refine their stems and petals to a hair-like thinness.

'Will you give us a prize?'

'O.K. A packet of *chips* at the bar; Janine's to be the judge. She's the only one who knows the names.'

The children disappeared round a bend in the path.

'Can you enjoy it at all?' Marc was teasing her.

'Yes. . . .' she laughed at her own confusion. 'Well, bits of it. It gets better as we get lower down.'

Janine smiled at her, sympathetic but detached. Hannah's suffering was so far from her own experience. Janine was one of those girls who snuff up the wild from a mountain crag, a springing, elastic girl, not a jelly.

As they rounded the corner at the point of the zig-zag, they saw the path ahead of them narrow to a ledge cut into the side of the rock face. A sudden cry, like a marmot, but more urgent and fearful, startled them. They could not see the children at all. Unable to stop herself Hannah called at the top of her voice, 'Sarah? Harry?'

She began to hurry, stubbing her toe harshly against a stone. At that moment Sarah appeared at the far end of the ledge. Her face was screwed up. She opened her mouth and began to scream.

'Stay there!' Marc shouted, starting to run.

Sarah continued to scream, her voice echoing shrilly back from the rocks, redoubling the terror. Marc flattened himself against the rock face and passed quickly along the ledge. Hannah copied him, vertigo momentarily displaced by a much greater fear.

Sarah was standing on a flat piece of grass where the path widened. She was gasping for breath, the screams dying in her throat, her arms sticking out stiffly from her sides. Marc put his hands on her shoulders and shook her gently.

'What is it, Sarah? What's happened?'

Sarah stared at him, her eyes fixed in horror. She seemed unable to speak.

'Where's Harry?'

Hannah was wildly searching the ground ahead of them. Sarah turned and pointed to the rock edge. Her arm had no joint in it. Stiff as a railway signal. 'He's . . . gone.'

Marc lay flat on the grass, grasping at tufts on either side of him, his head hanging over the edge. He shouted,

'Harry! Can you hear me? Are you all right?'

Again the echo. Only his own voice answering.

'I can't see him. There's a sheer fall. We'll have to get lower down.'

Janine was already running down the path to the next bend. Marc got up and hurried after her. Hannah was about to follow when Sarah suddenly threw her arms round her legs and clung to them as if that was the only way she could prevent herself falling.

'I didn't push him.'

Hannah cradled Sarah's head in her arms, stroking her hair. The child burst into tears, great sobs shaking her thin shoulders. Hannah crouched down and took out a handkerchief, wiping away the tears as they trickled down Sarah's hot cheeks. She forced herself to speak, her voice barely a whisper.

'Shall we go and look for him?'

Sarah's eyes searched her mother's for some sign of reassurance. Hannah tried to smile but it was as if her mouth was set in plaster. She stood up, holding Sarah's hand tightly, and began to walk along.

At the bend there was a clear view of the rock fall. Harry was sprawled on a boulder, flat on his back, his head hanging sideways. Janine crouched over him, her ear to his chest. Marc was clambering over some stones towards them. He bent down beside Janine and took the boy's head in both his hands, moving it gently to and fro. Then he stopped, kneeling by the body with his own head bowed. Hannah stood still. Very slowly Marc leant forward to pick him up so that now Harry lay in his arms, his head hanging like a broken flower below Marc's shoulder.

Letting go of Sarah's hand, Hannah began to run. Janine, too, began running but towards her, away from Marc. As they reached each other Janine stopped and put her hand for a moment on Hannah's shoulder, looking into her eyes with an expression of such sorrow that Hannah shook her head as if to ward it off. Janine passed her, running towards the path where Sarah was standing. Hannah's movements slowed down. Marc began to come towards her, carefully, across the stones. She was walking towards something unimaginable. Her steps got slower and slower till she could hardly move. Marc was standing in front of her. His eyes never left hers. They stood facing each other. As if something other than herself had taken control of her, she put out her arms in slow motion. She seemed to be outside her body, looking down on the scene from a great height. Marc lifted the boy into her arms. Weighed down, she sank onto the ground, her head bent forward towards Harry's and began to rock to and fro as if she was trying to rock him to sleep. His eyes were closed. How do I know someone isn't dreaming me? His head hung limply down. I don't know, Harry, I don't know. She closed her eyes. Someone is dreaming us both. She pressed her ear against his chest, listening for a sound that was no longer there. Only an unbearable silence. Then she heard a low moaning, like an animal in pain. It was coming from her own throat.

Marc crouched next to her and put his arm across her shoulder, holding it firmly. Little by little the pressure of his hand stilled her movements. She opened her eyes, whispering, 'Is his neck broken?'

Marc said, 'It must have happened instantly.'

Was he trying to comfort her? She turned sideways to look up at the rock face. 'What long moments . . . when he was falling . . .' She burst into tears, staring at the rock, her face screwed up. Marc put both his arms round her across Harry's body and held her gently, bending her head to his shoulder. Gradually she grew quieter.

'Let me take him.' He stood up and lifted Harry away from her. The boy's arm hung down in front of her face. In his tightly clenched fist were two yellow flowers.

'Sarah – don't forget Sarah,' Marc said.

She looked back to where Janine was kneeling on the path, her arms round Sarah. Sarah was staring over her head at her mother.

'Take her down to the hostel. I'll follow you.' Marc's voice was insistent, pushing her into the realisation of someone elses' pain.

She burst out, 'Couldn't we bury him here?'

Marc shook his head gently. She nodded, shaking the tears out of her eyes.

'I know, I know. But it's so terrible . . . poor Sarah . . .' She got up and began to run towards the child. Sarah broke away from Janine and rushed towards her calling,

'Mama, Mama . . .'

They put their arms round each other, clinging together. All at once Sarah stopped crying and said in a very matter of fact voice, 'He was trying to pick a flower. A yellow one. It was just below the ledge.'

Hannah nodded. She was past speaking. Janine began to walk down the path, leading the way back to the hostel. Hannah and Sarah came after her, their hands cemented together. Some way behind, more slowly because of the burden he was carrying, Marc followed.

12

Harry was lying on his back in the police morgue. That was the last she had seen of him. That afternoon Marc had carried him into the cold room and placed him on a marble slab. He lay there on his back, his eyes shut as if he was sleeping. So often he slept on his back. She would have liked to put a pillow under his head. The policeman took a white sheet out of the cupboard and pulled it over him. She wanted to scream, 'Don't'. Across the room was another slab draped with a sheet. The place had an unpleasant, aseptic smell. One of the smells of death?

They went into the office. Marc answered questions, so the man could fill in the right forms. For a foreign national everything had to be done in triplicate with a copy for the British consulate. The man's voice droned on. He did not look up. Hannah's eyes were on his feet beneath the desk. He wore curious openwork shoes of plaited brown leather. She was waiting for the words of accusation he ought to be speaking. She wanted him to stand up and look her straight in the eyes saying, 'J'accuse . . .' Where had she got that phrase from? It was what she was saying over and over again inside her head. Guilty. Guilty. She wanted someone to acknowledge it.

From above the office came the sound of a piano. Someone practising the opening bars of Beethoven's *Für Elise*. The piano was out of tune. Did the policeman's family live over the office? Small, white fingers, like his, on the ivory.

The man scraped back his chair and stood up. Was this the moment? Hannah's breathing became rapid, her anxiety growing minute by minute. But he said nothing of the kind. He merely stated that the police doctor was expected in an hour. He would fill in the death certificate after inspecting the *cadavre*.

When he spoke the word *cadavre* the suffocating feeling began. Why did it sound so much more terrible in French? She was thinking all the time that Harry was in the next room but also that Harry was not in the next room. She could not make the two facts come together. Where was he? It was as if he was lost and she should be looking for him. But where could she start? The police office was stifling. She swayed on the chair as if she might fall and Marc got up and put his hand on her shoulder.

The policeman was saying something. Her understanding of French seemed to have stopped abruptly at the word *cadavre*. It echoed round her head. Marc touched her hand.

'He says you needn't stay any longer. We can call for the certificate later and let him know what to do with the body.'

His face had the same concerned expression as when she lay sprawled on the ice and he bent to instruct her in what to do.

'Let's go, Hannah. You need a drink.'

They left the *gendarmerie*. Marc took her into a café and ordered coffee and cognac, holding her hand all the time as if afraid she might float away if he did not keep her moored.

'What did he mean, Marc, about the . . . body?' She could not say the name, not in connection with what lay under the sheet in the morgue.

'Drink some brandy. Put it in your coffee.' Marc pushed the glass across. 'Something has to be decided, Hannah, about the burial. It has to be in forty-eight hours. That's the law in France.'

Tears splashed from her eyes onto the paper table cloth. 'I . . . wanted to leave him in the mountains, I wanted to bury him there.'

Marc held her hand tightly. 'Do you want to take the body back to England?'

'No,' she cried out, 'dragging him about from place to place . . . I couldn't bear it.'

She looked down at the cloth where the tears had already been absorbed and prodded at the damp patch with her finger. 'Philip . . .'

Philip had revolved round and round in her mind for hours. What she had to tell him made it impossible for her to focus on him clearly. 'Philip . . . poor Philip. He doesn't know.'

Her finger had poked a hole in the paper. 'I can't send him a cable, it would be a terrible way for him to hear.'

'Can't you get in touch with him? Do you know where he's staying?'

She remembered the letter. On hotel writing paper. There must have been a telephone number. But what had she done with the letter? With sudden discomfort she remembered throwing it into the wastepaper basket. 'There's a letter back in the village. I could try to ring him up.'

'Where is he?'

'Benghazi. Libya.'

'Libya!' Marc looked at her in amazement. She had told him almost nothing about Philip. 'You'd better try that. We'll go back tomorrow.'

The thought that they could go next day lifted some weight off her, to leave these loathsome mountains behind, this place of horror. Suddenly she knew what she wanted to do.

'Marc, could Harry be buried in the village? Would it be allowed?'

Marc's face showed relief that she had been able to make a suggestion. 'Why not? You'd have to get permission from the mayor, and the priest at Saint Jacques, but that shouldn't be impossible. Elaine Pinet's the mayor. We could ask her.'

'Now. Could you ask her now?'

She half rose from her chair. Seeing her agitation, Marc went over to the telephone at the end of the bar. It must have been a bad line because he had to raise his voice. The facts of the accident rang loudly round the almost empty bar. The barman stared at Hannah curiously. She looked down, clenching her hands tightly together under the table. Only one thing seemed to matter – that Harry could be buried in the village. She wanted it passionately.

Marc came back. 'She says you're to leave everything to her. She's going down to see the priest tonight, she'll arrange for the undertaker who buried her husband to fetch the body from the police here. I've written the name down so we can give it to them.'

Hannah stood up and put her arms round Marc's neck. She began to cry. He held her tightly. 'There's one thing. She asked if Harry was Catholic. I said yes.'

Hannah pulled back to look at his face. He was attempting a smile. 'Oh, Marc, Harry was nothing. We're none of us anything.'

'It makes it easier for Elaine Pinet. I don't want to put her wrong with the priest.'

'Philip was brought up as one. But he hasn't been to church for years. Does it matter?'

'As far as I'm concerned, God, who sees all, will forgive all.' His smile was twisted. 'One mumbo-jumbo's as good as another.'

*

They're driving back to the village, Sarah and Hannah in the back holding hands. Whenever they are together their hands creep towards each other like small animals seeking comfort. Hands are best at this wordless communication. Sarah's right hand is lying in Hannah's left. Every now and then she looks up, searching her mother's face for some reassurance that the smashed bits of her world will come together again. Hannah's eyes cannot give it to her. Windows onto her own pain. Sarah winces and looks away. Hannah brings her left hand over to enclose Sarah's completely. The child leans against her and Hannah can feel some of the tension going out of her arm.

Janine and Marc are in front. None of them has spoken a word since leaving the *gendarmerie* with the death certificate. Hannah keeps looking at the backs of their heads. How uncannily alike they are, their hair the same dense black, the set of their necks. She feels numb. Everything going on around her just as before. Cars driving along the road. Farmers in their fields. In the towns they pass through, the shops are open, the streets busy. People jerk their arms and legs about, their mouths open and shut, they shake hands, go in and out of doorways, all in meaningless activity, like an old film speeded up. Why doesn't it stop? If only they could be frozen in mid-gesture so she could look at everything slowly and carefully and try to make some sense out of it.

Marc turns on the radio. It crackles badly, very distorted. The announcer speaks the news rapidly without seeming to pause for breath. A strike of air traffic controllers. Planes are being grounded or directed elsewhere. Marc twiddles the knob until he gets music – it sounds like Bach. He leaves it playing quietly. Bach sounding thinly, distorted, from far away across the mountains.

Hannah could not bring herself to read the letter again. She smoothed the creases sufficiently to see the address. Yes, there was a telephone number. What time would it be in Libya? They had been driving half the day, so it was already evening. She stood there uncertainly, wondering what Philip would be doing at this moment. She tried to see his face. 'Philip.' Even saying his name aloud could not bring it into her mind.

There was a knock at the door and Madame Pinet came in. She shook Hannah's hand. Her face expressed not so much concern as a kind of passive resignation. 'I know what it is to lose someone you love, Madame Straight.' She spoke slowly and formally. 'You have all my sympathy. It is even more terrible to lose someone so young.'

Hannah bowed her head and said quietly, and with the same formality, 'Thank you.'

Madame Pinet related her conversation with the priest. He could see no objection to the child being buried in the village. The payment for the plot would be made to him. He preferred the funeral to be early the next day as he had a wedding later on the other side of the valley.

Madame Pinet's tone was now one of calm practicality. Her large figure in its dark blue apron sprigged with tiny white flowers gave Hannah some kind of reassurance. She knew what to do. What was meaningless to Hannah was not so to her. A ritual that had to be attended to. She was trying to draw Hannah into it. She stood there patiently, waiting for an answer.

Hannah said, 'I have to telephone my husband.' What would she do if Philip did not like the idea?

'Of course. Naturally.' Elaine Pinet shook hands again. 'Come to the café later to tell me what you want to do. For a long-distance call I advise you to go down into the town. The local exchange is no good. It sometimes takes half an hour even to get through to my daughter in Marseille.'

Making this telephone call was the worst thing Hannah had ever had to do in her life. How would she start? What could she say to protect Philip from the despair she was feeling? Just one fact she had to tell him. Then the conversation would be over. She was an agent for his destruction.

Marc came into the kitchen with Sarah. 'Have you found it?'

'What?' She could not think for a moment what he meant.

'The telephone number. Did you find it?'

She nodded, pointing to the letter. He sat down at the table looking with distaste at the tea she had made. Hannah got up and poured him a pastis. Sarah picked up the jug and dribbled water slowly down the side of the glass. She liked to see the liquid turning cloudy.

'I'll drive you. We'd better go to the Hotel Moderne. I know the receptionist. At least you can sit down while you're waiting. It may take hours.'

'Marc . . . you don't need to come. I . . . I can go on my own.'

'Can you? You think you could drive?' He spoke roughly. She opened her mouth to speak then closed it again, shaking her head. She felt sick.

'Of course you can't go by yourself. Sarah and I'll come with you. You'd like an ice-cream, Sarah, wouldn't you?' He put out his hand to the child. Sarah, taking it quickly, returned a ghostly smile.

*

I'm standing by the telephone in the Hotel Moderne, in an alcove next to the reception desk. No door. Cigarette butts on the floor under my feet, a smell of stale smoke. I'm leaning against the wall because there's no chair. Countless other people must have leant there. A stain of grease on the brown wallpaper. Across the hall I can see Marc sitting with Sarah at a table on the pavement. This is what I remember. The door framing them like a photograph. Marc looks so tired. The first time I've noticed it. He still hasn't shaved. His mouth is set as if a weight were dragging it down, surrounded by prickles of black stubble. Sarah's shoulders are bowed. Neither of them moves. We've been here over an hour waiting for the call. At this moment I see them so clearly it's as if I am them.

What I've been longing for all day, for time to stop, has happened. I'm suddenly connected to them. The connection is the meaning. That's all. These are the two people I care about. A thread of reality up which I might be able to climb back to the ordinary world.

Hannah was slightly drunk. Three pastis on an empty stomach while they were waiting for the call. The receptionist, an elderly man with bad teeth, signalled to her as he shouted into his mouthpiece, '*Un moment, je vous la passe.*'

Hannah picked up the receiver. Her hands were sweating. 'Hullo? Hullo?'

'Hullo . . . this is Philip Straight speaking, who is that?' In spite of the crackle on the line she could hear his voice, faint but clear.

'Philip, it's me. Oh Philip . . .' She could not go on.

'Hannah? Is that you? Why are you ringing? Is anything wrong?'

'Philip, there's something I must tell you . . .' She stopped again, making an effort to control her voice.

'Hannah, what is it? . . . Hannah, are you still there?'

'Yes. I'm here. Philip, Harry's dead. He was killed in the Alps.'

'Harry? . . . Oh God, Hannah, what are you saying? I can't hear properly. Did you say something has happened to Harry?'

'He's dead, Philip.' She forced herself to speak with unnatural loudness. 'We were walking in the mountains and he fell. He broke his neck.'

His voice was suddenly muffled. 'Oh God . . . Harry.' A moment's silence then a strange sound as if he was breathing with difficulty. 'Hannah, are you all right, and Sarah?'

'Yes, we're all right.'

'Thank God. Hannah, I wish I was with you.'

'Philip, we have to decide about the funeral.'

'What did you say? I can't hear at all well.'

It was like a nightmare. She was almost shouting. 'About the funeral. Would you mind if he was buried here, in the village?'

'In France? You want him to be buried in France?' He sounded puzzled.

'I don't know. I'm so confused. But I think so. It seems the best thing. I'd like it to be done quickly. I don't want it all to drag on, it's too . . . painful.'

'I don't know how soon I can get a plane. I'm not sure how often they go to France.'

As he was speaking she noticed the receptionist pick up a newspaper and spread it out on the desk. The headlines caught her eye. She gasped, 'Philip, I forgot. There's a strike. I don't think you could get here. No planes are allowed to land.'

She had a feeling of immense relief. She had not realised how much she dreaded his arriving.

He was saying, 'I've been so busy I've hardly had time to notice what's going on in Europe. We're supposed to finalise the negotiations in the next few days.'

'Would you mind, Philip, if I go on with the funeral here? I can't face . . . bringing the body back, all that.'

There was a pause. He sounded doubtful. 'I don't know what to do. How will you manage on your own?'

'There are people here arranging it all. They're being very kind.'

'Hannah, what an awful situation. Are you sure you're all right?'

'Yes, I'm all right. I just want it to be over.'

'When would the funeral be?'

'Tomorrow.'

'Oh God, I wish I could be with you. I'll be thinking of you all the time. When will you come home?'

She had not thought about it.

'Hannah? Are you there? When are you going back to London?'

'I'm . . . not sure.'

'I'm pretty certain I'll be leaving here by next week. You'd better come back as soon as you can after the funeral, Hannah. I may get home before you. I don't like to think of you on your own. How wretched there should be a strike . . .'

There was a high-pitched buzzing on the line, obscuring his voice, then it went dead.

'Philip? Philip, can you hear me?'

Nothing. She waited a few moments, then put the receiver back, her hand shaking. She went over to the receptionist. 'I was cut off.'

'Do you want me to make the call again, Madame? We'd have to wait for a re-connection and pay the full price again.'

'No . . . no, I'd almost finished. It doesn't matter.'

'I'll check the cost of the call and tell you in a few moments.'

She went outside to the table and Sarah looked up anxiously. 'Did you speak to him, Mama?'

'Yes.'

'I wanted to talk to him too.'

Hannah touched her cheek. 'We were cut off. Something went wrong with the line.'

'When will we see him?' Sarah's mouth was quivering.

'Next week. He can't come here because of the air strike. He's going back to London.'

Marc looked at Hannah questioningly. She did not know what to say. She sat down with her arm round Sarah and pulled her close. Her head ached.

'Sarah, we're going to bury Harry in the village. Madame Pinet's arranging it.'

'In that little graveyard with the beads?'

Hannah nodded. Sarah's voice lightened.

'It's much nicer than where they buried Grandpa.' Philip's father, lying in a huge battlefield of marble monuments in North London. 'It's not so frightening. Harry liked it there. We played with the beads sometimes. And we buried a dead snake.'

*

Janine had prepared soup. They sat in Marc's kitchen to eat it. Her sympathy was unerring and delicate, sensed by the other people, unspoken. For the first time Hannah saw the little room off the kitchen where Janine slept. She had not known it existed. Kept exclusively for her use – a narrow bed and a cupboard, austere, like a monk's cell. It fitted Janine, her air of self-containment and simplicity.

Marc's expression, whenever he looked at his half-sister, was gentle. The savagery vanished. The one person he did not have to ward off. Hannah noticed it as if from a long distance away. She was getting more and more drunk. She held herself in check sufficiently to go down and see Madame Pinet and then put Sarah to bed. Sarah clung round her neck – something she had not done since she was a small child – and they squeezed each other tightly. Within a few moments of lying down she had fallen asleep.

Hannah went back to the kitchen. The wine bottle was empty and Marc had opened a bottle of *marc*.

'Sit down, Hannah, we're going to get pissed.'

She swallowed the spirit too fast and it rushed down her gullet like fire. She began to choke, bending her head to the table. Marc laughed. The oddness of the sound shocked her. She looked up. His eyes seemed to be entreating her. What for? She had never seen such a look on his face before. Is he asking me to forgive him, to absolve him She tried to smile. She could feel her mouth going into a contorted shape. Did it look like a smile? Marc's face slipped out of focus. Suddenly two faces. She turned her head slowly to look at Janine. Janine had two profiles, one superimposed but slightly to the side of the other. She shut one eye and the two profiles became one again. She opened it and they jumped apart.

'Why are you winking?' asked Marc.

'I'm trying to make your face come together. It keeps falling apart There's two of you.'

Janine got up to wash the soup bowls. Marc filled Hannah's glass 'Sip it slowly. Roll it round in your mouth before you swallow it.'

She threw back her head and gargled with it. Marc laughed more than ever. She let it trickle slowly down her throat a few drops at a time

Janine stood by the door to her room.

'If you'll excuse me,' she said quietly, 'I'm going to bed.'

Marc went over to her, putting both arms round her shoulders.

'*Merci, ma soeur.*' He rested his cheek against hers. '*Bonne nuit. Dors bien.*'

She went in, closing the door behind her. Marc walked across the room towards the stairs. 'Come on.'

To Hannah's surprise she found she could hardly stand. She lurched towards Marc with her arm outstretched to stop herself falling, then leant abruptly against the wall. 'My legs aren't working properly.'

He took her hand to lead her upstairs. She closed one eye to keep the steps in focus and propelled herself upwards, her other hand on the wall.

The room was dark except for the far end by the couch where the moon poured a milky light through the open window. She could see the moon quite clearly. Moons. Two of them. She shut one eye again. Moon. Only one. Marc, who had been walking just ahead of her, turned round abruptly and propped her against the wall. He started to kiss her violently, her mouth, her cheeks, her neck. He pulled her shirt open and fastened his mouth onto her breast like a child desperate for milk.

The sensation was extraordinary. She gasped and twisted in

144

response, hardly able to stand up. She started to slide down against the wall. He carried her over to the bed and stripped off the rest of her clothes and his own. Then he knelt down by the couch, his body pale in the moonlight. The movement of kneeling suddenly recalled the last time she had stood in the doorway and she pulled away in horror. He knew why immediately.

'Hannah this is real. It's not a show. The only real thing.'

She exploded with rage, digging her finger nails into his flesh. She kicked him in the stomach using all her strength to try to force him onto the ground. For a moment he was taken by surprise, then, with movements as violent as her own, he fought back. She was snarling like a tiger, without any control over her movements. He forced both her arms down by her sides, crossed them behind her back and with one hand gripped them by the wrists. Then he rolled on top of her, his weight pinning her to the ground. Her head was swimming, all her senses disorientated. Marc's eyes glittered in the light from the window. His breath came in gasps. With his free hand he made an entrance through her pubic hair for his penis, thrusting it inside her as far as it would go. He was locked on top of her, his tongue in her mouth which she had opened involuntarily as soon as his mouth came close to hers. He released her arms from behind her back and stretched them out on either side like a figure of crucifixion, his hands interlaced with hers. With the rhythmical movements of his body he began to overcome her struggle till, in spite of herself, her legs twined round his back holding him as close to her as she could. She wanted to keep him there forever.

The sun rose at five-thirty. Thirst had woken her early and she went downstairs to drink two big glasses of cold water. She walked out towards the cemetery and sat on the wall watching the sky turn slowly from grey to pink to pale blue to brighter blue. The daily transformation from dark to light, this inescapable circle, seemed suddenly extraordinary. The timelessness she had longed for was here, in the slow rising of yesterday, in the slow rising of tomorrow. If she could only link up with that red ball hanging so heavily over the rim of the distant mountains as she had connected to the two people framed in the doorway of the hotel.

The rage of the night before had gone. She put her hand to he sore cheeks where Marc's stubble had rubbed. With surprise she realised that it was not anger with Marc that had burst her open – he was only the trigger. The anger belonged to everything that had happened, the hardness of the rocks, the humiliation of her own power lessness, anger that nothing could be changed, now or ever. It was the never that filled her with such despair.

Giving way to her rage had shifted something, as if a knot had loosened slightly inside her. She felt oddly grateful. How had Marc transformed her fury? Just by accepting it? She had never allowed herself to be as angry as that in her whole life before. She had never she reflected, been as drunk. She had wanted to destroy everything near her. If anyone had been as angry as that with her she would have shrivelled up like a leaf in the fire.

She looked down at the neatly-marked plots in the cemetery Generations encompassed in so small a space, a patchwork of earth that could absorb any amount of tears. They could flow forever into the indifferent ground.

13

The priest wore white vestments. Elaine Pinet whispered to Hannah that normally he would have worn some black but the child, being so young, allowed the wearing of white. The coffin looked very small on the stone floor in front of him. Madame Pinet had got up at six and, assisted by Georges, swept out the church and dusted the altar and the two front rows of seats. It was no longer used for regular services. She had not had time to clear the cobwebs from the high window at the back. They hung like dusty hammocks through which the sun could hardly penetrate. Marc had lit two candles to lighten the dimness and Henri Bonnieux carried in a bunch of sunflowers from his own plot. Their glow of yellow lit up the interior of the church more brightly than the flickering candles.

Henri and Marc stood on one side of the coffin, Georges and Leo on the other. The hearse had been parked in the square since ten-thirty, the driver and his assistant standing in the shade by the church wall fanning themselves with black hats. A very hot day. At five minutes to eleven the priest had arrived on a small motor cycle with a boy sitting behind. He nodded briskly like a busy executive and hurried into a small room at the side of the church followed by the boy carrying his bag. Elaine Pinet had taken particular care over the dusting of this room.

Within five minutes they appeared again, the priest walking slowly now and with dignity, the boy carrying a censer. Harry would have liked the smell, thought Hannah. He loved burning joss sticks in his room. The boy looked a little older than Sarah. Below the rim of his robe you could see the heavy mountain boots all the boys in the villages wore. Hannah had promised Harry a pair to take back to London. The presence of the boy interested Sarah.

'He's from Saint Jacques,' she whispered. 'I saw him in the procession at the *fête*.'

The priest stood facing them. He began to intone rapidly in a low key without the usual emphasis of speech so Hannah found it hard to catch the sense. Then she heard, '. . . prepare ourselves to celebrate the sacred mysteries . . .'

The words jumped out at her – she had never thought of a church service like that – relieving some of her discomfort about the whole business of a Catholic funeral. As near as anything could be to what she was feeling herself. The priest went on, Elaine Pinet at her side murmuring the responses, but Hannah hung on to those words as if they could give meaning to the whole ceremony – some part of the mumbo jumbo to which she could respond. The sacred mysteries.

They knelt down, Henri Bonnieux painfully lowering himself to his knees clutching Marc's arm. The priest picked up a wafer from the table, holding it with the silver chalice and lifting them both into the air. The boy rang a small bell. Then the priest turned while the boy poured wine over his fingers into the cup. The bell rang again. The priest genuflected towards the altar. He was singing. Hannah heard Madame Pinet beside her responding: 'We proclaim thy death, Lord Jesus, we celebrate thy resurrection.'

Henri Bonnieux's voice came in after the others, hesitant, the thin voice of an old man. Georges joined in the Amen. By following a second after Elaine Pinet, Hannah, too, could say the Amen.

'Amen. Amen.'

For a brief time as a child she had been sent to a Church of England school. On various Holy Days they had walked in a crocodile wearing maroon felt hats and maroon and blue striped ties to the local church. The prayers had been taught them earlier in the week. Hannah's greatest embarrassment was the creed:

'I believe in God the Father Almighty, Maker of Heaven and Earth and in Jesus Christ His only son our Lord who was conceived by the Holy Ghost, born of the Virgin Mary, suffered under Pontius Pilate, was crucified, dead and buried. On the third day he rose again from the dead. He ascended into heaven, and sitteth on the right hand of God the Father Almighty from whence he shall come to judge the quick and the dead. . . .'

Not that the words were hard to remember – even now they were imprinted on her memory – but how could you say you believed in all hat? The words had stuck in her throat. Paradoxically, it seemed worse to be telling a lie in church. Then, all of a sudden, she devised solution. She would miss out the first two words – surely no one would notice – and then loudly and clearly she could join in the rest. The relief was enormous. Remembering it now as she murmured the Amen she wondered how it could have mattered so much. What xtraordinary scruples in a child of ten. Sarah's age. Sarah, holding er hand tightly, echoed her murmur with a whispered 'Amen'.

The priest began the Lord's Prayer. Without thinking Hannah oined in, in English. 'Thy will be done on earth, as it is in heaven . . .'

Elaine Pinet turned to smile her approval. This was the one prayer Hannah had always liked. Even nowadays under the cold eye of the headmistress she could say it without distaste. A prayer whittled down to the essentials. Sufficient, in its simplicity, for all occasions. Give us this day our daily bread and forgive us our trespasses . . .' Did you need any other?

Elaine Pinet, Claude's parents and Henri Bonnieux stepped forward to line up in front of the priest. A moment later, to Hannah's surprise, someone else joined them. Molly. She was wearing the same green skirt she had worn that day Hannah had seen her in the café. But now her blouse was clean and round her neck hung a string of heavy green beads. Of course, Hannah remembered, she knows what's going on better than I do. She may not understand all the words but the gestures must be the same. A great many gestures, the priest continually bowing, lifting things up, bells ringing. Now the audience is going on stage. Like when the magician at a conjuring show invites people to help him. They feel special, participating in he magic.

Sarah whispered, 'What's Molly doing? Why's she standing there?'

'They're taking communion.'

'What's that?'

'I . . . I can't explain it now.'

Not now or ever. A kind of spiritual cannibalism? Would Sarah understand that? It must mean something quite other to the people standing there, something outside my knowledge.

Like watching a show. And yet, at the same time, she was glad of it. If not this, what else could she have done? What else was there for people like her, belonging to no religion, unable to speak with conviction about anything except that sense of mystery?

She was touched by all the people in the church just being there Elaine Pinet had offered her this ritual. Hannah accepted it gratefully

Everyone knelt down in silence, Hannah in slow motion, a little after the others, Sarah holding tightly onto her hand. Side by side staring straight ahead at the coffin. The priest's smock touched the wooden edge. Through the open door of the church came the sound of doves. Everyone stood up again. Now the four men turned to heave the coffin onto their shoulders, Marc and Leo in front, Henri Bonnieux so bent that only his hand touched the wooden under surface. The weight was taken by the others. Slowly they started down the aisle.

How odd there's no organ music. I've never been to a church before without music. I prefer it like this.

As they passed, Elaine Pinet beckoned to Hannah to join her behind the coffin. The only person dressed for the occasion – a black suit black stockings and shoes, a black straw hat. She had offered to lend Hannah a black veil but Hannah could not bring herself to wear it She remembered her grandmother's big hat with the black muslin veil that hung down all round her when she went to collect the honey from the beehives at the bottom of her garden. Like a witch dressed for a rite. Unrecognisable. Hannah did not want to frighten Sarah by altering her own appearance.

They followed the coffin slowly towards the cemetery. By the angle of his frail, lined neck, brittle as a vine stem, she could see that Henri Bonnieux was feeling the strain. The small procession walked straight through the iron gateway, up the central path and turned right to halt beside a freshly dug plot of earth. The bearers lowered the coffin slowly onto the ground as the hearse driver hurried forward to fasten two broad canvas straps round it. Then the priest started to speak again and the boy by his side passed him a container from which he sprinkled Holy water onto the coffin while the boy swung the censer He stood over the grave with his hand lifted to bless it and the four men lifted the canvas straps and lowered the coffin gently to rest at the bottom of the pit. All the time the priest was speaking rapidly ords and gestures indissolubly linked. He was doing it all too fast. Hannah could not take it in.

Madame Pinet picked up a handful of soil and threw it into the grave, earth hitting the wood like falling rain. Everyone else bent to throw earth onto the coffin, then Hannah, and last of all Sarah, following the gestures of the others like an echo.

The sound of earth on the coffin is absolute. Each person with his handful of earth burying Harry. The final sound.

Sarah, seeing her mother's tears, began to cry herself. The priest said his last prayer and stood in silence for a moment. Then he turned and put one hand on Sarah's head while with the other he shook hands with Hannah. My daughters, he said, my daughters, murmuring words that were meant to be of comfort. For a moment he allowed himself to slow down, letting his eyes rest on Hannah's. It seemed to her they had a look of curiosity. She nodded, afraid of sobbing out loud if she tried to speak.

He turned away down the path, the boy following. Then Elaine Pinet shook her hand and one by one all the mourners came up to her. She tried to smile, to thank them for being there, for their courtesy, their kindness. She remained standing with Marc, Janine, Leo and Molly. Molly was trying to wipe her tears away with the back of her hand. She sniffed loudly. All at once she came up to Hannah and threw her arms round her neck. Hannah was dazed. She did not know what to do next. Molly turned round to Leo.

'Lend us a hanky?'

Leo searched in his pockets and found one. Molly bent down to wipe Sarah's face. Then she wiped her own and blew her nose. Marc put his arm round Hannah and began to lead her towards the gate. As he passed his father's grave and Helen's he bent to pick a sprig of rosemary. He held it under his nose for a moment then passed it to Hannah.

'Tomorrow when Georges has finished we'll plant something.'

'Georges?'

'He's the grave digger. He has to fill it in.'

*

Marc swung the bucket upside down and the last drops of water fell onto the earth. Sarah went off to pick flowers. She wanted to stand them in a glass jar next to the rosemary and lavender bushes they had planted.

Marc asked, 'Do you have to leave straight away?'

'Tomorrow. Philip's expecting me back. I would have had to go anyway at the end of the week. Term begins. I'll have to start my job.'

Her voice was low and depressed. She was afraid to go back, afraid of all it would mean. Harry's absence. A weight she could not put down. She remembered when she was fourteen coming round from an appendix operation, thinking, this is only a nightmare, this unbearable pain. In a moment I'll wake up and everything will be all right. Then, as she became fully conscious, realising the nightmare was reality.

Panic-stricken she suddenly wondered if she would ever see Marc again. Whatever it was that had started between them might be buried under this damp earth.

She looked across at his bent head as he concentrated on pressing the earth round the base of each plant with his foot. I love you. The words startled her. They rose silently inside her head. She did not open her mouth. I want to give you everything that is in myself, to get to know you as well as any human being can know another. I accept you as you are. I accept everything about you.

She put her hands together and clenched them tightly, gritty with earth. She was surprised to find she cared so much about something living. All her feeling had been with the dead. The first thing to learn is not to intrude. Marc will never open the door wide onto himself and say 'Come on in'. Sometimes, by accident, it might be left slightly ajar and then I could slip in and walk about very delicately trying not to disturb anything, ready to leave at any moment.

With his head still bent Marc said casually, 'You'll come back?'

'Do you want me to?' The question slipped out. The opposite of what she intended.

'The house is yours whenever you want to use it. I hope you can help me decide what to do with Helen's papers. You know more about them than I do now.'

Her heart was thumping in agitation. 'Where will you be?'

'Here for a bit. Then Paris. I've got an exhibition in October. I hope to sell enough to last me through the winter.'

'What if I was here . . . all the time, living in the house?'

He shrugged. 'Why not? My aunt liked it.'

She shouted at him, 'I'm not your aunt.'

He looked up for a moment, startled, an expression of pain in his eyes. All at once it came to Hannah in a shock of insight that he did not know how much he was confusing her with his aunt. Is that the only reason he likes me, if he does like me? A space he needs filled, an ache inside him. I know what it's like. I know after four days.

Managing to control her voice, she asked quietly, 'What do you want to happen?'

Again that shrug. 'I want what happens to happen.'

What an extraordinary answer. How casually he accepted the idea of her living in the house. Not a matter of any great weight, not a matter of threat or anxiety. Could she ever take things as easily as that without worrying if they would work out or not, each day an experiment in living? As so often with Marc she found herself thrown back again onto herself. He was not going to take any responsibility. Why should he?

*

She cooked the odds and ends of leftover food for supper. Spaghetti, two hard boiled eggs, a tomato. Sarah ate with her usual concentration. Hannah could only manage half an egg. It was as if all her saliva had dried up. The food remained dry and lumpy in her mouth.

There was a bottle of wine left. She was tempted to open it and drink it all to liquefy the desert inside her. She forced herself to shut the cupboard. She must not get drunk. Still a lot of clearing up to do.

After Sarah had gone to bed Janine came in.

'You're going tomorrow?'

Hannah nodded. 'Yes. It'll take me two days. I don't feel up to driving very fast.'

'Could you give me a lift as far as Paris? We could share the driving.'

Hannah put out her hand to touch Janine's, smaller, soft and brown.

'Are you sure you need to go back? You're not just doing it for me?'

153

Janine shook her head. 'I'm supposed to stay with my mother
Brittany. But I have to go to Paris first to fetch some things. I'
nothing with me, only a rucksack.'

It was a relief that Janine would drive with her. As if some part
Marc was coming on the first stretch of her journey. The drivir
would make her jittery, she knew. She was afraid of having an acc
dent. She must take Sarah safely back to Philip as soon as she coul
That was what he must be needing more than anything else. She d:
not allow herself to think beyond that.

Helen Grant's papers were in rough order. She had divided the
according to subject. Not easy. One book flowed into another, the
were so full of cross references. To think out a way of publishir
them would be a long job. There would have to be a framework eve
if the notes could be presented as they were. The oral records we
the most interesting to Hannah, yet their resonance came partly fro
the context into which Helen Grant suggested they might be put.
was this that would require so much research. Was she capable of i
She would have to read as much as Helen Grant herself. A long jo
One she would have to come back here for. When would she be ab
to?

She began to stack the note-books neatly along an empty shel
Suddenly she had the feeling that someone was looking in on he
She went to the window and pressed her face against the glass. A fe
feet away a figure was staring towards her. Georges. She felt oddl
afraid. He did not move.

She turned away in agitation. She could not shut the shutters with
out opening the window. But that would be too pointed. Somethin
inhibited her from offending him. He was vulnerable. You could nc
treat him like anyone else. Perhaps he wants something. Waiting fc
me, she thought. How long has he been there?

Nervously she opened the front door and stepped into the shadow
square. The enormous dark sky, pierced with stars, dwarfed he
dwarfed the stone houses, the church, the figure of Georges walkin
towards her. A weight pressing down on them. He started to spea
stammeringly, his voice oddly high-pitched for a man, almost girlis

'*Madame . . . Madame . . .*' He was thrusting something toward
her. A basket.

She reached out to take it. '*Merci, Georges.*'

'For your journey. Marc told us you're going away . . .'

His voice faltered and died away. Hannah held the basket towards
e light from the window. A pungent, animal smell, two goat cheeses
sting on a bed of leaves. Beside them a sealed jar.

Hannah heard steps behind her and Marc's voice. '*Bonsoir, mon
cle.*' He patted him with the same rough affection as he did Bi-
che. Georges shuffled his feet like a child, grinning. Hannah put
it her hand.

'Thank you, Georges. I'll think of you and your father when we're
ting these in London.'

His hand was curiously damp as if he was sweating. He went back
his house.

In the kitchen Hannah picked up the jar. 'What's this?'

Marc held it up to the light. 'Toad's eyes pickled in goat's blood.'

Hannah snatched it away to inspect it herself. 'Could it be cherries?'

Marc nodded. 'Cherries in alcohol. My grandfather's speciality.
ou're honoured to get some. Helen loved them. As a child I was
lowed one after lunch on New Year's day.'

Hannah put the jar back in the basket. As she did so she noticed
mething underneath it. 'What can this be?'

Two small pieces of polished vinewood were bound tightly to-
ether with long, twisted grasses. They fitted into the palm of her
and. Marc touched them lightly with his fingers.

'A little memento from Georges.'

'What for?'

'I don't know. To protect you? Only Georges knows. Maybe he
els bad about . . . what happened. Some kind of . . . responsibility?
e all do.' His voice was harsh. 'You. Me. Perhaps Georges too. You
member those stones by your door?' She nodded. 'God knows
hat he thinks he did. He must be worried about something happen-
g to you and Sarah.'

Marc put the mannikins back in the basket. Hannah was trembling.
Marc, I'm afraid.'

'You believe in this sort of crap?'

'No . . . I suppose I don't. But . . . they make me uncomfortable.'

'It's up to you. Do what you like.'

'Poor Georges.' His damp hand. How awful to be in that state of

155

permanent fear, everything threatening. At this moment she cou
almost imagine what it must be like. 'Are you ever afraid, Marc?'

There was a long silence. He was staring at the basket.

'Yes.'

'What of?'

Again silence. Then he said, 'Of people wanting something fro
me I can't give them.'

What a clear warning. His face looked bitter.

'When I was a child my mother wanted me to be everything to he
There was no one else. I suppose I had to . . . justify my father
death. Expiate her guilt. She wanted me to be perfect, always goo
always loving. I could never give her what she wanted. I was s
afraid of disappointing her it suffocated me. I think I was afraid mo
of the time. Until she met my stepfather. I hated him. I was tormen
ted with jealousy. But the relief was tremendous. I behaved so bad
she had to send me to live with my aunt.'

He went over to the cupboard. 'Anything to drink?' He took o
the remaining bottle of wine. 'Châteauneuf. That'll do. Let's take
up to the balcony, Hannah. You bring the glasses.'

'I don't want to get drunk. I haven't finished clearing up.' Sh
wanted to make love with a clear head, a gentle goodbye.

'You won't. Just a glass or two. Come on.'

She took two glasses out of the cupboard and followed him. Whe
she reached the top floor he was putting two chairs on the terra
facing the invisible view. They could see nothing except clusters
dotted lights where villages clung to the slopes of distant hills. In th
valley the two-eyed lights of cars speeding down the main road.

He turned to put his arms round her, holding her very close, h
face in her hair. She pressed her breasts against him, moving the
slightly from side to side against his chest.

'Hannah . . . my beautiful Hannah . . .' his voice was sad. 'W
can't make love.'

She leant against him, not moving away, her hands still holdin
the glasses, as he went on, 'There's something I have to tell you.' H
released himself gently, reaching for the wine. 'Sit down.'

She held out the glasses for him to fill. Her eyes were graduall
getting used to the darkness but she could not see the expression o
his face. What was he going to say? That he could never see he

ain? Was that why he'd come up here? So she could not see his
ce?

He sat on the edge of the parapet, half turned away.

'I've got V.D.' His voice was flat. Slightly harsh. The words
nned her. Something she had never even thought of. Outside her
perience. What did it mean?

'You're shocked.'

'I've . . . never known anyone before who . . .'

'Yes, you have.' He sounded embarrassed.

'What d'you mean?'

'Molly.'

'Molly?' She felt sick. 'You mean it was Molly who . . .?'

'Unless it's you.'

Now she was embarrassed. 'I . . . I don't think so.'

'Hannah . . .' He took her hand, leaning forward. Could he see her
pression better than she could his? Such light as there was, from
e stars, fell on her face. 'Does it make me . . . disgusting?'

She shook her head quickly. 'Marc, why does it mean we can't . . .'

'I don't want you to catch it. There's just a chance you might not
ve got it yet. I only noticed yesterday.'

'You mean I might . . . I might have it already?'

'Probably.' His voice was bitter.

'Then why can't we . . .?'

'No. Then you'd be certain to get it. I couldn't do that deliber-
ly.'

'I haven't . . .' she didn't know how to talk about such a thing. 'I
ven't noticed . . .'

He interrupted, sensing her awkwardness, 'You wouldn't. Women
ten don't know they've got it until it gets bad. Molly probably
esn't.'

'You mean she's spreading it around without knowing?'

'Very likely.'

'Oh God! How horrible!'

'It would be more horrible if she did know.'

'What will you do?'

'Go to the doctor. Lay off for a few weeks till I've got rid of it. It's
t serious, you know. I've had it before.'

'Oh!' She looked at him sadly.

157

'One of the commonest things there is. A social disease,' sounded ironic, 'passed on among friends. It's unpleasant. A bo That's all.' He held her hand lightly in his palm. 'Come on, Hann: it's not the end of the world. Let's say it's a . . . hazard of my way life.'

A hazard of his way of life. She tried to keep her voice steady. meant, what will you do about Molly?'

He shrugged. 'That's up to her, isn't it? I've told Leo. He w pretty irritated. I saw him this afternoon. He said he'd take her to t clinic at Avignon. I didn't see Molly. She was at La Corneille's ha ing her French lesson. Ludicrous.'

'What is?'

'Molly, La Corneille, the whole thing. Leo's crazy. He's bor€ that's his trouble. He needs some new amusement the whole tin And, of course, he's always looking for copy.'

'What shall I do?'

'What about?'

'About whether or not I've got . . .'

'Have a check when you get back to London. Go and see a doc' or go to a clinic. I don't know how they organise it there. You c ask someone. Ask a friend.'

Who?

'I'm sorry to have landed you in this,' he sounded bitter, 'on t of everything.'

She had the shakes again, her whole body beginning to judder

'Hannah, what is it? Are you cold'

She shook her head, her teeth chattering. 'Marc . . . do you thi we could lie on the bed for a bit? I need . . . just to lie down wi you.'

He led her over to the bed. She bent to fold up the white cover and hang it on the chair. Then she lay down stiffly on her bac Marc's fingertips moved lightly over her arm then her face, as if was trying to draw the tension into himself. The trembling grew le It came in spasms. He lay down with his arms round her and beg to rock her body to and fro like a baby's. She tried to think of n thing. To be here, now, with him for the little time there was left

*

Another day of brilliant sun. She would never get used to it, the
ality of the light. She was standing with Sarah beside the grave.
rah had wanted to water the plants before they left. Their survival
s a matter of great importance to her. How quickly the human
yche entangles itself in unlikely objects, she thought, strands of
pe weaving themselves in and out of the spikes of lavender. Just
shes they had grubbed up yesterday and replanted. Already for
rah they meant far more.

They had been up since seven. The house was all ready to leave.
nnah could not bring herself to close the shutters. She wanted to
member it as it was, open-eyed, living, to keep that image of readi-
ss in her mind. A house she could come back to, Marc said. The
certainty of it all overwhelmed her. This is not final, she kept say-
; to herself, nothing is final. Then the realisation came back.
rry . . . that is.

They went back to the house and she shut the front door, leaving
 key in the lock. Henri Bonnieux was returning with his goats
m their morning walk. Suddenly they began to hurry forward
th alarm, their udders flapping, legs striking out at awkward angles.
o's car was coming into the square. Molly jumped out, excited and
ppy. The same green beads she had worn at the funeral.

'I came to say goodbye. You won't forget to go and see Mam? Tell
r I'm all right, that I'll try and send her some money one of these
ys.'

Her movements were awkward as a young bird's. Everything is
ginning for her, thought Hannah. She's free. She's staying here.
n going. Molly's eyes lingered on Hannah's for a moment as she
d, 'Leo's taking me to Avignon this morning. I've never been.'
e looked quite unconcerned. ' 'Bye, Sarah.'

She gave the child a hug, hesitated for a moment then leant for-
rd to touch Hannah lightly on the cheek with her lips. She smelt
isky. Was it Patchouli? A bit like incense. She got back into the
r. Leo waved his hand out of the open roof like a drowning man.

Elaine Pinet had brought them ham rolls for the journey. Janine
s putting her rucksack on the back seat next to Sarah. Too bulky
 go in the boot. Marc came up the alley, his hair on end, rubbing
 eyes sleepily. Janine kissed him goodbye, and Le Vieux and
orges, then she shook hands with the others, Madame Pinet and

Claude's parents. Hannah took their hands slowly each in turn. S[he]
came to Marc. He put his out in mock formality, smiling, as if it w[as]
a kind of joke, saying goodbye in this way. She touched it for [a]
second then turned to jump into the car. Janine was standing by t[he]
door looking at her questioningly.

'Shall I drive?'

Hannah nodded. She could not see for tears. Janine started t[he]
engine quickly and guided the car through the narrow lane towar[d]
the road to Saint Jacques past the cemetery gates.

14

was evening as they drove into London. Rush hour. Drizzling just
ough to use the windscreen wipers, with cars stuck bumper to
umper all through the city. People queued at the bus stops under
eir umbrellas, their faces patient, resigned. They had stood there
sterday. They would stand there tomorrow. Hannah felt as if she
as being sucked into a dark tunnel. Something there waiting to
wallow her up. The car would find its own way without her needing
direct it. An old dog, nosing its way home.

When she shut the front door behind her the house had an alien
nell, musty, a little damp. Not her house. Perhaps she had forgotten
hat the smell was like. She went into the kitchen. Smaller than she
membered. How badly it needed painting. Automatically she went
fill the electric kettle. Beside it an unopened box of airport whisky
nned down a note.

> Darling – got back at lunch time. Felt too restless to hang
> around so I've gone to the office. Ring me when you get in. Long-
> ing to see you both,
>
> P

She read it twice, standing very still.

'Sarah, he's back.'

'Where? Where is he?'

'At the office . . .' She hesitated. 'Do you want to ring him?'

'Oh, yes!'

Hannah's hands were shaking as she poured boiling water onto the
ıstant coffee. She opened the whisky and topped up the mug. A
ttle Scotch courage, that's what she was needing. She drank deeply
ith both hands round the mug. Then, abruptly, half the coffee
ɔilled onto the table as she put the mug down with a jerk. One of

Harry's pictures was pinned on the kitchen wall. A man walking the rain under a yellow umbrella.

'He's coming, Mama, he'll get a taxi. He thinks you'd be too tir to fetch him,' Sarah reported, smiling all over her face. 'Isn't it love to be home?'

Philip's case was on the bed upstairs, unpacked, a pile of dir washing on the floor. Waiting for the service industry to begi thought Hannah, stuffing things into the laundry bag. By the tin she had unpacked her own bags, exhaustion and whisky combined make her head swim. Moving Philip's case she lay down, trying relax, slowly working on each part of her body in turn – clench yo toes, relax your toes, tighten your leg muscles, relax your leg muscle squeeze your thighs together, relax your thighs . . . She had got far as her arms when she heard the front door.

'Hullo? Anyone at home?'

'Daddy! Oh, Daddy!'

'Sarah, how are you?' He must be hugging her. 'How's my puss cat?'

'I'm all right. I'm hungry.'

'So am I. Where's Hannah?'

'Upstairs, I think.'

He was bounding up the stairs. Hannah sat up too quickly, swing ing her legs over the edge of the bed. She felt dizzy. He pushed ope the bedroom door.

'Hannah!'

A strange God come down from the sky, his face brown and gleam ing, hair half-bleached from the sun. But a God in pain. Deep line either side of his mouth. He was still wearing his cream-coloure tropical suit. She tried to stand.

'Hannah, are you all right?'

How like Harry he was. Wave after wave of dizziness made he sway. She blacked out and fell back onto the bed.

When she came to she was lying against the pillows covered by blanket. Her skirt had been taken off. Philip was sitting in a lo chair by the window with Sarah on his knee. How often she had sa in that chair nursing one of the children when they were babies and woke up in the night crying for milk. Philip was cradling Sarah, his face strained as he looked out of the window. Sarah's eyes were on her mother's face. She whispered, 'She's awake. Her eyes are opening.'

'Hannah?' Philip stood up. Hannah felt as if she was floating, not quite there, coming back from a long distance. 'How do you feel?' His voice was worried.

'I don't know,' she said faintly, 'a bit odd.'

'Shall I get Dr Coates?'

'No, for Heaven's sake. I'll be all right. I'm just tired, that's all.'

'You must be. I blame myself. I should never have let you do that drive by yourself. It must have been a terrible strain.'

'She didn't do it by herself,' said Sarah. 'Janine did some.'

'Who's Janine?'

'Oh,' said Hannah, 'a girl we met. She wanted a lift to Paris.'

'We stayed the night with her,' said Sarah excitedly. 'I slept on the floor. Paris was lovely. I saw the Seine.'

'Hannah,' Philip leant forward and kissed her very gently on the forehead, 'I'm so glad you're back. I've been so worried, thinking of you on your own, having to . . . cope with everything.'

Hannah nodded with her eyes shut, her head going up and down like a puppet. 'It was all right. It's . . . over.' Impossible to look at him.

'Do you want to sleep?'

She shook her head.

'I'm hungry,' Sarah said loudly. 'Can't we have something to eat?'

'So am I. What shall I get you, Hannah?'

Now he was safely at a distance she could open her eyes again. 'Anything. I don't feel hungry.'

'You must have something. Sarah and I'll make it.'

Sarah was pulling him by the hand saying, 'I've got a surprise for you. Come downstairs.'

He looked towards Hannah, his eyes puzzled, reluctant to go out of the room. She lifted her hand and waved towards the door.

'Go on. Don't worry about me. I'll come down in a moment.

He went out, closing the door very quietly as if she were an invalid. Her new role?

As the light faded outside the window she half dozed, staring at the huge plane tree at the bottom of her neighbour's garden, each leaf edged in black. How odd that the dimmer the light the more clearly the shape of the tree stood out. A beautiful tree. Some of the house holders complained that it kept out too much light. They wanted it lopped. It towered over the rows of terraces, a giant relic of a time when there were no houses here, only grass and trees with perhaps cows under them. She stared at the tree as if seeing it for the first time, black branches gesturing towards the sky. What were they saying? Tree. The essence of tree. It existed. The idea of people wanting to cut it down filled her with terror. One by one its arms sawn off. Deformed, like herself. She clamped her hand over her mouth to stop herself screaming aloud. Then she forced herself to get out of bed. Standing, she could not bring the room into focus. What am I doing here? Why this room? Why me?

Philip and Sarah were eating scrambled eggs, Sarah chattering about the village, explaining her map. She did not mention Harry. Philip asked no questions. Was he keeping them until she had gone to bed?

Hannah asked, 'The contract – did you get it, did the plans go through all right?'

'Yes.' He looked pleased. 'The last few days were hectic but we brought it off. The Minister was enthusiastic. It fits in nicely with his long-term development plan, as I thought it would.'

'I'm so glad.' She got up, automatically clearing the plates. She could not eat.

'I'll put you to bed, Sarah,' said Philip. 'Coming, pussy?'

Sarah had suddenly flagged, her head nodding over the table. As Philip carried her upstairs she lay back in his arms, smiling.

Hannah caught her foot against the basket Georges had given her. She put it on the table. What should she do with the cheese? The vine leaves had begun to curl at the edges. She lifted them up and suddenly saw the mannikins. She had forgotten them. Two sticks tied together. Why had they made her so afraid? Dry sticks. She was about to put them in the rubbish bin. But something prevented her. The car had not crashed. They were safely back. Instead she went into

164

he garden and stuck them in the damp earth, hidden behind a
hrub.

She stands looking into her lighted kitchen. How many thousands
of hours has she spent round that stove, in front of that sink, washing
that floor? Nobody there. An empty room, lit like a stage set waiting
or the actors to enter and get on with the play. A man comes in.
Elegant, a certain presence. He must be the protagonist, surely? He
glances round the room as if surprised there is no one there. He's
looking for someone. His wife perhaps? He goes out, calls offstage,
comes in again. He stands leaning both hands on the table, looking
tired. He stares straight out at the audience. Of course he can't see
them because they're in darkness. He rouses their sympathy by the
droop of his shoulder, the sadness in his mouth. He glances at the
basket on the table, examining what's inside. It makes him smile.
Something he likes. He takes out a small, round, white object and
sniffs at it, smiling all the time. He cuts off a slice, placing it on his
tongue with the tip of the knife. He's savouring it slowly, staring at
the audience again. An idea seems to come into his head. He raises
his eyebrows into an exaggerated arc, and, still holding the knife,
advances to the extreme front of the stage. He is very near the audience. He calls out loudly like a man in a house of ghosts who comforts himself with the sound of his own voice.
'Hannah, are you out there? Are you in the garden?'
He's calling someone onto the stage. In contemporary productions
this is often done. Designed to blur the distinction between actors
and audience, to encourage participation. A woman steps onto the
stage. She is wearing a blue denim skirt. Her black hair is dishevelled.
It needs washing. Still holding the knife, he puts both arms around
her and bows his head down beside hers.
'Hannah, I was worried. I thought you'd disappeared.'

If she could only tell him everything that had happened. Her tongue
was like wood. He dropped his arms and walked back to the table.
'I'm glad you brought the cheese. Better than I remembered. Is it
from that same old man, what did they call him – *Le Vieux*?' She
nodded. 'Sit down and have some with a glass of whisky. They'd go
well together.'

'Is Sarah all right?' The child. A safe coinage to exchange between them.

'She's reading. Back to the cosy world of Tolkein's Middle Earth I guess she needs it. She'll put out her light soon.'

'Does she seem . . . all right?'

She could not keep the anxiety out of her voice. He put his hand over hers.

'She's fine. Her same beautiful bouncy self.' He paused, then went on, 'Does she . . . talk about it?'

'No.' She took an envelope out of her bag. 'The death certificate. You'd better have it.' Philip was unfolding the paper inside. She clasped her hands together tightly. 'We were walking in the Alps with the girl Sarah told you about and . . . her brother.' She did not trust herself to use Marc's name. 'Harry and Sarah were ahead of us, picking flowers. Sarah said Harry was trying to reach a flower on the ledge below the path. We found him on the rocks below.'

'He was dead when you found him?'

'His neck was broken.' The weight of Harry's body in her arms. A dead weight. That was how you referred to it.

Philip looked as if someone had stabbed him, afraid of what the wound might mean. He put his hands on her shoulders. 'Hannah, we must help each other. We must comfort each other.' She nodded, her head down. She did not know how. 'We'd better go to bed. You must be exhausted. I know I am. Don't talk any more now. Let's leave it.'

She nodded again. With a slight pressure on her shoulder, Philip eased her out of the chair and turned out the light. She went upstairs with him following behind. Sarah's light was out. She undressed privately in the bathroom and got quickly into bed. Philip was unpacking his sponge bag.

'Do you want a sleeping pill?'

'Yes, please.'

He handed her a glass of water and a small white pill. There were two eyelids closed in sleep etched onto the surface. She swallowed it and lay down facing outwards, her back towards the middle of the bed. A signal they had devised years ago to indicate when one of them did not want to make love. Philip kissed the back of her neck and turned out the light.

She was woken by Sarah pulling up the blind with a snap. Next to er the bed was empty. She sat up guiltily.

'This won't buy a bonnet for the baby.' Her grandmother's idiotic hrase, one that always made Sarah laugh. She wished Sarah had nown her. 'Where's Philip?'

'Gone to the office. He had an appointment. He overslept. Why idn't you get up?'

'Too tired. How about you? Did you sleep all right?'

'Of course I did, my bed's lovely, much softer than the one in rance. Get up, Mama, you're lazy. We've got a lot to do.'

'What?'

'Fetch the cat and the tortoise and . . .' she turned away '. . . Iarry's mice.' Her friend Janet was looking after them.

Philip rang up. He was sorry to have had to rush off. Was she all ght? There was such a backlog of letters he didn't know how he'd ver get through them. He might be late home. He hoped she didn't ind. The panacea of work. He would work harder than ever now.

Her own problem nagged at her. She did not want to think about . Physically, she felt all right this morning. Those two eyelids had ragged her into a deep sleep. Could there really be anything wrong?

She took her hand-mirror into the bathroom, locking the door. She rouched, holding the mirror so her genital parts were reflected in it. ike a sideways mouth slightly parted, lips over inner lips, moist, rownish-pink on the outside, paler within. No rashes that she could ee, nothing to suggest disease might be spreading into her most pri- ate inner recesses. How could she find out? Go to her G.P.? What a opeless idea.

Only on the back of a door in the women's public lavatory in 'iccadilly Circus tube station did she ever remember seeing a notice bout V.D. and that was years ago. Where, in God's name, were hese things advertised? Or were they too disgusting for society to dmit publicly?

Of course, there was always Jim Finnigan. He would be sure to now. She imagined his face as she walked into the staff room saying,)h Jim, I think I caught V.D. in the holidays. Or should she say lap? More the sort of word he would use. I've got clap. I'm sure you know the right place to go for treatment. Can you offer me some claptrap to get me out of the claptrap?

Marc had said ask a friend where to go. Going downstairs to the telephone she tried to make herself ring up Margaret at the Citizen Advice Bureau. There was no one else. She lifted the receiver, then put it down again. Impossible. She stared at the squat pile of directories. Somewhere inside them must be a clue to the information she needed. You could find out anything by telephone nowadays. She took the A–D book and looked up 'Clinic'. Nothing remotely useful 'Clinic for Nervous Disorders'. 'Clinic for Dental Repairs'. 'Clinic Nursing Home'. Almost as a joke she turned to the S–Z. Ven . . . To her surprise there it was. An entry in black type. 'Venereal Diseases A list of clinics headed by 'NHS Information Service – a recorded announcement'.

When she dialled the number a cultivated male voice, like a Radio 3 announcer, spoke soothingly into her ear:

'Venereal diseases are transmitted by sexual contact with an infected person. There are two main venereal diseases called syphilis and gonorrhoea. Syphilis usually shows itself in both men and women as a pimple on the area of the sex organs. The pimple breaks down and becomes an ulcer which isn't painful but is associated with enlarged glands in the groin . . .'

She did not appear to have that. The voice went on to gonorrhoea In women gonorrhoea might have no obvious signs but this did not mean the infection was not present. The voice ended by urging her to go to her nearest clinic. No, she thought, not the nearest, that was in the local hospital only a few blocks away, according to the list. A bit too near. There was another not far from her school. She would go there next week, when Sarah was safely back at school.

It's much worse here than France. So many more things to remind me of Harry. I keep thinking he's about to come into the room.

I heard noises coming from the room above. Harry must be playing with . . . The thought congealed in mid-air. Out of the window I could see Sarah and her friend Janet rolling on the grass. Then heard the noise again – a kind of knocking. Intermittent. You hold your breath when you're afraid.

Outside his room I listened with my head bent against the door something moving inside, a soft banging. I threw the door open suddenly. Nobody there. The noise was coming from the window – the wind blowing a lantern he hung there last Christmas against the wooden frame.

I keep wondering who opened the window.

By the time Philip came home from work, late, as he had warned her, Hannah had been unable to resist having two glasses of whisky. He went first to say good night to Sarah, already in bed. When he came down he only glanced at her glass saying, 'I could do with a drink myself. I've been dictating all day. Valerie stayed late to help me.'

His secretary. A young graduate hoping to rise to better things. She certainly would, Hannah had often thought. She was always ready to stay late. Since she joined his staff a year ago Philip had been able to get through far more work. He was talking of promoting her to be his personal assistant and getting someone else to do the typing.

Feeling guilty about breakfast, Hannah had made an effort with the supper. Moussaka. Something Philip liked. They sat either side of the table, three foot of wood between them. It seemed like three thousand miles of desert. That pale sand Philip liked so much spread out all over the kitchen. The worst thing was not being able to look at him. To screen the agitation inside her, she fed him with details about the funeral, how kind people in the village had been, especially Madame Pinet. Facts, not feelings. He seemed dazed by them, uncertain how to take her, but determined not to comment on her behaviour. He had always been able to bide his time. Watchful, wary, hunter after bird.

As soon as they finished eating he went into his white room and put on a record. Then he sat on the sofa, adjusting the velvet cushion behind his head, closing his eyes. She brought in two cups of coffee and put them down on the smoked glass table, noticing as she did so that the glass was dusty.

I'd better dust . . . Oh, there it is. The reflex. I'd better dust it tomorrow. Pat, it comes out. Years of conditioning. Pavlov's bitch, guilty when the saliva doesn't run at the sound of the bell. Does Philip have these reflexes? In the office, possibly, not at home. His territory's divided. There are things he doesn't bother to think about

at all. His job's important. Mine isn't. He has a career to worry abou
I don't. So that I'll have the time and the energy to empty the ru
bish, carry the dustbin out into the street on a Thursday, look aft
the children, do the washing, clean the house, buy the food and pr
pare it for eating, dust the glass table. Haven't I a duty to open
this brave new world to him?

Her bitterness surprised her. Where had it been all these year
Why hadn't she minded these things? She had not minded anythi
it seemed. Not felt much at all. Anaesthetised. The love song
Hannah J. Straight.

> *Let us go then, you and I,*
> *When the evening is spread out against the sky*
> *Like a patient etherised upon a table . . .*

The patient is coming to. She seems to be getting angry.

She sat down, staring across at Philip. Remote. A fine-boned, sens
tive face. Thank God his eyes are closed. When he's puzzled they'
exactly like Harry's. What on earth does it mean to love someon
The only definition I can think of at the moment is having an affe
tionate curiosity about the totality of another person. Philip has ha
no curiosity. Can I say I've had much about him? Not enoug
Mutual dependence. No questions asked. A matching of frailties.

She remembered reading the phrase somewhere. It came back no
as something painfully appropriate. Suddenly it occurred to her th
the anger she was feeling was a cover up for something else. Was sh
trying to find reasons for disliking Philip so she would not feel
guilty? She closed her eyes in self-disgust. Accessory after the fac
There must have been collusion for things to turn out as they had.
was a conspirator in my own subjugation. No adult human bein
could oppress another without the connivance of the victim. Ho
odd to call it oppression. Not what it had seemed like. It had seeme
like . . . security. Then why don't I want this security any mor
The price is too big to pay. It has almost bankrupted me.

If only I could talk to Philip. The fear of hurting him paralyses m
He's never encouraged unpleasant confessions. Self-censorship ove
the years has gone too deep, now, trying to be the kind of wife
wants. Or I think he wants. Could that be what he's doing too? Try
ing to be the kind of husband he thinks I want? When did the mask

170

put on become our only faces? A relationship sustained by pos-
sions, a house in common, a car, half-squeezed tooth-paste tubes,
ty under-pants. Trivia. I'm walking in a forest of tall trees. When
ap on the trunks they're hollow. The least storm will bring them
shing down.

Hannah tried to let herself be carried along with the music.
zart. Philip's unfailing antidote. The Symphonia Concertante for
lin and Viola. This time it worked for her too. An effortless
icism about the playing, so stylised, so precise. Listening became
ind of meditation in which she could forget herself.

When the record ended she waited a few moments before opening
eyes. When she did, Philip's were on her face. He smiled. For the
t time she was able to manage a half-smile back.

A moment of connection. The most I can allow myself. I know
at he meant when he said 'We must comfort each other'. It would
a solution for him. Discords can end in making love. But not
nces. What was unspoken remains.

The thought of infecting him fills me with despair. I can't let him
ch me. The most fastidious of men who always washes after
king love. To contaminate him with something he couldn't wash
ay. It would destroy him.

15

At school Hannah found they wanted her to work full time. Th[ey] had decided to set up a special 'refuge' for some of the more distur[bed] and backward children, the chronic truants, to take the pressure [off] them. A small unit, just two teachers. Nick Gates would be one of the[m.] The Head of the Remedial Department, Mrs Calloway, explained[.]

'It's not only teaching I had in mind, Mrs Straight. I was hop[ing] you could do more in the way of contact with parents. The probl[em] seems to lie as much with the family situation as with the ability [of] the child.'

Hannah was so taken aback she could not think what to say. S[he] was obscurely flattered. One part of her wanted to respond imme[di]ately but the rest of her held back, hedged in by uncertainties. N[ick] Gates grinned at her. 'Come on in. The water's fine.'

Mrs Calloway went on, 'It won't start immediately. We'll tak[e a] few weeks to get things organised. For instance, we haven't [yet] sorted out the premises. So could you think about it and let me kn[ow] what you decide in a week or so? It would be a great advantage [to] have someone the children already know rather than having [to] advertise. That's why I hope you'll be interested. Sean Mal[one] would be one of the group.'

'Dick the Prick is King' it said on the corrugated iron fence next [to] Molly's house. The front door was open. Hannah rang the bell. S[o] out of order. She called out, 'Mrs Malone?'

Sean came along the corridor. When he saw Hannah he blushe[d] looking shy.

'Hullo Sean, how are you? Is your mother in?'

'Yeah, in the kitchen.' He led her into the back room and sat do[wn] immediately, his face turning to the flickering light from the te[le]vision like a sunflower to the sun.

Molly asked me to come and see you.'

Molly?' Mrs Malone half rose from the chair where she was feeding the baby on her knee from a bottle. 'Where is she? Is anything wrong?'

No, she's . . . all right. She's still in France. I saw her there. She wants to stay. She's been offered a part in a film.'

Our Molly in a film?' Mrs Malone stared at her in amazement. 'I can't credit it!'

It may mean quite a bit of money. She said she'd try to send you some as soon as she could.'

She'll not be coming back, then?'

Not . . . for a while.'

Mrs Malone's face was sad. 'I knew she'd be leaving us, but I didn't think it'd be that soon.' She shifted the baby to rest his head more comfortably in the crook of her arm. He sucked with the absorption of an addict, eyes closed, his small hands gripping the bottle. 'You can't blame her. She's better out of it. We're in such trouble I don't know what to do for the best, and that's the truth.'

Perhaps there's something I can do?'

Mrs Malone looked at her unbelievingly. 'I'm in too deep for the Holy Mother herself to get me out of it. He's gone.'

Who . . .?'

Kevin. My husband. Inside. Been put away for two years.'

In prison? Oh no!'

Mrs Malone's voice was bitter. 'We're better off without him. Sean,' she jerked her head towards the door. 'Keep the kids out will you? I want to talk to Mrs . . .'

Straight,' Hannah said.

Sean,' his mother shouted, 'turn that blessed thing off.'

He got up reluctantly, shoulders hunched, and went out, slamming the door. Mrs Malone switched the set off.

When I married him I didn't know what he could be like with the drink inside him. I've been that afraid sometimes, I've run out in the middle of the night to the neighbours. But I've always gone back. Where else to go, was there?' Her voice sunk so low Hannah could hardly hear it. 'Two weeks ago he was laid off. It was his own doing. He lost his temper with the foreman. There was a bit of a shindig.

173

Then of course the foreman wouldn't take him back. I was out at
clinic with the two little ones at the time. Sean was off the L
knows where. Just Irene at home with the other three. She's g
like that. She'll mind them for me.

'It seems Kevin came back when the pubs closed with a skin
He came straight in here where Irene was sitting with the kids .
Her voice was flat, no feeling left in it. 'He dragged her into the fr
room and tried . . . he tried to interfere with her. Irene's a big g
Just turned fourteen.' Hannah's stomach turned over. 'She star
screaming. The boys were trying to pull him away so he picked
little Mick and threw him right across the yard. His head smash
against the wall. If my neighbour hadn't heard the commotion a
come over the back fence he might have killed the lot of them.'

'Oh God!' Hannah covered her face.

'When I got back they were all down at the station. They'd tak
Michael to hospital. He'd a fractured skull and his arm was brok
in two places. Irene was with one of those police women. She had
whole story out of her.'

Hannah stared at Mrs Malone, the tears streaming down her fa
The other woman looked up, her eyes resigned, almost dead. 'Y
needn't cry, Mrs Straight. It was better he should be known for w
he was. I could never have taken him down there myself. I've t
much pride.'

She got up, holding the baby against her chest to bring up
wind. When she stood straight, Hannah could see the bump of l
hip bones under her brown skirt.

'What are you living on?'

'Social Security.'

'Is it enough?'

'We have to manage. The trouble is the back rent. I didn't kn
he wasn't paying it. The money was going on drink and the hors
Now all this street's coming down and I don't know if the G.L.C
give us another house. We been on the list five years for a new pla
But the woman up at the Welfare says there's no hope of that. T
most we could get is another dump like this. They don't go givi
new places to the likes of us, not big families, not with rent owir
And now there's no wages coming in.' The baby belched gent
dribbling curds over its chin. 'If I don't get a place the council w

174

ve to take the kids and look after them. I could manage with the
oy in one room. It's Sean I'm worrying about. He's in trouble.'
  What for?'
Thieving. He was with a gang of lads from the flats. They were
t bored in the holidays they got up to all kinds of devilment. I
In't know what was going on. They've put him under a supervision
ler. If he gets in any more trouble they say he'll have to be sent
ay. They said he was . . . out of control. Now with school starting
in I'm worried in case he doesn't go regular. You know what he's
e. Sometimes I think the teachers don't care if he's there or not.'
Hannah leant forward saying, 'I'll do everything I can to help him.
. . I may be working there full time this term.'
  What about your own kids? Molly told me you had two of them.'
Hannah hesitated. Then she said quickly, 'My son was killed in
ance. In an accident.'
The other woman stared at her. 'God rest his soul!' She spoke
tly, 'I should never have bothered you with my troubles.'
  Sympathy was like a rope between them. Hannah said awkwardly,
arry . . . my son . . . he had some pet mice. I don't know what
n going to do with them now. I know what Sean's like about
imals. Perhaps he'd like to look after them?'
  Mice!' Mrs Malone shivered with revulsion.
  I don't mean bring them here,' said Hannah quickly, 'I mean he
lld come home with me sometimes after school if he wants to.
ere were three of them when we went away. There's more now.
ey're always having babies.'
  Like me!' Mrs Malone's face was bitter. 'There'll be no more of
t, thanks be to God! I've learnt all I need to know about men. I've
d my bellyfull.'
  The literal meaning of what she had said suddenly occurred to
em both at the same time. They looked at each other for a moment,
en burst out laughing. It was as if Mrs Malone had not had the
portunity for a long time. She laughed weakly, rocking to and fro
the chair, gasping for breath.
  A little girl came in, sucking an iced lolly. She stared at her mother.
  'hat's up, Mum?'
  'Nothing, Sandra.'
Hannah got up. She said she would come again the following week.

175

On the way out she hesitated. 'Would you like me to write Molly?'

'No,' Mrs Malone shook her head. 'What's the use in sending bad news? She's better off as she is.'

Sandra switched the television on and sat down in the seat Hann had just left. The lolly had stained her mouth green.

'Goodbye,' Hannah said.

An advertisement flashed onto the screen. As she walked down t passage a voice murmured,

> *Fry's chocolate creams –*
> *Everyone deserves a little piece,*
> *Fry's chocolate creams –*
> *They turn relaxation into an art!*

*

Philip had brought various invitations home with him, for priv views, drinks parties of colleagues and so on, saying, 'I don't know you'd be interested in any of these?' He picked out one card a passed it across. 'I thought we might go to this, he's a useful man keep in with. Sounds rather good value.'

It read: 'The Deputy Chairman of the Greater London Coun Mr Michael Gaythorn, and Mrs Gaythorn, have asked me to say t it would give them very great pleasure if you and Mrs Straight co join them for dinner at the Royal Festival Hall on Wednesday 1 September and afterwards in the Ceremonial Box for the second h of the concert (Wagner – Overture to the Meister Singers; Dvora Violin Concerto in A minor).

'If you are able to accept perhaps you would be so good as to arr at the Main Entrance to the Hall at 7.15 p.m., where you will be m and escorted to the Restaurant. For your guidance Mrs Gaytho will be wearing a long dress and Mr Gaythorn a dinner jacket.'

It was signed by Mr Gaythorn's Assistant Private Secreta G.L.C.

'Shit on Mr Gaythorn's dinner jacket,' said Hannah quietly.

176

Philip jumped up. 'Hannah, what's the matter with you?' He was angry. 'Why do you say that?'

'Shit on him!' she shouted, 'and on Mrs Gaythorn's horrible long dress, and shit on his assistant private secretary and the G.L.C. and the whole fucking lot of them!'

Philip's face had gone white. 'Must you speak like that in front of the child?'

'Why not? Why shouldn't she know what shit is? She may step in it sometime!' Hannah was looking Philip openly in the face, her eyes blazing. 'If you want to go to things like that, then go. But don't ask me to come!'

Sarah was staring at them. Hannah could not bear the frightened expression on her face. She turned and rushed up the stairs to throw herself onto the bed, weeping uncontrollably. She kept thinking of Mrs Malone, Mrs Malone. How could she help her? The first time she had been close to another woman for years and felt her troubles as deeply as her own.

The week-end was strained. Now it was Philip who avoided looking into her eyes. What had he seen there? He kept his distance as if afraid of being burnt. On Saturday and Sunday he went to the office for several hours, taking Sarah with him. She came back with note books, paper clips, carbon paper.

'Valerie was there,' she said to Hannah. 'She's nice. She bought me crisps and a shandy. It's got alcohol in, you know. Do you think I'll be alcoholic like you?'

16

A painful conversation with Sarah before school. She's sipping
drinking chocolate.

'Why haven't you taken Daddy his cup of tea? Aren't you go
to?'

'Oh . . . well . . . I forgot.'

'I'll do it. Let me do it.' She jumps up, puts the kettle on, tea
into the cup, two sweeteners. Her chocolate's getting cold. 'He m
be sad if he doesn't get a cup of tea. He's used to it. Anyway,
know he can't get up without it.'

If I abandon the ritual will she take it on? Am I just passing
oppression from me to her? She goes upstairs in slow motion, tak
care not to spill a drop. He hates sloppy saucers. The conditionin
beginning. No, that's not true. It began years ago. How can I s
it?

She comes back, eyes shining.

'He's awake. He's drinking it. He'll be down soon. He says h
take me to school.'

The longing to serve the person we love. It's in our blood.
when it's done with love what can possibly be wrong with it?
thing. Until the spontaneity goes. No longer an expression of
but an obligation of duty.

I don't want any two mornings to be the same. Sarah does
much the same as she can possibly make them.

Hannah had a bath, washing herself thoroughly as if she c
scrub away all sign of disease. She put on clean underwear. As
was shutting the front door the telephone rang. A deep foreign v
Arab?

'Is that the residence of Mr Philip Straight?'

'Yes.'

'This is Yasser Mahmoud speaking. I'm ringing from London ⸤port.'

'Oh, yes?'

'When I met Mr Straight and his charming assistant in Benghazi he ⸤d me to be sure and phone him if I came to the U.K.'

'Mr Straight's not here. I'll give you his office number.'

⸤She told him the number and put down the receiver. Who did he ⸤an – Philip's charming assistant? That Libyan engineer who was ⸤ping him? She puzzled over this as she wrote the name Yasser M. ⸤ the telephone pad. She did not know how to spell it. She presumed ⸤ilip would know who it was.

⸤The hospital was a huge Victorian brick building, the entrance ⸤amped with modern lettering over a stuck-on vestibule. She went ⸤ the counter marked 'Enquiries' and said softly through the grill, ⸤an you tell me where the V.D. clinic is?'

'Speak up, dear, I can't hear you properly.'

'I'm looking for the V.D. clinic.'

⸤A woman at the next grill turned to stare at her.

'Through the swing door, out into the courtyard and it's on your ⸤t.'

⸤She followed the directions but she could find nothing saying V.D., ⸤ly a sign for 'Physiotherapy' and an arrow with 'Ambulances' over ⸤ Then in the far corner she saw the words 'Special Clinic'. Could ⸤at be it? The notice was attached to a small, concrete hut like a ⸤blic lavatory. Special. A word for presents and treats, for every-⸤ing cherished and out of the ordinary. A disease that was ⸤ecial.

⸤There were two entrances – 'Male Clinic', 'Female Clinic'. Imme-⸤ately inside the door a woman sat in a small glassed-in office.

'Come in and shut the door. Are you a new patient?'

'Yes.'

⸤She stamped a pink card with a number.

'This is your card. Bring it with you every time you come. I'm not ⸤ing to nag you about anything else, dear, but be sure to bring it ⸤ery time. Just wait in reception till you're called.'

⸤She sat on a red plastic chair next to a black girl with an Afro hair ⸤yle. The girl smiled at Hannah as if they were fellow losers in the ⸤me game. They sat in silence. Posters pinned to the wall offered

free contraceptive advice to anyone over sixteen. One had a ca:
board cutout of a man with a gun. He was shooting above his head
a stork carrying a baby. The caption said, 'There must be an eas
way.'

A grey-haired woman in a white coat called Hannah from a si
office. Endless questions – age, general health, married?

'Yes.'

'You're living with your husband?'

'Yes.'

'When did you last have intercourse with him?'

'Not . . . for some time.' The doctor looked up, fiddling with I
glasses as if she was focussing a microscope. 'He's been abroad.'

'Now, why have you come to us? Have you any reason to beli(
you might be infected? Have you been with anyone else?'

Hannah stared back at her. Why the hell should she feel so e
barassed and awkward? She was beginning to get angry. 'Why (
should I be here?'

The doctor scribbled something in her notes. Hannah leant f
ward trying to read the writing upside down but it was too small. S
could imagine some eager researcher poring over these recor
extracting little nuggets of statistical information about the mo
health of the nation.

'We'll examine you in a moment. You're not menstruating I p
sume?'

'No.'

'When was your last period?'

'I'm not sure. It must be about . . .' Hannah stared at the docto
bent head in consternation. With so much on her mind she had r
calculated it so exactly before. 'Over five weeks ago . . . or more.

The woman looked up. 'Is your cycle normally regular?'

'Yes . . . I think so . . .'

'Have you any reason to think you might be pregnant?'

'No, I . . . It never occurred to me.'

'What contraceptive method do you use?'

'A loop.'

'They're not entirely foolproof, you know. Conception can oc(
in about two per cent of cases.'

The idea was so extraordinary Hannah could not take it in. T

ctor said briskly, 'We'd better get on with the tests. Are you aller-
to penicillin?'

Hannah whispered, 'No.'

Right. Go into the cubicle next door.'

A nurse with silver-buckled belt invited her to remove her skirt
d pants. 'Can you produce a specimen for me, dear?' She went
tfully to the other side of the curtain.

Hannah peed into a wide glass container. Some spilt on the floor
cause her hand holding the container was shaking. 'I'm sorry,' she
d, as the nurse came back in.

Never mind. These accidents do happen. Just sit up on that
uch.'

The couch had metal foot rests sticking out at each side. She was
ected to slide her bottom to the edge of it and splay wide her legs
reach the foot-rests. The doctor came in, sliding her hands into
stic gloves, and directed a spotlight between Hannah's legs. The
rse handed her a thin metal rod with a twisted loop at the end.
nnah braced herself, gripping the sides of the couch with both
nds. It looked like an instrument of torture, a horrible wire exca-
or. She felt something cold and hard inside her as the doctor
atted to the nurse across her legs.

'That recipe you gave me for chocolate sauce – I tried it at the
ek-end. It's delicious.'

'I'm glad you like it. It's always been a favourite with my kiddies.'

'My husband's the one with the sweet tooth. I don't indulge him
a rule, only on Sundays as a special treat. He has to watch his tum.'

he nurse passed her a fresh instrument. 'Move your tail a little
ver, will you?'

She stuck something so hard up Hannah's bottom that she cried
t, 'What are you doing?'

'Just routine checks. Keep still.'

It hurts much more up the arse. Can you get it there as well?
nnah felt the humiliation of the dehumanised.

The nurse said briskly, 'You can get dressed now, dear.' Then she
tracted some blood from Hannah's arm and told her to wait outside.

These damned shakes. Why did she always get them when she was
ghtened? She sat on her hands to keep them still and stared at the
or. An endless wait.

181

'Mrs Straight, come in, will you.' The doctor shut the door beh[ind] Hannah. 'Sit down. I'm afraid the tests are positive.'

'What . . . what is it?'

'Gonorrhoea. All too common these days. You'll have to under[go] a course of treatment. Luckily we've caught it in the early stages. I['m] wondering about your partner. Do you think we might be able [to] contact him?'

'What?' said Hannah, getting up in fright, 'You mean my husban[d.]'

'No, no. Whoever it was passed the infection on.'

'He knows.' She sat down again. 'He told me to come. Anyw[ay] he's in France.'

'Right then. I'll give you an injection now and you'll come ba[ck] for another at the end of the week.'

Hannah sat with her shoulders bowed. She felt as if someone w[as] dropping huge boulders on her head, one by one. The doctor sto[od] up.

'We're rather busy this morning so if you wouldn't mind standi[ng] up I'll give you your injection.' She put the needle in. 'We wo[n't] know about the other test until this afternoon. I've sent a specim[en] over to the hospital lab.'

'What test?'

'Pregnancy. You can come back later to hear the results.'

17

annah realised from the expression on Philip's face there must be
mething very wrong with her appearance.

'Hannah, you look ill. You're terribly pale.'

She put her hand up to her cheek. 'Do I? I feel a little . . . odd.'

'You must go and see Dr Coates. I should've insisted on it last
eek. Can't you go tomorrow?'

'I have to work tomorrow. There'll be children waiting.'

'Can't you miss it? Surely it doesn't matter?'

'No. No.' she said quickly, 'I don't want to. Perhaps I'll be better
tomorrow.' She sat down, feeling very tired. 'Oh, by the way, a
an rang you from the airport. Yasser something. From Benghazi.
e said he met you there.'

'Yasser Mahmoud, was it?'

'That's right. I gave him your office number.'

'He's in the Ministry. Nice fellow, quite friendly to me.'

She asked curiously, remembering, 'Who did he mean by your
arming assistant?'

Philip said casually, 'I suppose he meant Valerie.'

'Valerie?' She paused in bewilderment. 'Was she there with you?'

Philip was looking in the fridge. She had not prepared his snack.
e said with his back to her, 'She was a great help. I sent for her
hen the going got rough. We had to rewrite the whole damned
asibility study.'

Hannah felt dazed. If she could only fit this information into place,
ut her mind was too full already. What else was he not telling her?

'Do you want some salami?' asked Philip.

'No. I'm not hungry. I'll have coffee.'

'Hannah, you're not eating. I'm worried about you. You're not
ourself.'

The tap was running noisily.

183

'Who is myself?'

'What did you say?'

'Nothing.'

'The strain on you has been terrible. I'm sure Dr Coates co[
give you something to help you over this difficult time.'

'What? What could he give me?'

'Hannah . . .' He took her hand, 'Don't get worked up. I mea[
sedative of some sort, something to calm you down, Librium, Valiu[
whatever these things are called. You're so on edge.'

Her hand was limp in his. A dead paw. 'I'd rather not take a[
thing. It seems an . . . evasion, somehow.'

'Hannah, for God's sake! There are some things we have [
evade.'

'Is that how you manage?'

'What do you mean?'

'By evasion. Do you evade things?'

'Don't get at me, Hannah. I've had a hell of a day.'

A restless night. Continual nightmares. I'm trying to wind u[
ball of wool. The cat pounces on it and tangles the thread, bitin[
with her sharp white teeth. I wake up sweating. I've lost the thre[
I've lost the thread of the loop. How could I have got pregnant?[
little thread is supposed to dangle down. The Family Planning g[
me a booklet:

> 'The loop is inserted when it is thin and straight. For this it[
> slipped into a hollow plastic tube approximately the size of t[
> cervical canal leading from the vagina to the uterus. The tube[
> then gently inserted into the cervix and the loop is pushed throu[
> the tube into the cavity of the uterus; once there it curls up in[
> its memory shape, leaving the thread showing outside the cer[
> in the vagina. For this procedure women need remove only low[
> underclothes and shoes.'

If the thread has gone, what's happened to the loop? Will [
entangle itself with the . . . foetus to make it deformed? And t[
gonorrhoea – what damage will that do? Why didn't I think of t[
before? I could have asked if there was any danger. I must get
these questions sorted out. It must be Marc's. That's what I have

clear in my head. It must be Marc's. I haven't slept with
lip since before he went to Libya. So it couldn't be his, could

low easy it was to feel superior to Molly, to think her a fool to
e risks. Now I'm in the same state. My body has betrayed me. It
pened without my intention. Am I my body? A machine
grammed to reproduce itself. We can't control it. No, that's wrong.
can. Not the starting, the conceiving, but we can do something
top it. Molly did. She aborted the process going on inside her.
lly stopped that bit of the machine and I helped her. Is that why
rry was killed? So I would know the meaning of a child's death?
ng beside Philip, I can't think properly. Questions scream inside
head. I must keep them quiet. I'm afraid he'll hear my thoughts
think them too loud.

he got out of bed. The room was airless. Like a sleep-walker she
nt downstairs and into the garden to grub up the two twisted
nnikins from behind the shrub. One was stained dark brown with
th from the middle down. As she held them in her hand it
urred to her with horror that the two grotesque figures were not
and Sarah as Marc had supposed, but herself and Molly. Every-
ng that had happened seemed to start with that first spontaneous
mise she had made to Molly, sitting by the couch. One moment
involvement with an unknown girl had led her into this labyrinth
disasters. But what was their origin? Was she, somehow, partly
ponsible for them, explosions detonated by the fuse of the buried
she had denied for so long? The chaos, the powers of darkness
was so afraid of, might be inside her.

linded by tears. In certain states clichés, worn-out phrases, like
songs, take on their original meaning. They reverberate in your
nd, over and over, as if they contained all that was to be said at
t particular moment. Blinded by tears.
I know what it means now. At first the tears are inside you, not
uefied but congealed in a heavy mass. They begin to swell, press-
; against the walls of your body as if to burst it open. The pressure
comes more and more unbearable. It rises from your belly through
ur chest. Your neck aches, the skin of your face is distended with
rs. Then they begin to seep slowly out of your eyes. Blinded by

tears. You can't see where you are. Water flows silently down y
cheeks. Blinded by tears.

The words sounded in my head – blinded by tears – over and o
again. Gradually another meaning began to come into my mi
Tears can stop you seeing into yourself. Tears are a veil to put
tween yourself and an anguish that is too much to bear. They so
nothing, they dissolve nothing. You are blinded with tears a
moment when to see clearly would be unbearable.

This account is getting more and more disjointed. It no lon
hangs together coherently. Whole moments in the days that follow
are lost. Misery shatters continuity.

I go back to the clinic. The nurse does the injection. I like
better. She doesn't give off an odour of moral distaste. Perhaps sh
too used to it all. I like the particular deep blue of her uniform. Re
ful. In the middle ages they believed certain shades of blue co
calm mad people. The blue glass in King's College Chapel in Ca
bridge. Translucent. A heavenly blue. Could they see God through

The nurse's hair is drawn back neatly under her cap, exposing
white neck. So clean you could eat off it.

'Nurse,' the words rush out in a jumble, 'do you think it, I me
. . . you know . . . the disease, could it affect the . . . the embryo

I can't say baby. I'm not going to say baby.

She's taken aback. She clearly doesn't want to say anything.

'I don't think so, dear. Not if we get rid of it. It's only when t
mother is badly infected at the time of the birth that it can dama
the baby's eyes. And that's a long time off, isn't it?'

On the way back I saw painted in black capitals all across the ra
way arches:

ABORTION NEGATES HUMAN DIGNITY AND WORTH!
FLUSH OUT THE BUZZARDS OF PAGAN DOGMA NOW
   COME IN TO ROOST!
DEPOLLUTE YOUR PLAYGROUNDS OF CYANIDE MORAL
   TRASH!
STOP THE MENTAL RAPE OF KIDS BY PERVERSE SEX
   INSTRUCTION!

STOP TORTURE BY EXPERIMENTS IN THE NUTHOUSE!
NOBODY SPOKE: THE STONES CRY OUT
OUTLAW THE CRIME – ABORTION
KILL THE PAGAN HAG – SEX PERVERSION!

Who is that message for?

However hard I try to fight it down, one part of me longs for this
oy. If I let myself think of it as a baby I'm filled with such awe I
gin to tremble. Why do I contemplate, even for a moment, des-
ying this new life? Because I'm diseased. My body is poisoned.
n the link in a chain of horror.

I seem to be spending a lot of my time in the bathroom. The only
or I can lock without it seeming too odd. The only privacy. What
es Philip think I'm doing? Suffering from Portnoy's complaint –
sturbating among the mice?

Harry's pet mice are still kept in here. They smell fusty and odd.
e used to let them out to play in the bath without fear of their
aping. He got into the bath himself and let them run about all
er him. A new litter has just been born. I can't help staring at them.
w pink embryos lying in a heap on top of each other. They are
rn before they're completely formed, their eyes covered with a
embrane so you can't see the full shape or colour of them, only a
rk shadow beneath the skin. Is the human embryo like that? A
embrane over the face, shadowed, unformed, unseeing?

I look at these small, vulnerable shapes as if I'm looking into my
n belly. Oh God, help me to decide what to do. I fold my hands in
eaningless prayer. A reflex action. The hands come together of
eir own accord. A prayer to King Mouse. I'm obsessed with the
ea of abortion. Something inside me screams whenever I think
out it. I mustn't wait like Molly did till it becomes a baby. I
ustn't think of it as a baby. A pink, gelatinous substance, without
eling, without identity.

Hannah sat in the locked bathroom rocking to and fro on a hard
air, unable to decide what to do. No time. No time. She was racked
tween the two hands of the clock, turning, turning. The machine
as functioning wrongly. It must be serviced by the doctor and the
irse. If she wanted to interfere yet more crucially with its functioning

187

she would have to take it to yet more doctors and nurses. Sp
alists in termination. What a terrible word. Molly cried out
through the operation.

The tension was unbearable. She got up suddenly and unloc
the door. Sarah was asleep. Light came into the hall from Phili
room where he had gone to work after supper. She stood in the do
way without him hearing. He was sitting at his black lacquered d
studying some papers very intently. The lamp shone onto his b
head. This is the man I am married to. This is the man I have li
with for twelve years.

'Philip . . .'

He went on reading for a moment before looking up. 'Mm . .

'I have to tell you something.'

He leaned back in his chair, stretching his arms widely and yaw
ing.

'I'm pregnant.'

He sat up stiffly in mid-yawn. 'Hannah, what are you saying?'

'I'm pregnant.'

She could almost hear the computer humming away inside
head. She stood there waiting for the print-out.

'I don't understand. When . . . I mean, how long . . . how pre
nant are you?'

I could lie. How many thousands of women in this situation m
have lied their way out of it. He's waiting for precise information
he'll know how to react.

'About six weeks.'

'But . . . it's eight weeks since I . . . went to Libya.'

'Yes.'

He stared at her. 'You mean, it's . . . not mine?'

She shook her head. What a relief to meet his eyes, not to have
evade them any more. She wanted to step forward and put her han
each side of his face and hold it gently but the anger in his eyes fro
her.

He said bitterly, 'I thought it was . . . Harry's death that was ma
ing you so strange, while all the time . . .'

'I didn't know.'

'You didn't know what?'

'That I was pregnant, until a few days ago.'

'How could you be so careless, so irresponsible?' He was shouting with anger, hands flat on the desk. 'All that business you went in for with the family planning, I thought that was meant to be foolproof.'

'You mean the loop?'

His mouth twisted. The subject was distasteful to him. Female plumbing. 'Whatever the hell you call it.'

'So did I think it was.' Her voice was jittery. 'Two per cent. I must be one of the two per cent.'

'Oh God!' He stood up and went over to the window with his back to her, his voice strained as if he was trying to keep a tight control over it. 'How serious is it? I mean was it just an . . . affair or something more permanent?'

'Permanent?' She sat down on the sofa, her legs weak.

'Does he – whoever he is – want you to live with him? Do you want to leave me?'

'We didn't talk about it. We . . . didn't talk about you.'

Philip turned round incredulously. 'What d'you mean, you didn't talk about me? Didn't he know you were married?'

Why do his gestures look so stagey? It's me that has rehearsed this scene, not him. Is he feeling less than he thinks he ought to?

'Yes. He knew that. He's . . . not the sort of person who asks questions.'

'What sort of person is he, may I ask?'

'He was the landlord, of that house we took.'

'Some rich old Parisian?'

'He's not rich. He makes jewelry.'

'How old?'

'I'm not sure . . . about twenty-eight.'

'Oh God, Hannah!' He spoke with contempt. 'The bored older woman on holiday falling for one of the natives.'

'I . . . didn't do it to hurt you. It . . . just happened. I suppose you would call it an accident.'

'Like Harry's death!'

Hannah felt herself go slowly red, as if he had slapped her across the face. Philip suddenly collapsed into a chair. 'I shouldn't have said that.' He put up his hand to support his head, closing his eyes in exhaustion. 'I suppose that's why you haven't let me touch you. I thought you were having a kind of . . . nervous breakdown.'

Can I tell him any more, thought Hannah, staring at his bow[ed] head? No. I can't. It would be even more degrading for him. 'Phili[p,]' she said softly, 'please help me. I don't know what to do.'

He waited for a long moment and then said, 'Why did it happe[n?]'

How could she give an explanation? She did not understand [it] herself. 'You . . . weren't there.'

He pressed his fists into his eye sockets. 'That's what I keep sayi[ng] to myself over and over again about Harry's death. I can't get it o[ut] of my mind. I wasn't there. If only I'd been there!'

'Don't, Philip! You musn't blame yourself. It's me, I'm the . . .'

'Why did it have to happen? Why Harry?'

Her voice shook. 'Must there be a reason?'

He looked up suddenly. 'Couldn't we go back to how we we[re] before?'

'Go back?' She looked at him in astonishment. 'Harry's dead.'

'I mean, you and I . . .'

'Nothing's the same, is it?'

There was a pause, then he said, 'At least you know where to g[o.]'

'What do you mean?'

'After your experience with that girl.'

'You mean . . . I should have an abortion.'

He looked at her icily. 'Am I supposed to pretend it's mine, go [to] the office saying – isn't it great, my wife's having another baby, co[n]gratulate me, won't you?'

The savagery in his voice transfixed her. His image, his reputatio[n.] Nothing must threaten that. She began to feel very frightened, li[ke] someone drifting out to sea in a boat with no oars. 'I know it's n[ot] logical but I . . . can't bear the idea of an abortion. It seems . . . wrong.'

His voice was sarcastic. 'You didn't have the same scruples abo[ut] that wretched girl, what was her name – Molly?'

'No,' she whispered. 'I know.'

He got up and began to walk up and down with his hands behin[d] his back. 'How can I tell you what to do? All I can do is point out t[he] consequences of the various courses of action open to you. You we[re] never very good at thinking things through.'

'No.'

'I'll spell it out. There are only two choices. One: you decide to [go]

ead and have the child. In that case I wouldn't expect you to go on
ing here. What you do would be your concern. It would be the
d of our marriage.'

She leant forward as if to speak but he went on, 'Let me finish.
wo: you face up to having an abortion and we carry on as best we
1.' His expression was bitter. 'I'm thinking of Sarah. Have you
ught about what it would mean for her or is it just yourself you're
rrying about?'

Hannah said miserably, 'I'm worrying about all of us. Whatever I
will be wrong. There is no right thing to do.' She looked at him
kwardly. 'It's not just my decision, it's . . . his as well.' She stum-
d over the words, beginning to talk too fast. 'I need to see him,
ilip, to talk to him. If . . . if I had a child it would be . . . his child
well as mine.' Anything she said was bound to hurt him more.
ils in the coffin of their dead marriage. 'I want to go back there. I
uld fly to Marignane and hire a car.'

'Rather an expensive trip, won't it be?' said Philip coldly.

'I'll pay for it. If you could just lend me the money till the end of
e month when I get my pay.'

'I don't see how you could afford it.'

'They've asked me to work full-time at the school.'

Philip stared at her. 'A full-time job? Would you want that?' He
unded alarmed.

'I'm . . . not sure. I'm thinking about it. I can't dec . . .'

'There's something I ought to show you,' Philip interrupted. He
ened his black briefcase and took out a letter from Jerome. He had
t that Tunisian contract and he wanted Philip to come in on the
b and form a new partnership with him. International Consultants.
'I rang him up today to get some more details. I wanted to talk it
er with my staff. It's a fantastic opportunity.' Some of the usual
oyancy came back into his voice. 'If I agree to go in with him I can
ut them all on more permanent contracts. I can start paying Valerie
my personal assistant and office manager and get a new girl for the
utine work. It would mean a great deal to all of us.'

Hannah said awkwardly, 'I'm glad. I know you always wanted to
ork with Jerome.'

'But there's another side to it, Hannah. It would mean going to
unisia for at least three months.'

191

'Why are you asking me? You don't usually consult me about yo
absences.'

'I thought you might like to come. It won't hurt Sarah to m
school. I've been . . .' he looked away '. . . worried as hell about y
since I got back. After what you've told me it seems an even bett
idea. It might help you to forget . . . all this sadness.'

Forget all this sadness? Sadness did not end. There was alwa
more.

'It's a nice place, not like Libya.'

'Valerie didn't mind Libya?'

Philip flashed at her, 'Libya's no place for children, you kno
that.'

She sat upright, clasping her hands together. To her surprise s
found they were sweating. Like Georges'.

'I think you should decide regardless of me. Do what you want
do. Will what I say affect your decision that much?' She must n
destroy anything else for him.

'It may affect what I say to people at the office.' He sounded ve
formal. 'Who's going to work on the Tunisian project and so for
who I take with me.'

He looked uncomfortable. Was he trying to tell her somethi
else? She thought, he's lining up his insurance policy. He's not goi
to feel insecure, even for a moment. Perhaps the new company w
offer him better terms than the old. I'll give him a no claim bonus
take with him. I'm not going to make any claim. Not ever. I'll p
the damages myself.

He sat down again at the desk. 'I have to finish this report fo
meeting tomorrow. I'd better get on with it.'

Marc, I didn't think I'd be writing to you. I remember y
warned me you were no good at answering letters – a tenuous co
nection, didn't you say a letter was? You needn't answer this o
because I'll be there soon after.

You were right about the infection. I have got it. But ther
something more important. I've found out I'm pregnant. I would
be writing to you except that I'm sure it's your child. It could
be anyone else's. (A hazard of my way of life.) Please don't thin
expect you to do anything about it, or hold you responsible – wh

ludicrous word in this connection. I don't. It's just that I'm finding it very hard to know what to do. I have to decide whether to go on with it and I need to talk to you before I finally make up my mind. I'm not saying I'll do what you say but I must know what you want to happen.

I'll fly to Marseille next week and drive straight to the village. Is the headstone ready? I'd like to put it up while I'm there. *Agréez, cher Monsieur, mes sentiments les plus mysterieux,*   H

18

'Up, up and away!'

Sitting in the plane, the catch-phrase from old Superman films keeps coming into my head. Up, up and away. Philip's ready for that. Jerome's proposal means there's nothing now to hold him back. His career is made. Philip as Superman. He doesn't need me any more. Not me especially, not the kind of person I'm becoming.

I have this creepy feeling that for Philip it's the role that matters, not the person in it. Someone else would be better for him. I can't do it any more, that supporting part. Valerie would be better. The old cliché. The secretary who becomes the mistress, who becomes the wife. Perhaps that isn't really happening. I'm making it all up. Are they different roles or just the same one under different titles? Valerie is paid now to be supportive. Her job. She probably likes it. She's being sucked in, entangled unawares as I was, wound round and round with intricate dependencies. Will she like doing it unpaid? Where do her frailties fit?

As Philip's work gradually became more demanding, I hid away those parts of me that didn't suit his needs. When he came home he was tired. He needed everything to be regularised, reassuring. Why did I think his work so important? Why did I sustain the mythology?

Over the last year, since Valerie came into his office, more and more late nights working there, more and more time abroad. Did she go with him every time? The odd thing is I didn't even realise what was happening. Stuck in my own roles – wife, mother, part-time teacher – skating busily on the surface like a water-boatman. Inside emptier and emptier. I remember my grandmother reading me William Blake. Her mentor. She liked to think of herself as his spiritual wife, walking naked in the garden. *The same dull round, even of a universe, would soon become a mill with complicated wheels.*

It's that same dull round Marc's determined to avoid. The mill with complicated wheels that grinds you into nothingness, the nothingness that is the absence of feeling. I let myself be bounded. I have no right to blame Philip. With another person he might not be the same. With another person I'm not. If we met in ten years' time would we even recognise each other?

*

At Marignane the air smelt of pine woods. Such a lovely autumn day, hardly autumn even. Here it was more like late summer. She hired the cheapest car possible, a Renault Four. It took her a little while to get used to the push-me-pull-me gears and driving on the right again. She wanted to get there as fast as possible. Her fantasy raced ahead. Letting herself think even for a moment that Marc might want her to stay and have the baby there filled her with such crazy joy she could not control it. She slid the window open and began to sing into the breeze, one of her grandmothers's songs:

> *The water is wide, I cannot get o'er,*
> *And neither have I wings to fly,*
> *Give me a boat that will carry two,*
> *And we will cross, my love and I.*

Her grandmother seemed to know only melancholy songs. She sang them in a high keening voice while she was doing the washing up. She liked, she once told Hannah, the mixture of voice and water. The one enhanced the other. Hannah tried to get the same effect by singing into the wind.

As she turned up the road to Saint Jacques she drove like one of the old inhabitants, without hooting, as if every turn of this beautiful, winding road was familiar – the grey, lichen-covered rocks, the humps of lavender, the ruined walls bounding the fields on either side. And then at last she could see the village. She was on the level stretch of road that led only towards that cluster of houses and nowhere else. She slowed down to savour the pleasure of anticipation. In a few moments she would see Marc.

She turned up the track that skirted the village and drove into the square. The house was just as she had left it, standing in sunlight with the lower shutters open. She got out of the car, hardly daring to breathe. Doves murmuring from behind their wire mesh, the trickle from the fountain. She walked almost on tip-toe down the alley towards Marc's door, wanting to surprise him.

It was half open onto the cool green kitchen. Nobody in there, the tap dripping slowly onto an unwashed, yellow plate in the sink, a knife and fork beside it. She felt like a detective looking for clues of his presence. What a beautiful plate. He must have just eaten off it. Egg congealed on the surface. On the table a brown cup half full of coffee. One cup. He must be alone. She had been afraid he might have someone with him. She put out her hand to feel the outside of the cup. Still warm. Over her head she heard someone walking about. He must be there. In a moment she was jumping lightly up the stairs, two at a time. She knocked at the studio door and without waiting for an answer pushed it open.

'Marc! Marc, I'm here!'

Janine was standing in the middle of the floor holding a broom. 'Hannah! I didn't think you'd get here so soon.'

Hannah looked wildly round the room. 'Where's Marc?'

Janine took a step towards her, saying, 'Come and sit down. I'll get you some coffee.'

Hannah had gone rigid. 'Where's Marc? Isn't he here?'

Janine said quietly, 'He left at seven o'clock this morning. He had to take all his things to Paris for the exhibition. The gallery sent a telegram yesterday and said if he didn't get them there by today it would be too late for the catalogue. He always leaves things too late.'

'This morning? He was here this morning?' Hannah could feel the panic rising inside her. 'Why didn't he send me a telegram? Why didn't he stop me coming?'

Janine looked embarrassed. 'I don't know. He was terribly busy. He didn't stop all yesterday. In fact we had to go on packing things up till five this morning. He only had a couple of hours sleep before he left.'

'I could have gone to Paris.'

'He did say something about Paris, that you might come there.'

'Today? Did he mean I ought to go today?'

Janine shrugged. 'I don't know. He didn't say. He just said . . . he might see you there sometime.'

196

Hannah leant against the wall to stop herself falling.

'Why didn't you go with him?'

Janine said gently, 'Marc . . . asked me to stay here to see you. I'm not going back to Paris yet in any case. I'm going to Corsica in a few days.'

'Did he tell you why I was coming?'

Janine's restrained expression told her nothing.

'He said you wanted to put up the headstone for the grave. He left you a note with the address of the *maçon*.'

Of course. She'd mentioned the headstone in her letter. Did he really think that sufficient reason not to stop her coming? Perhaps he thought she was rich, that the fare meant nothing.

Janine put out her hand awkwardly and touched her on the arm. 'Please sit down, Hannah, you look so tired. I'll get you some coffee.'

She pulled her gently towards the couch. It's no joke, thought Hannah, that smells can be aphrodisiac. To sit in this room and feel passion for a sheepskin. What could be more humiliating? Her longing for him was unbearable.

'Where did he leave it?'

'What?'

'The note.'

'In Aunt Helen's house, I suppose.'

Hannah jumped up and started down the stairs.

'Wait, Hannah! The house is locked.'

Janine picked up the massive key from the work bench and handed it to her.

The note was on the table.

Hannah – in a terrible hurry. Sorry I have to go before you get here. Janine will explain. The *maçon* is Jules Villaret, 35 Rue St Saturnin, a turning off the main road out of town. I saw him in the market last week and he said it was ready. Don't know what to say about the other thing. You ask what I want to happen. I want what happens to happen. That's all I can say. If things are too difficult you'd better not go on with it. I wouldn't want to influence you. I think only you can decide.

Why not come to Paris for the exhibition? I'll send you a card. This is for you.

The note was weighted down at one corner by a silver collar in th
shape of two snakes, their heads meeting at the centre. The necklac
was supple and gleaming, an intricate design of hammered silver
each scale a separate link in the chain. Hannah picked it up. Cold a
a real snake. He's opted out, she thought. Mercury, quicksilver
slipping between the fingers. He conducts the souls of the dead to th
infernal regions. They have to find their own way out. Is there one

She fastened the necklace round her neck. He left me his snakes
She felt empty of all emotion. A head full of air. She went outside
legs walking towards the cemetery of their own accord. The gate
creaked stiffly. I am inside the room of the dead. You know one of the
company here. Down the path and turn right.

The earth that had been damp when she last saw it was dry now as
the surrounding plots. No name. Nothing to give it identity. The
lavender in the middle looked withered. She remembered Marc saying lavender doesn't transplant well at this time of year. The roots go
too deep. They don't like being disturbed.

Should I go to Paris? Today, if there's a plane, or tomorrow morning? She put her hand up to her neck feeling the silver band. A
collar, she thought, nothing but a dog collar. I'm like a dog running
after its master, grovelling on the ground for a touch of his big toe.
Suddenly she exploded with anger. To hell with him. She ran out of
the cemetery back to the car and got in, driving back along the road
she had come by. He's afraid, she thought, just like anyone else.
Afraid of getting involved. Tiny little fingers clutching at him from
inside my womb like vine tendrils. He wants to chop them off.

She drove very fast, brushing the tears out of her eyes with one
hand, to get to the *maçon* before he closed his workshop. At least she
could do that. She remembered another verse of the song she had
been singing earlier:

> *I leaned my back against an oak,*
> *Thinking it was a trusty tree,*
> *But first it bended and then it broke,*
> *And so did my false love to me.*

In front of her, before the turn in the road, a tractor was crawling
along. She hooted to make it pull over. The driver waved her on
without turning round. She was half-way past when she realised her

mistake. A blind corner ahead. Round it at full speed came a grey *Deux Chevaux*. It was too late to pull back. The tractor driver turned his head towards her, sunlight flashing on his glasses as he shouted something. She braked hard, trying to steer the car onto the narrow verge. At the wheel of the *Deux Chevaux* Madame Corneille's horrified face was coming straight at her, beside her in the passenger seat a waterfall of red hair. Hannah turned the wheel as hard as she could and the Renault shot over the edge, grinding across grey stones as it lurched down the steep slope and crashed upside down against a rock.

The most peculiar sensation. Very hard to breathe. Was she alive or dead? Pinned down by something pressing hard against her chest, like a butterfly stuck with a pin. Part of God's collection of the once living? The feeling of returning into her own body came with waves of pain, circular waves whirling her round and round on the end of a rope of pain. From far away a faint voice saying her name – Madame Straight, Madame . . . an odd, frightened voice, like a girl's, yet not a girl's. She had heard it before. With an enormous effort she forced herself to focus on the voice and try to answer. She opened her eyes. Georges' face, his mouth half open and moist with spittle, was very close to hers. Upside down. Eyes magnified into eggs of watery blue. A thin sound came from her throat and then the wave washed over her again.

*

I've never been in this room before. Whose is it? The walls are papered with brown and green flowers. The bed's very high off the floor. The floor tiled with square, red tiles. She put the evidence together carefully in her mind. It must be France. Those tiles. The bed has a white metal rail. What a beautiful gold mirror. Scalloped edges like a golden shell. Someone lying in the bed in the mirror.

She tried to lift herself up in order to see better into the mirror. She could not do it. Her body felt as if it had been punched all over. The figure of a woman moved into the edge of the mirror.

'Madame Straight?'

She turned her head slowly to the right, nervous of any movement. A woman in a blue checked overall, her bony face smiling anxiously, stood beside the bed. Hannah had seen her before a few times - Mademoiselle Terrain, the farmer's daughter. She started to speak but the woman shook her head. Hannah was speaking English. Of course, the woman couldn't understand. Straining to concentrate her mind she started again, in French.

'Where am I?'

'At our house, at the farm.'

'How did I get here?'

'Georges Bonnieux carried you. He got you out of the car. It was the nearest house to the accident.'

Hannah sank back into the bed. Unbelievably soft. Perhaps it was made of feathers. She remembered the pressure on her chest, pinning her down. It was gone. She wiggled her fingers experimentally. Yes, they moved. They didn't even hurt. It was her arms and chest that ached so much, particularly one side. But she could breathe. Suddenly a feeling of horror came over her - the faces just before the crash.

'The other car - was anyone hurt?'

'No.'

Mademoiselle Terrain shook her head. Madame Corneille had scraped the wing of her car badly against the tractor. The English girl had bruised her head on the windscreen. Madame Corneille had taken her to the hospital for a dressing. Madame Corneille was angry, Georges said, very angry. That idiot English woman, she had said, driving like a mad person. She would sue her.

'Georges is afraid of her,' said Mademoiselle Terrain. 'But then,' she shrugged, 'he's afraid of everything. We were surprised he found the courage to get you out of the car. You were trapped by the steering wheel. He had to climb through the door on the other side. You were upside down.'

There was a knock at the door. Mademoiselle Terrain went out. Hannah could hear a murmur of voices, then she came back saying, 'My mother sent for the doctor. May I bring him in?'

Hannah nodded. Mademoiselle Terrain opened the door wider to admit a neat, bald man. Hannah again tried to raise herself on the pillows but he gestured to her to lie still. He drew a chair up to the edge of the bed and lifted her wrist to take her pulse. Hannah saw to

r surprise that her arm was encased in a long, white sleeve. She
)ked down at her chest. She was wearing a cotton nightgown but-
ned up to the neck. She turned a puzzled face to Mademoiselle
errain.

'Whose is . . .?'

'It's mine,' Mademoiselle Terrain said with embarrassment, 'I
)pe you don't mind. My mother and I changed your clothes.' She
ushed. 'They were . . . torn.'

Satisfied with her pulse the doctor turned back the covers as
Mademoiselle Terrain slipped discreetly out of the room. He rolled
ne white gown up to her armpits and began to examine her limbs
arefully one by one, testing each joint in turn. When he came to her
nest she gasped with pain as he touched her rib cage. He pressed
ghtly with his fingers.

'Does this hurt?'

'Yes,' she cried out.

He worked from one side to the other. The left side was much more
ainful than the right. He rolled her over gently on the bed and went
ver her back. Then he turned her again and smoothed the night-
own into place.

'You're very fortunate, Madame. Nothing but some badly bruised
ibs. Rest in bed for a few days. Keep warm. What about your head,
loes it ache?'

'Yes. I feel . . . very strange.'

'That's to be expected. You've had a mild concussion.' He exam-
ned her skull carefully. 'There's a large bump on the left side. If you
nave severe headaches or any unusual symptoms in the next few days,
please let me know immediately.'

He stood up as if getting ready to leave. Hannah's anxiety was
growing every minute. 'Can I ask you something?'

'Of course, Madame.'

'Before the crash I was . . . I was going to have a child. Could it
have been affected by the accident? I mean, do you think I'm still
pregnant?'

'Do you wish me to examine you?'

She nodded. He opened his case and took out a packet of plastic
gloves. The old routine. She tensed herself for the probing fingers as
he pressed his other hand on her stomach.

'No abdominal pains?' She shook her head. He squeezed gentl
moving his fingers around inside her. 'There's no bleeding, no si
that anything has been disturbed. Have you ever had a miscarriag
'No.'

'As far as I can tell everything is as it should be. Babies are not
easy to dislodge, you know. But I advise you to stay in bed for
least a week, to be on the safe side.'

He smiled at her, a dry, reassuring, little smile. She began to cr
Tenderness overwhelmed her, for the unborn baby, for Harry, f
Sarah. She had nearly killed herself and the baby. That it should st
be there seemed a miracle.

The doctor stood holding his bag, waiting. Of course, this
France. He wants to be paid.

'How much do I owe you?' she asked awkwardly.

'Fifty-five francs, Madame.'

She looked round for her bag.

'I'm afraid I don't know where my purse is. It may be still in th
car.'

He bowed. 'Don't worry, Madame, the Terrain family are ol
patients of mine. I'm sure I can trust you to send the money to m
surgery.'

He shook hands and left the room. A little while later Mademoisell
Terrain came back carrying a cup.

'I've made you a *tisane* of camomile. Good for the nerves. It wil
help you to rest.' She put it on the bedside table. 'Is there anythin
else you want? I must see to the hens before it gets dark.'

'No thank you. Unless ...' Hannah looked towards the window
that was tightly closed '... unless I could have the window open?'

Mademoiselle Terrain opened it wide, saying, 'I closed it to keep
out the smoke.'

A heady smell filled the room, a smoky sweetness, unlike anything
she had smelt before.

'What are they burning?' asked Hannah.

'The old lavender bushes,' replied Mademoiselle Terrain. 'My
brother's pulled them all up from the big field. The planning permission came last week from Avignon for six holiday villas. They're
going to start building in the new year.'

She went out, closing the door quietly.

I'm looking out of the window across to the cluster of houses that rms the village, walls propping each other up, literally. *To settle in is village of the heart, my darling, can you bear it?* Auden's question. arc can't. He doesn't want to be anyone's prop. A bird of free ght, like a swallow, touching wings with other birds around the arch the church, migratory. I don't feel angry any more. What I love is hat he is. Why did I allow myself to think he'd be any different m what I know him to be? *Only you can decide.* Couldn't I have cognised that in London?

All those years with Philip, abdicating my life to someone else, inking he could give the meaning to my existence, that he could ke the responsibility for my happiness or unhappiness – what a load put on someone, an intolerable load. All Marc has done is give me ck to myself. What's left of me. To want what happens to happen. hat does he mean? Not letting yourself manipulate or be manipu- ted?

There was a community here in this village but it's dying. Helen rant saw that. Even Monsieur Terrain has finally been persuaded pull up the lavender. In her notes she was trying to piece together continuity that's almost broken. It remains in the person of one old an – *Le Vieux* – and his son who is deranged. How odd. It was eorges who rescued me.

Marc said I could come back whenever I wanted, to work on the tes. I'd like to get them into a form that could be printed. I like search. I even know how to do it. Something to thank the Professor r. Only this time the book, if I could shape it, would be for myself d for all the people who once lived here, for Helen Grant, for arc's father, for . . . Harry, to link them to the living, to Marc, to e child.

I suppose Philip will go to Tunisia. He must know now our pendencies are over.

He asked me why it happened.

I was in a box. The lid blew off.

If I'm going to have this child, I'll have to support it. A commit- ent. Is that what I was looking for? I can take on that full-time job the school. Start from there. I'll need the money. Teachers get paid leave to have their babies. I think I could learn something from working with Nick Gates. He isn't afraid of chaos. What was it he said he was doing? Eliminating negatives. It makes me want to laugh. I can't. My chest hurts too much. Negatives of my old self. Hard work to eliminate them all. What remains may have a continuous battle just to survive, trying not to be afraid of not knowing what's going to happen. Embracing the uncertainties, as Marc does.

The dream is over. I must try now to stay awake. Harry's question I never could answer – how do I know someone isn't dreaming me? I still don't know how to answer except to say perhaps it doesn't matter as long as you're not asleep within the dream.

It was getting dark outside. Hannah lifted herself painfully a little higher on the pillows to get a last view of the distant mountains before night fell. Through the window drifted the smell of burning lavender.